MERRY & BRIGHT

HARTBRIDGE CHRISTMAS SERIES
BOOK 6

N.R. WALKER

BLURB

When given the opportunity to make his dream of owning his own bookstore come true, Winter Atkins couldn't say yes quick enough. Moving to Hartbridge, Montana, with his favorite aunt is the adventure he needs to start over. And leaving behind a string of unhappy boyfriends because of his asexuality, Winter is all too happy to shelve the idea of dating forever.

Deacon Clark has never fit in. Autistic and neurodivergent, he excels in his studies and at his father's veterinary clinic, but his social skills are lacking. He's attracted to men, but his bluntness and aversion to being touched have made dating impossible.

When Winter brings an injured cat into Deacon's clinic, it sparks an unlikely friendship; something both men need more than they realize. Hartbridge's Christmas Cupid has his work cut out for him this year. But with the help of two newly orphaned kittens, from friendship, the strongest bond forms.

COPYRIGHT

CAUTION WARNING

The author wishes to advise of the death of a stray cat in the very first chapter of this book, which the main character accidentally hits with his car.

Reader discretion is advised.

MERRY AND *Bright*

N.R. WALKER

CHAPTER ONE
WINTER ATKINS

"MR. WINTER ATKINS," the realtor said. "Please sign here."

He slid the paperwork in my direction, pointing to the sticky note with an arrow. I gave my aunt Rowena a quick glance, unable to hide my happiness and excitement. She grinned right at me, encouraging me to seal the deal.

I scribbled my signature, and Ro gave my arm a squeeze. "Well, we're doing it!" she said. "No going back now."

No, there wasn't.

There was never any going back.

Once I'd quit my job, packed up my small apartment back in Boise, and said goodbye to my friends, there was no going back.

I mean, I could, if I had to.

But I didn't want to. I wanted this new adventure to work out.

I needed it to.

Ro had invested some of her inheritance money in this new venture. She'd invested in me. More than my mother, Ro's sister, had. To say my relationship with my mother was strained was an understatement. Had been since as early as I could remember, since I was obviously gay and she couldn't deal with it.

She never disowned me or kicked me out. But her parenting came from a sense of obligation, not out of love. I learned all too well that her love came with conditions.

Whereas my aunt Ro welcomed me with open arms. She used to take teen-me aside and tell me it was okay to be me, it was okay to be gay, to be figuring shit out. I was basically the child she never had.

She'd been my saving grace.

Then and now.

Ro and my mother's uncle had died and, not having any children of his own, left them a sizable amount of money and stocks. My mother had never mentioned the money to me—not that I'd expected her to—but Aunt Ro wanted a change of scene, and something to dump some dollars into for tax purposes. She'd been to Hartbridge before and had fallen in love with the tiny town. And given I'd been a book-store manager for years, we found an ideal location, and I'd just signed the lease.

This was really happening.

She'd also found an old farmhouse a few minutes out of town, which we'd moved into just two days before. And I wanted to clean the store and paint the walls before the contractor guys installed the shelving and service counter next week. So, when I say it was *happening*, I meant it was *all* happening.

We took the keys and went to the store that was now ours. I parked out back, my hands trembling as I unlocked the door, and we stepped into the empty store. The glass front faced a paved road closed to traffic that met up with the river, just off Main Street. Directly across from us was a coffee shop run by the youth center as a training hub.

"It's going to be amazing," Ro said. "And the installers will be here on Monday, right?"

I nodded. "Yep."

"Then let's get to work!"

I laughed. She'd always been such a doer. I knew it would be pointless to tell her not to worry, that I could do it on my own. I didn't expect her to help me, but hanging out with her was always fun. We'd always gotten along so well, and I enjoyed our time together. We often just hung out because we enjoyed each other's company. Even when I was a kid, she'd hated being called aunt or aunty and had insisted I call her by her name.

She was five feet and three-quarter inches. That three-quarter inch was important, apparently. She had dark gray curls to her shoulders, Kermit-green chunky glasses and a brilliant smile, usually painted a bright red. She had a bright aura, she was smart as a whip, kind and gracious, and her energy was contagious.

I adored her.

The fact she was putting her trust in me made me even more determined not to let her down.

I wasn't worried. In fact, I knew we could do this. I knew my industry. I knew the book market. It was a great location in a great little town. Everyone I'd encountered so far had been friendly and welcoming, and it was inclusive.

There were pride flags in the youth center window, and the man at the hardware store who'd helped me choose the paint yesterday was clearly gay. I don't like to judge or assume, but when I'd asked for a neutral, warm white, he'd smirked at me, grabbed my arm, and said, "Ooh, I know just the thing." He'd handed me a swatch of different whites. "These have a warm undertone. Ren thinks I've learned about paint colors from him, but honestly, I learned everything I know about undertones and complexion from Drag Race."

I'd laughed at that. "Love that."

He was a bit fem, had a dark beard, an accent I couldn't quite place, and a wedding ring on his finger. I had no idea who the Ren was that he'd mentioned, but I figured from the way the tall guy behind the counter had smiled at him that it was probably him.

Everyone seemed so friendly here. It was such a pretty town, nestled in the mountains by the river. I couldn't wait to see it in full winter mode. Ro told me there was a Christmas festival in the town every year, and while that sounded fun, given it was mid-November already, it told me I didn't have much time to get this store up and running to capture most of the Christmas trade.

So, Ro and I got busy painting walls. Plus the pre-cleaning and cutting in and everything else, and by the end of the second day, the awful, dirty sepia yellow was gone, and 'First Snow' warm white was in. It looked fresh, clean, and inviting.

It felt so good.

Good to be productive, good to get the ball rolling. Good to start this new chapter of our lives.

"Okay, I'll head off first," Ro said. Then she stretched out her shoulders and arms. "Ugh. I need a hot bath. But I'll stop by the pizzeria first and pick up dinner. We're not cooking tonight."

The old farmhouse had one of those old-fashioned deep baths that was made for soaking tired and aching bodies.

"Sounds perfect," I said. "I won't be long here. Just gonna put a second coat on the windowsill."

"Okay, darling," she said, waving me off as she headed out to her car.

I finished the windowsill and, standing in my new

empty store, I took a minute to look around. I was so freaking happy. This was going to be the best thing that ever happened to me. A fresh start like the fresh coat of paint.

I intended to bury myself in work for the foreseeable future. No exes to run into to remind me how I was so lacking, how my being asexual was a fault or something they could fix.

No siree.

I had zero intention of making those same mistakes twice.

Or a third or fourth time, as the case may be.

This was my chance to start over. Build the business of my dreams, and get to live a fulfilling life, happily single forever, surrounded by books.

Cozy town, cozy bookstore, cozy me.

That was the plan.

And I couldn't wait.

Locking up the store, I pulled on my coat and went out to my car. Found my favorite playlist, which I'd aptly named Best Songs for Being Gay. I cranked up the volume. Queen began to belt out "I want to break free" and I was giving it my best karaoke special, reversed out of my parking spot with enough vigor to make Freddie Mercury proud, and felt a thump and heard a godawful screech.

Even above my own godawful screeching.

I hit the brakes and shut the engine off. There was only silence, and I was almost too scared to get out . . . but then I saw a cat half drag itself to the side of the building.

Oh no!

I jumped out and ran over to it. It was not good. Lying very still and its back legs were . . .

Dear god.

I took off my coat and bundled the cat up, carrying it to my car. I drove off again, this time without the vigor and the screeching, but with extra panic and sobbing. There was a vet clinic we passed on our way from home, so I thankfully knew where it was.

There were still a few cars in the lot, and the lights were on inside.

Thank heavens.

I grabbed the bundle of coat and cat and raced it inside. There was a lady behind the reception counter, and she stood up when she saw me. "I hit a cat," I said, crying, and I'm surprised she understood me.

"Come this way," she said, quickly ushering me through a door.

A man in a white lab coat appeared and took the bundle from me, and I was all but pushed back out of the room.

So, not knowing what else I should do, I sat in one of the waiting room chairs and waited. And cried, and wiped my snotty nose, and despite how badly my hands were shaking, I sent Ro a text.

> Will be late. I hit a cat with my car. I'm at the vet

Her reply came through immediately.

> Oh no! Need me to come down?

> No, it's fine. Just waiting to hear

> Okay. Let me know if anything changes

She was such a godsend. I cried a little at her kindness, wiping away a tear.

I couldn't believe I'd hit a cat. Was it under my car when I'd gotten into it? Did I not see it in the backup camera?

And I'd been having such a good day . . .

Still a decidedly better day than the poor cat was having.

And of course, that made me start crying again.

Then a man came out of the door, holding my coat, folded neatly, his expression sad.

And I knew. I knew it was bad news.

Didn't stop me from asking though. "Is the cat . . . did it . . . ?"

He shook his head. "She couldn't be saved."

I slumped back in my seat and cried, my face in my hands. "I killed her. Oh my goodness, I killed a cat. I'm a terrible person. Does she have an owner?" I looked up at him. "Oh no. Does she have an owner? Was she microchipped? Who do I have to go break the bad news to? I just moved here and someone's going to hate me already."

He fidgeted with my coat he was still holding. "There was no microchip. From the condition of her coat and weight, she was likely a stray."

"Well, that's good," I said. I mean, it didn't make it any better, though I was relieved I didn't have to go tell some poor child I'd killed their beloved pet. Or a little old lady's only companion. I wasn't sure which would be worse. "Well, it's not *good*. That poor cat. I think it was under my car when I got in. I don't know. I didn't see it. It was an accident, I swear. I'll pay the bill, whatever the cost. That's fine."

He made a face, though it was hard to tell through my tears and snot-sobbing, then he sat beside me and handed me a tissue. He waited until I had some composure.

"I'm sorry," I said lamely. "I've never killed anything before."

He didn't say anything, and when I looked at him, I could see he was uncomfortable. He was a little wide-eyed, unsure of how to react or where to look. He handed over my coat and stood up.

"We are closed for the day now," he said.

Oh.

Well then.

Right.

A little rude perhaps, but at least I got the message.

"Okay, sure," I said, dabbing my tears as I stood. "Thanks, I guess." I walked to the door, giving him one last look.

He shifted his weight, fidgeting his hands. He looked uncomfortable but sad. He was only young, I realized now that I took better notice of him. Twenty-something, short ashy-brown hair, blue eyes.

He squinted, uneasy, glanced at me before focusing on the wall instead. "'Death is not the opposite of life but an innate part of it,'" he said softly.

Then turned on his heel and walked out.

I stood there, blinking at where he'd been, until I remembered that he'd asked me to leave.

I went home, was met by Ro with a big hug, wine, and pizza. After I'd told her everything that had happened and had another good cry, I couldn't help but think about what that guy had said.

I'd heard it before; I was sure of it. I just had to place it . . .

"I'll be damned," I said, rushing to my bookcase. I pulled out one of my favorite books ever and flipped through the pages.

"Death is not the opposite of life, but an innate part of it," I read out loud. "What the hell."

"What is it?" Ro asked me from the door.

"That guy. The vet," I replied. Well, I'd assumed he was the vet. He had a white coat over scrubs, but he could have been a cleaner for all I knew. Not that it mattered. He'd had the awful task of giving me bad news. I held up my well-read, well-loved copy of *Norwegian Wood* by Haruki Murakami. "He quoted this."

She stared at me, a slow spreading smile at her lips. "Uh-oh."

"Uh-oh what?"

"I thought you'd sworn off men forever."

"I did. I am," I replied indignantly. "I mean, yes. One hundred percent. I have sworn off dating, sworn off being disappointed by men who don't understand me, sworn off men who . . ."

"Who quote one of your two hundred most favorite books ever."

My eyes met hers and I let out a pathetic whine. "Yes. Even then."

"That wasn't very convincing, Win. Try it again, this time with meaning."

I stroked the cover of my book as if I'd hurt its feelings instead of my own. "Yes. Even then."

CHAPTER TWO
DEACON CLARK

"HOW'D IT GO?" Dad asked me, a gentle hand on my shoulder, just for a moment, just for as long as he knew I could allow.

He knew my limitations.

"As expected," I replied, taking my coat off and hanging it neatly.

"Come in and have some dinner," Mom said from the kitchen. "I made grilled fish."

My place was set at the table, and when I slid into my seat, she put a plate in front of me, my knife and fork at nine and three o'clock, glass of water at ten o'clock. The fish looked good, the vegetables not touching.

"Thank you." I took a few mouthfuls. "A man brought an injured cat in," I told Dad. "It didn't make it."

Dad frowned and sat opposite me. "Oh. Do you want to talk about it?"

I wasn't quite sure what he wanted me to talk about. Not all animals could be saved; we both knew this. It was the first thing they taught in veterinary school. It was the first thing Dad had taught me as a young child when I would help him at his veterinary clinic. It was an unfortunate fact of life.

I took another mouthful of dinner and shook my head. "No."

"Okay."

"The man was quite upset."

Dad winced. "Was it his cat?"

"No. A stray, I think. Not chipped. Poor condition." I sipped my water. "Though there were enlarged nipples. I believe it was nursing."

Dad's lips formed a thin line, a telltale sign that this was not good. In this case it meant there was a litter of kittens now on their own.

"I didn't tell the man that," I admitted. "He was distraught enough."

"You didn't know who he was?"

I would have said if I did.

"No."

Dad inhaled deeply and let out a sigh. His smile was not his happy one. "You did the right thing. I'm sorry I wasn't there tonight to help you with that."

I shrugged as I swallowed another mouthful. "It's fine."

Mom gave my shoulder a quick squeeze. "Well, there are some mini apple pies from the diner. I can heat one for you if you like?"

I put my fork down. "No, thank you. It's not necessary." They were both looking at me as if they expected me to say something else. "Mrs. Gilbert is bringing her Pomeranian in tomorrow at nine. She said he's not himself, which is probably directly related to how many treats she gives him."

Dad nodded, and this time his smile made his eyes shine. "There's a good chance. I'll remind her again that one treat a day is enough."

We sat there for a long few seconds.

My parents were very outwardly caring and loving people, and I knew they tailored their concern for me with gestures of service and kindness. I loved them very much, but I wasn't good at small talk.

In fact, small talk made me uncomfortable. I wasn't any good at it, and I didn't like how people looked at me waiting for my input.

I stood up and put my plate straight into the dishwasher and made myself hold eye contact with Mom. "Thank you for dinner."

She grinned. "You're welcome, love."

"I'll go shower now."

Dad poured himself a glass of milk. "Our show starts at seven. Don't forget."

How could I forget something we did every single night? Regardless, I nodded, happier now. "Okay."

I went to my room and closed the door, feeling immediately at ease. The relief of it, I felt in my bones. It was quiet, and it smelled right. My single bed in the corner with the blue covers was perfectly made, just as I'd left it this morning. My notebooks and pens sat on my desk, exactly as I'd put them; not a thing out of place. As I knew it would be, but I still liked to see it.

I showered quickly in my bathroom and wore my winter pajamas when I redressed, hanging my towel neatly on the rack to dry.

And as I sat on my bed to put my slippers on, my eyes went to my bookcase. Neat rows of my favorites, the ones I'd first read from the library but needed to buy, to have for my very own.

To one book in particular.

I slid it out of its row. Its red cover with the white circle and the black lines of legs that look like trees.

Norwegian Wood by Haruki Murakami.

This book, this perfect book. Words that stayed with me long after I'd finished it. Words that resonated with me. That plucked a string inside me.

I've read a lot of books. Fiction, non-fiction, and text-books, of course.

Manga and yaoi. I'd found those when I'd gone to college . . . I didn't own any physical copies though, only digital.

I loved all books. Some more than others.

But I'd read *Norwegian Wood* more times than I could count, and it resonated with me even more, every time.

I'd quoted this book today to the distraught man who'd brought the cat into the clinic.

I wasn't entirely sure why, which wasn't a feeling I liked. I rarely offered my opinion or words of comfort, unless asked. He hadn't asked me, but I'd felt compelled to offer something.

He was so upset, and more often than not, I found people's outward display of emotions disconcerting. But with this man, I wanted to help him, which admittedly usually ended badly— my father typically intervened in situations such as these—but I'd said to this man the first words that came into my head.

Words that helped me process the reality of veterinary science—understanding my father's profession and the path I'd chosen to follow—and appreciate the fact that we helped more than we lost.

Death was a part of life. I knew that. It wasn't easy, but it was the undeniable truth. I couldn't offer any words on loss or the pain which accompanied it because it was not my loss to bear.

But I wanted to comfort that man with words that I myself had found comfort in.

I wondered briefly how he was. Was he still sad? And

the kittens who were now fending for themselves. Were they warm? Were they crying for a mother, a source of food, who wasn't coming back?

"Deacon," Dad called out. "Our show's about to start."

I slid the book back into its place and found my dad in his favorite chair with Mildred, our bulldog, by his feet. I sat in my usual spot, unsure how to broach the subject.

"Everything okay?" Dad asked me.

"I'd like to find the kittens," I said. "From the stray that was brought in. I should have asked the man where he'd hit her with his car, then I could have gone to see if I could find them. There's no way of knowing how young they are, a few weeks perhaps, and they might not be able to fend for themselves. I should have asked him, and I didn't. I feel bad that I didn't ask. I didn't even ask his name. He said he would pay whatever fees we charged, but I didn't think to get his name. He was so upset, I . . ." I shrugged. "I thought it best if I just let him leave."

Dad gave me a warm smile. "We can ask around tomorrow and have a look at the cameras at work. We might see his car, and we can find him that way. Don't feel bad about the kittens. They weren't your primary concern at the time."

"I should have thought about it, but I didn't. As a veterinarian, I'm supposed to think of these things."

"We'll see what we can find out tomorrow. I'm sure those kittens are in their little hideout, warm as toast. We can start looking tomorrow."

I trusted his judgment, so I tried not to think about it and to enjoy our 7:00 p.m. ritual.

His attention turned to the TV. "Ooh, okay, it's about to start."

Every night we watched reruns of *Antiques Roadshow*,

guessing how much each item was worth. This little game we played was one of my favorite things.

The show began, and I tried to stop thinking about the kittens, which of course, meant I thought about them more. My mind did this to me often. Trying to *not* think about something usually made it the only thing I could think about.

Dad did his best to distract me, and the guessing games were fun. I appreciated his efforts, but I was relieved when it was time for bed. It meant I could lie in my room—my favorite place—surrounded by my things, where it was quiet and contained, and stare at the ceiling. I could think about finding the kittens tomorrow. My mind kept replaying the scenario of the sad man and how upset he'd been, how I'd tried to comfort him by quoting Haruki Murakami.

And of course, the more I tried to *not* think about him, about his kindness and his sad eyes, the more I thought about him.

I slipped out of bed, slid my copy of *Norwegian Wood* from the bookcase and took it back to bed with me.

I'd read it a few dozen times, and I could have very easily began at page one, immersing myself in the gentle words. There was a pattern, a cadence to the writing that I connected with, and yes, reading it over would have been easy and would have stopped me thinking about the man from the clinic.

But for reasons I didn't quite understand, I didn't want to stop thinking about him.

So I slipped the book under my pillow, switched my lamp off, and closed my eyes. I pictured in my mind the man and the way he looked at me when I'd quoted those words to him.

His kind face, the way his sad eyes met mine.

I couldn't get the image out of my head, but for another reason I didn't quite understand, I didn't even mind.

CHAPTER THREE

WINTER

I ARRIVED at the shop early. The contractors would be installing the shelves and the service counter today, and I was excited for the store to start taking shape. My first delivery of books would be arriving later this week and I needed the store operational by December first.

I had a week.

I parked my car, trying super hard to *not* remember the carnage I'd caused last night, ending that poor cat's life. It was an accident, a horrible, awful, no-good accident, but still . . .

I felt bad.

But being busy would help me forget about that and help me forget about the man at the vet who'd quoted one of my favorite books.

Okay, so I had a hundred favorite books, but it was up there. It was on the list.

And he'd quoted it to me, unprompted, just off the top of his head.

His six-foot, brown-haired, handsome head. With his alarmed wide blue eyes, awkward stance, and slight grimace, he was still handsome. And I was the king of awkward and social ineptitude. I was used to getting weird looks from guys and making them feel uncomfortable. Not in a creepy way. Just in a what's-wrong-with-you kind of way.

Just another day for me, I'm afraid.

A knock at the door scared the daylights out of me and I let out a very manly squeal, thankful Aunt Ro wasn't here yet. She'd have thought that was hilarious. As it was, the guy peering at me through the front door laughed.

Great.

Seeing his coat had the company logo on the front, I opened the door. "Morning," I said.

"Didn't mean to startle ya," he said, far too cheerfully. "Are you Winter Atkins?"

"I am. Come in." I gave him room to walk in. It wasn't freezing out, but it was cold enough. "Please tell me you have all my shelves and my service counter," I said.

"We sure do," he replied, just as a rather large white van backed up to the front of the store.

I wanted to clasp my hands together and say *yay!* like a manga schoolgirl character, but remembering my high-pitched squeal just a minute ago, I clapped my hands together and said a very masculine, "Good stuff," instead.

His two staff began bringing gear in as I went over the floor layout plans, confirming everything was correct, then seeing they were more than capable—and seeing my very fabulous service counter in the middle of the store, waiting to be put in its final resting place—*and* after watching the first of the shelves being installed, I got out of their way and went in search of coffee.

It was too early for the café across the road so I walked up to the diner. It was a testament to the classic retro American diners from the 1960s, though I was sure this was all original. It was warm and busy, the staff friendly, and it smelled amazing. No doubt the baked goods in the cabinet and the man I could see in the kitchen pulling out trays of muffins were to thank for the delicious aromas.

The waitress, an older lady with hair a copper color that I could only describe as courageous, greeted me with a motherly smile. "What can I getcha, love?"

I liked her immediately. "The largest coffee you're legally allowed to give me, and two of the lemon blueberry scones, please."

I thought Ro might like one when she came down later. Or, if she was late, I could totally eat both and not tell her . . .

Just a few short minutes later, I was walking back to the store. It was off Main Street, just before the turn to the bridge, central to everything. I just couldn't get over how picturesque this town was.

Like a freaking postcard.

The main street was lined with old-fashioned awnings, planter boxes, gorgeous window dressings, with the mountains as a backdrop. It was stunning. And the people all smiled and waved.

My cynical city-self would almost think this was a dystopian nightmare if I didn't love it so much.

I was going to be happy here. I just knew it.

I had a skip in my step as I headed back to the shop, mentally running through everything I still needed to do. I had the new computer and point-of-sale system at home already, waiting for the service counter to be installed. Then I could set up the cataloging software, the accounting software, and tweak the website some more.

I could hear the drilling and banging as I got closer, smiling at how close it all was to coming together, and I noticed the man from across the way putting some tables out in the sunshine.

"Morning," he said when he saw me.

He was in his forties, at a guess, with grayish hair and a warm, wide smile.

"Oh, hi," I replied.

We kinda met in the middle of the road, and he nodded toward my store and the worker inside it. "It's all happening here today," he said.

"Yes," I said, maybe a little too excited. "Shelving and my brand-new sales counter."

"A bookstore, right?" he asked. "Pretty sure that's what I heard."

"Yes! The Fox and Fables Bookstore. I'm very excited."

He held out his hand. "Name's Gunter Zuniga."

I had to shove the scones under my arm so I could shake his hand. "Winter Atkins. Most people call me Win."

"Nice to meet you." He was handsome and had striking blue eyes. "I see you've found the diner okay?"

"Oh yes," I said, holding the bag of scones as proof. "I've already convinced myself the lemon and blueberry scones are calorie-free."

He chuckled. "I run the drop-in center here and the café." He gestured to the closed store on the end, opposite mine. "Well, it's more of a training center for teens. Café's only open four days a week. Helps kids get some experience in the food service and retail industry. There aren't many jobs in small towns, so it helps them get a foot in the door when they venture out into the real world."

"I love that. What a great initiative."

"Yeah, the kids love it. It also gives them a place to hang out."

"The spot by the river here is just lovely," I said. "This town is so pretty."

"Ah, you've fallen under the Hartbridge spell," he said with a grin. "Have you just moved here?"

I nodded. "From Boise. My aunt and I live out on Cottonwood Road. She found an old farmhouse that's more work than whimsy, but as long as she's happy."

He grinned. "I bought a fixer-upper myself. If you need any advice or help . . ."

I snorted at how cute that was. "Oh dear god, no. I won't be doing any of the fixing. Believe me, nobody wants that. My aunt Ro does the fixing. I'm more of a hire-a-professional kind of guy."

He chuckled warmly. "Fair enough."

Noticing the pride flags in his center window, I figured now was as good a time as any . . . "I appreciate the pride flags," I said. "I will admit, when we were looking for locations, it made me feel welcome. So thank you for that. I know it means a lot for teens to see it as well. I worked at a big book retailer for years, and having that visibility is so important."

His face lit up. "It really is. It's part of the reason I opened this center," he explained. "I never had that growing up, and I have to wonder what difference it would have made if I had."

So he was queer . . .

Good to know.

A man carrying a box came down the sidewalk. He had sandy-grayish hair, wore navy trousers, a gray woolen sweater, and a dimple pierced his cheek when he saw us.

"Ah," Gunter said. "I could have come up and got those."

"It's no problem," he said, handing the box over to Gunter.

Gunter looked between us and made introductions.

"This is Rob O'Reilly. He's the town doctor, just around the corner."

I held out my hand. "Winter Atkins. The bookshop is mine. Well, it will be. Once it opens."

Doctor Rob grinned at me. "Gotta say, I was very happy to hear we were getting a bookstore."

"Thank you. I'm excited to be here."

"Just moved here?" he hedged.

Before I could answer, Gunter replied for me. "He has just moved to town, just in time for Christmas. And he was just commenting on the pride flags and how that made him feel welcome . . ."

They smiled at each other as if there was an inside joke I wasn't privy to.

"Is that a problem?" I asked, not entirely sure where I stood on the line between acceptance and mockery.

Gunter grabbed my arm. "Oh no-no, no problem. No problem at all. Believe me. You're in good company here. I'm gay."

Rob nodded. "And I'm gaaaaay. Like *gay* gay."

"Oh, am I being sequestered into some queer sex cult? Because you should both know, that while I am also *gay* gay, I'm also very asexual and not really interested in debauchery. I'm not being judgmental or anything. It's just not my thing. So if there's, like, meetings or something, as far as involvement, I can take down the minutes or make flyers, but I'll leave the immersive experiences up to you."

They both stared at me for a second, then both burst out laughing. "Tell me," Rob said, "have you met Hamish at the hardware store, by chance? Pretty sure you'd get along."

"Dark hair? Beard?" I asked and they both nodded. "Yes, briefly; he helped me pick out a paint color. I did get queer vibes, not gonna lie. Is he ace or does he make the flyers? Not sure what you mean when you said we'd get along."

Gunter laughed at that. "No, you're just alike, that's all."

Oh.

"Uh, Mr. Atkins," one of the workers called out from the doorway to my shop. "You have a noise."

A noise?

"What do you mean I have a noise?" I asked, my voice a mix of squeak and shrill. "What does that even mean?"

I went to the door, not brave enough to step inside, and stuck my head in. "A scary noise?"

One man was kneeling down by the wall, his ear perked, listening. He nodded. "Did you hear that?"

Not over the sound of my thumping heart and wild imagination, no.

We were all quiet again, and then I *did* hear something. Very faint, very small.

Another worker came in from the back door. "There's a gap in the subfloor, but I can't even get an arm through."

I went inside, not sure what the hell was going on. "Your arm through?" I asked. He put his arm into the crawl-space willingly? "What exactly are you trying to reach?"

Then we heard it again. A tiny little cry.

"Sounds like you've got critters in there," he said.

Critters?

"What kind of critters?"

"Kittens, by the sound of 'em," he replied.

Kittens.

Oh no.

The stray cat.

I put my hand to my forehead, and Gunter was beside me then, concerned. "What's wrong?"

"There are kittens stuck under the floor," I said. "Oh

god. Last night I ran over a cat. I rushed it to the vet but it couldn't be saved. I think I killed the momma cat, and now her babies are stuck."

"The white cat that hangs around the back?" he asked.

"You know it? Oh my word, was she yours? I'm so sorry! I tried to save her, but she must have been asleep under my car or hiding, I don't know. I didn't see her until—"

"No, she was a stray," he said. "The kids would leave food out for her sometimes, but she wasn't too friendly." Then he looked at the workers. "And there're babies stuck in there?"

They both nodded. "I was drilling the brackets in for the shelves and heard something."

"How do we get them out?" I asked, trying not to panic. "I don't know if I can start cutting holes in walls."

The guy who'd tried to stick his arm through the gap shook his head. "Nah. Through the outside would probably be easier. Gonna need an angle grinder though."

An angle grinder? I wasn't even sure I knew what that was. I mean, I knew what Grindr was . . .

"Could Soren do that?" Gunter asked Doctor Rob.

I hadn't even noticed Rob was in the room, but he took his phone out in a flash and grinned as he spoke into it. "So I know firemen rescue cats from trees, but what about from crawlspaces or walls?"

Firemen?

Oh god.

Rob chuckled. "And an angle grinder . . . Okay. Yep, the new bookstore across from the rec center . . . Okay. See you soon."

He disconnected the call and smiled. "They'll come take a look."

"Firemen?" I asked, trying not to show how horrifying that was. "We don't need the whole flashing-lights and sirens thing, do we? Loud and attention-grabbing so the whole town comes to see really isn't my thing."

It actually made me feel a little ill.

Rob and Gunter both laughed. "Ah, no, they're just around the corner," Gunter said.

Then my aunt Ro arrived, curious about the small crowd in the store and why we were all looking at the wall and why one man had his ear pressed to the floor.

"What are we doing?" she asked. She looked fabulous with her bright green glasses and matching sweater today.

"There are kittens stuck," I said. "Orphan kittens."

She put her hand to her heart. "Oh." Then she realized, her gaze shooting to me. "Oh."

I grimaced. "I know."

Then two very fit, very gorgeous men in Hartbridge Fire Department coveralls jogged into the shop.

"Oh," I muttered. "Well, this isn't terrible."

"No, no, it's not," Ro whispered.

Gunter chuckled beside us, and Rob was grinning. Fireman number one went to him first. "What have we got? Kittens stuck, you said?"

Doctor Rob gave him a nod, then he turned to me. "Soren, this is Winter Atkins. He owns the bookstore. Winter, this is my partner, Soren."

Partner . . .

"Oh," I said, clueing in far too late. I looked between Gunter and Rob. "I thought you two were . . ."

They both shook their heads. "No," Gunter replied. Then he waved me off. "I'll explain it all later."

Okay then.

It was determined that yes, going into the crawlspace from the outside would be best, and yes, the angle grinder was required. But Fireman Soren and fireman not-Soren made short work of that. Soren got down on his belly and, armed with a box, went in while not-Soren held a torch. He shuffled in until only his legs and boots remained, and after a few minutes of grumbling, grunting, and an expletive or two—while we all stood there, watching—Soren shuffled backward and not-Soren helped pull him out. He got to his feet, covered in dirt and spiderwebs, grinning, holding the box.

"There were only two. Unless one wandered off, but I couldn't see any others," he said, handing the box to me.

Inside were two very dirty, very tiny, very cute little orange-and-white kittens. "Oh my goodness," I whispered. They were scared and meowing for their momma. "You poor little babies."

"Oh, they're just the sweetest," Ro whispered beside me.

"Thank you so much!" I said to Soren, not-Soren, and to Rob and Gunter. "Thank you. Oh, these babies must be so hungry. I should take them to the vet. Get them checked over and learn what to feed them." I looked at Ro then. "I have to keep them. I'm the reason they're orphans."

She put her arm around my shoulder and nodded. "I know."

"I'll take them now," I said.

"Yes, yes. I'll stay here until you get back."

"Thank you."

Fishing the keys from my pocket, I unlocked my car and carefully put the precious box on the passenger seat. Then before I got in, I checked underneath my car for any more cats, which my entire audience found funny for some reason. Then I drove out.

The vet clinic was busier than I'd expected. Not that I'd given one single thought to how busy a small-town veterinarian clinic should be. But still. There was a man with a cat in a carrier and a woman with a golden retriever who was doing his very best to smile at everyone.

So cute.

"Can I help you?" the receptionist asked, looking at the box more than me.

"Uh, yes. I don't have an appointment, sorry. I came in last night with the cat that . . . succumbed to its injuries"—I cringed at the two people in the waiting room—"but here I have two kittens that I'm fairly certain are the babies to the . . . now dearly departed momma cat."

Recognition flashed in her eyes. "Oh yes, last night. I remember."

"Yes. It was horrible and I still feel really bad. But these little babies were stuck under the floor or in a wall. I'm not entirely sure. Some firemen had to come get them out." I put the box on the counter and opened the lid so we could see the two little kittens. "They're very young."

She nodded. "Hmm. Were you just dropping them off?"

Dropping them off?

"What? No, no. I want to keep them. I mean, I'm the reason they're orphans so it's only right, right? Out of guilt or moral obligation, I suppose. I was raised Catholic, so both probably."

Someone snorted, and when I looked up, there was a man smiling at me. He was around fifty, at a guess. Handsome in a dad-next-door kind of way. And he was wearing scrubs with the vet logo on the breast.

"Hello," he said, coming over to look in the box. "What have we got here?"

"Two little baby orphans," I said. "The very nice fireman had to cut into the subfloor thing to pull them out."

He lifted one out, and it gave the cutest little squeaky meow. "Orphans, you say?"

"Well, yes. I brought the momma cat in last night, but

she didn't . . ." I winced again. "It was my fault. She must have been hiding under my car but I didn't check. I actually didn't even know checking for cats was a thing I should be doing, but anyway . . ."

He smiled. "Ah, I know someone who'll be very happy to see these little ones."

He does?

"You do? Do they have an owner? Oh goodness, did I kill someone's cat? Please tell me I didn't. Oh my." I put my hand to my forehead, not feeling the best.

Still smiling, he nodded to a door off the waiting room. "Come this way."

I took the box with the one remaining kitten and followed the vet into the room. There was another door, which he opened and called out, "Deacon? Room two, please."

I scooped up the second tiny kitten, holding it to my chest. "Is Deacon the owner?" I asked, trying to put on my bravest face. "It was a terrible accident—"

"No, no," the vet said, just as Deacon came into the room.

I stared at him.

Deacon. Deacon was the guy who'd quoted *Norwegian Wood*.

He stood there, as awkward as I felt. He noticed the kittens we were holding and his wide eyes went to the vet. "Are these . . . ?"

The older guy handed the kitten over to him, then gestured to me. "I think so. This gentleman said he brought the injured cat in last night."

Deacon looked at me for a second before giving the man a nod. "Yes."

"He said these kittens were nearby?"

He looked at me to clarify his question.

"Yes," I said. "At my store. I'm opening the bookstore on Short Street, and that's where I hit the momma cat. Then today we heard little meows under the floor, so the fireman had to cut the siding to get them out. There were only two. They're very young, so I thought I should get them checked. They've been a whole night without their momma, which means no food, and I don't know how to look after them. So I thought I'd bring them here to get them checked out and maybe some information on what to feed them, because I have no clue."

Deacon blinked at my word-vomit, and the older guy smiled and took some pity on me. "Deacon here was worried last night there might have been kittens left behind because the mother was feeding. We checked the camera footage this morning to see if we could find your car, maybe find out where you'd hit the cat. But we couldn't see anything, and we didn't get a name."

"I was a bit of a mess last night. I've never killed anything in my life, and Deacon quoted *Norwegian Wood,* and it's one of my favorite books, and anyway my name is Winter Atkins."

Deacon was staring at me. Like, *staring,* staring at me but not at my eyes. Almost as if he'd picked a spot at the outer corner of my eye, or maybe he was staring at the space between us. I wasn't sure. His cheeks were a little pink.

The older man looked at Deacon for a long beat, then back at me, and he smiled. "Okay. Well, Mr. Atkins—"

"Please, call me Winter. Actually, most people call me Win."

His smile became a grin. "Well, Win, I'll leave the care of these two little kittens up to Deacon. Who is my son, by the way. He's very capable of caring for animals and at quoting favorite books, apparently." He stopped at the door and gave me an amused look. "It was very nice to meet you, Win."

Then he was gone, and it was just me and Deacon. Who was still staring at me, but not *at* me, and still had pink cheeks.

"You know Haruki Murakami?" he said.

"Yes. I love books. All books."

"Same," he said quietly. "I . . . I don't know why I quoted that. I almost quoted a jisei . . ."

Oh my god.

"Jisei? Japanese death poems? You know what those are?"

His eyes met mine, ever so briefly. "Of course."

Of course?

Because *of course,* everyone can quote Japanese death poems by rote.

"I have three books of them," I volunteered. "Quite remarkable, actually. Admittedly, I have a lot of books and a lot of favorites, but *Norwegian Wood* in particular would be in the top twenty at least. I knew what you said was familiar, so when I got home, I pulled out the book and found it. I was surprised, to be honest. I wasn't expecting . . . that."

"Hmm." He winced as if my rambling caused him physical pain. "Winter is an uncommon name."

Ah, the curse of my name.

"Yes. It is."

His blue eyes were piercing, and for a brief moment, he met my gaze, then looked at the kitten I was holding. He then seemed to remember he was holding the other one. "I'm glad you found the litter," he said. "I was worried last night. I wanted to go looking for them but didn't know . . . I didn't ask your name, and I should have. It was an error on my behalf."

"No," I said. "I was a blubbering mess and had just

delivered that poor cat to you, right at closing time. My offer to pay for any charges still stands. And these little ones. I'll do my best to look after them, but I don't know the first thing about kittens this young."

"Hmm," he said, holding up his kitten, looking it over. "I'd say four weeks old. They appear healthy, if not a little underfed and dirty. It is young to be without their mother, so they will need proper care. Feeding every five or so hours, and adequate heating. A water bottle perhaps, though body heat would be best."

"Body heat?"

"Yes, they rely on their mother's body heat for temperature regulation."

"Sure, but how would I do that?" I had visions of me with two kittens stuffed down my shirt. "Because that's . . . I don't know . . . I mean, I guess I can . . . like *down* my shirt? I'm not sure that's entirely good for them . . ."

He blinked, his eyes meeting mine, concerned, then he looked at my shirt, even more concerned. "Down your shirt? Why would you do that?"

"You said . . . you know what? Never mind. I can google better ideas."

We both stood there, not speaking for a long, awkward moment, until the kitten I was holding let out a squeaky meow.

"Oh, you poor little baby," I said, cuddling him to my chest. Then I looked at Deacon. "Can we please feed them? I don't know what to give them or how to feed them, and they must be starving. And scared. And sad."

He looked at me, then at the door, probably wishing his father would come back in and save him from me. Then, without a word, he turned and walked out the door he'd come through, taking the kitten with him.

Okay then.

Before I could wonder how long I was supposed to stand there before I went looking for help, the receptionist, who it turned out was also a veterinary assistant, came in with the kitten and a set of digital scales.

"Deacon's just getting some milk to temperature, but first we need to weigh these little ones," she said.

I hadn't even thought of that. "Oh, okay. Yes, that's a good idea."

She weighed them both and was typing all my details into the computer first as Deacon came back in with a cute little bottle. He showed me how to best feed them, letting me do it as he watched on, correcting my hand for the angle only once.

They were both so hungry. And *they*, as it turned out, were two little boy kittens. He explained how much of the special milk to give them, how often and how to test the temperature, what to look out for, how much weight they should gain every day, how to clean them, and a long list of what not to do. He was very efficient with details. Conversation, not so much. Admittedly, neither was I. But once he had factual information to talk about, he was a different guy.

"Okay," the vet tech said, still at the computer. "Your account's all set up, and all the information for these two is done. We just need names."

"Names?" I asked. "I have to name them?"

They both stared at me. "It's generally how it works, yes," she said.

Deacon seemed to find something funny. He had a nice smile.

"I've never named anything before," I admitted. "It's a big responsibility."

I mean, do I go with a literary great name? Leo Tolstoy

didn't seem a great choice. What about book boyfriends? I have plenty of those.

"Merry and Bright," Deacon said.

"Pardon?" I wasn't sure what he was referring to.

He pointed to the box the kittens were in, the box I'd brought them here in. It looked like a Christmas decoration box, but on the front, near the bottom, were indeed the words *merry and bright*.

The vet tech began typing. "That'll do for now. Don't worry," she said. "If you think of something else, just let me know when you bring them in next week for a follow-up and chipping."

Deacon was clearly very pleased with this. "Merry and Bright," he said their names as he wrapped each kitten up in the old scrap towel and put them back in their box. "Good Christmas names."

Merry and Bright.

I wasn't entirely sold on those names but they were kind of cute, and we were heading into the holidays. These two little souls entrusted into my care for the coming winter months. They'd surely have died if we hadn't found them and rescued them.

If I hadn't been the cause of their orphaning.

So maybe a little Christmas spirit was in order.

"Good Christmas names, indeed."

CHAPTER FOUR
DEACON

"SO, the appointment with Mr. Atkins went well," Dad said. We were at the table having dinner. "Glad he found those little kittens, huh?"

I nodded. "Very. They wouldn't have survived long, especially with the cold coming."

He ate a forkful of food and took his time chewing and swallowing. "Winter's an unusual name, isn't it?"

"It is."

"He seems very nice," Dad added. He was watching me. For what, I wasn't sure.

I nodded as I ate some dinner. "This is very good, Mom. Thank you."

"You're welcome, darling," she said. "You both worked hard today by the sounds of it."

"Winter's an unusual name, don't you think?" Dad said. Back to this again . . .

"Yes. I told him that, though I'm sure he's heard it before. He didn't seem surprised."

The way they both stared at me made me think perhaps

I shouldn't have said that. Either to Winter or that I shouldn't have told my parents I'd said that. I wasn't sure.

"Perhaps telling someone their name is weird isn't polite," Dad said gently.

"You just said his name was unusual."

"But not to his face," he said, then he sighed. "But you're right. I did say it was unusual. And I shouldn't have said that either. But anyway, he seems very nice. And he's opening a bookstore. That'll be great for the town."

"I'm looking forward to it. I think he said he wants to open on December first. There'll be a grand opening."

"He'll have his hands full with a new business and two very young kittens."

I didn't mention what Winter had said about shoving them down his shirt because I'd like to think he was joking. Sarcasm was often lost on me and I'd learned that people often used it carelessly. Winter had looked horrified when he'd mentioned the shirt-stuffing and he said he didn't think that would be good for the kittens, so I trusted that he wasn't about to try it.

"I named them," I said. "The kittens. He said he'd never named anything and it was a great responsibility. Though I'm not sure that was true, given the fact we have customers with pets named Catrick Swayze and Droolius Caesar."

"True." Dad chuckled. "So what did you call them?"

"Merry and Bright," I said with a smile. "It was on—"

"On the box they were brought in," Dad said, smiling. "I noticed that. Very cute names, Deac."

"He'll probably change them," I allowed.

He studied me for a while. "And he mentioned that you'd quoted one of his favorite books. That's pretty cool that he likes the same things you do. Especially your books. I didn't think anyone knew about those Japanese books."

"Those books are a study on the final acceptance of

death by Samurai. It's not morbid as it is more a study of the human psyche." I noticed Mom give him a curious look, and it was random that Dad would keep mentioning him. I didn't do well with innuendo or hints. He knew this. "Are you trying to make a point?" I asked. "You keep talking about him. I saw many clients today."

"No, no reason," he said, though I wasn't sure I believed that. "It's just that he was very nice and he said you'd quoted a poem. I thought you were a bit shy around him, that's all."

Shy?

"How was I shy?"

He sighed and eventually gave me a warm smile. "I thought you might have liked him, that's all. You seemed a little struck by him, and I was just curious. Maybe you and he could be friends, at least. You have some things in common, and he's new to town and about your age."

"He's two years older than me," I said. He'd given his driver's license, so . . . "He's twenty-eight."

Dad smiled. "Anyway, I thought we could go to the grand opening of his bookstore. That sounds fun, don't you think?"

A weird thrill ran through me. Excitement, but also an uneasy jittery feeling I wasn't sure I liked or not. The thing was, I did like Winter. He was cute, and he cared for those two little kittens so much already. My parents knew I liked guys, but I hadn't acted on it, not since my early years at college, and that had been an experience I wasn't eager to experience again.

But friends would be okay.

Nice, even.

Someone I could talk to about books. I didn't have anyone like that in town. Mrs. McPherson loved reading, and Mr. Humphries loved history books, but there was no one my age.

I gave a nod, ignoring the heat in my face. "Yes, to the grand opening. Though if there's a lot of people . . ." I made a face. "Maybe later in the afternoon."

Dad smiled as if this made him extra happy for some reason. He collected our empty plates and took them to the sink. "Oh, Deac, just so you know, it's totally acceptable to call a client and ask for an update on their pets. I do it often. So if you're worried at all about how those little kittens are doing or if he has any questions—he did mention a few times that he's not experienced in such things—maybe a phone call couldn't hurt."

Mom joined him at the sink and gave him a nudge, but I'd had enough conversation, enough interaction for one day. "I'll go shower now," I said, getting up from the table. "Leave the dishes, please. I'll do them after our show. I'm out of time." I checked my watch. Goodness, it was later than we usually finished dinner.

I quickly went into my room and closed the door, unsure why my heart was thumping.

The time differential? I was normally showered by the time our show came on, and I didn't like being late.

Or all the talk about Winter, and my dad telling me he could tell I'd liked seeing him today? Which was the truth. I'd never been able to hide my reactions. I knew other people had better control over that, and I knew other people cared about that.

The truth was, I did like Winter.

He was cute and gentle, and he loved books. But it couldn't be anything more than that. I didn't want it to be anything more than that, regardless of what my father alluded to. Or perhaps he hoped I'd make a friend and nothing more.

I wasn't sure, and I didn't want to ask.

I didn't want to make Winter uncomfortable in the way I knew I often did. It was never my intention, but I'd been told several times in my life that I did make people uncomfortable sometimes, so it was usually best for everyone if I stayed away.

But I could call Winter. As my father had said. It would be within my professional duty to check on the kittens. So instead of focusing on seeing him again, I steered my train of thought to perhaps calling him.

Yes. I could call him.

Not tonight, of course. But tomorrow. To see how their first night went. To ask if he had any questions or if he needed any advice or suggestions.

Yes, now *that* I could do.

In fact, having made the decision that I would call him tomorrow made me happy, and not stressed about seeing him again or asking if he'd like to be my friend.

After my shower, I was getting dressed in my warm pajamas and slippers when Dad called out. "Our show's about to start, Deac."

I hurried out to the living room, seeing the dishes were done. "Oh. I said I'd do the dishes. It's my job to do the dishes."

"It only took me a few seconds," Dad said. "But I'll make a deal with you. You can make us a cup of tea during the ad break. Deal?"

I relaxed then and smiled as the intro music of *Antiques Roadshow* began. "Deal."

I WAS MORE nervous than I thought I'd be. In fact, deciding to call Winter at a respectable 10:00 a.m. gave me a few hours in the morning to make myself regret eating breakfast.

I did see clients at the clinic, and that was a good distraction, but the looming phone call was always on my mind and made me quite useless. I found it difficult to concentrate, and I kept watching the clock.

Ten o'clock was so far away, and then it was coming too soon and I wasn't prepared enough. Or ready.

And my tummy ache was getting worse. That jittery feeling was back, and I was certain now I didn't like it. It made me anxious and that made me irritable and—

My dad took my hand, and I only realized then I'd been tapping my pen on the stainless-steel table.

I hated this feeling.

I pulled my hand free and let out a deep breath.

"Deacon," Dad said, his voice serious. "I'll need your help at ten when the Paul's bring their ferrets in, so it would be best if you could call Mr. Atkins now."

Of course I'd told him I'd call Winter at ten.

"Now?" I looked at my watch. It was only 9:42 a.m.

"Go on, his number's right here," he said, pointing to Winter Atkin's details on the computer. He must have pulled them up because I hadn't . . .

Had I really been that distracted?

"I don't like this feeling," I said.

"I know," he said gently. Then he used his boss voice. "Call him now, please. We have clients waiting, and the Pauls will be here soon."

Right. Yes. Work.

I had work to do.

Call Winter.

He's just another client. No different from any other.

Except he was.

He liked poetry, and he knew the works of Haruki

Murakami. He'd said it was a favorite, and I had to wonder what other books he liked.

And he was cute. He was shorter than me by at least two inches, had short brown wavy hair, bright brown eyes—when he wasn't crying—and a gentle smile.

I had to call him.

My phone suddenly weighed ten pounds, my tummy twisted, and I felt both hot and cold.

Dad's voice welcoming a client into his examination room spurred me into action. He needed my help at ten, so I had to do this now. I had a job to do, so I entered Winter's number into my phone and hit Call.

He answered on the second ring, and it sounded like he dropped the phone. There was a clunk and muffled sound, then a bright, "Hello, Winter Atkins speaking."

I froze.

"Hello?"

I blinked, my mouth suddenly dry. "Ah, yes," I said. Then I had to clear my throat. "Winter, this is Deacon Clark. Deacon, from Hartbridge Veterinary Clinic."

"Oh, Deacon," he said. Then it sounded as if he'd fumbled something again, he mumbled again, and this was clearly not a good time.

"I can call back," I said, knowing I probably wouldn't be able to. "Or my dad can."

"No, no," he said. "It's fine. I'm just trying to feed Merry, and Bright is a hungry little hippo. Let me just put him back into the basket."

There was a muffled sound, then he was back. "Okay, that's better. How can one little kitten be such a bully to his brother? Here you go, Merry . . . That's better . . . Good boy."

I was smiling, my tummy ache suddenly all but gone.

"Sorry, Deacon," he added. "What can I do for you? Is everything okay? Did I forget to pay for something?"

"No," I replied. I could see his account was paid in full. "I was just calling to follow up on the kittens, to see how they were doing, and to ask if you had any questions."

"Well, I think they're okay. Eating well. Bright is a big bully and poor little Merry gets trampled all over. Me, on the other hand, slept for a total of two hours. How do parents do this? It's been one night." He sighed. "Ignore me. I'm just being dramatic. Aww, little Merry finished his bottle. Give me one second."

It was quiet for a bit, then he was back again. "I appreciate you calling. I do have some questions, but I just received my first delivery of books and I need to get them entered into my computer system, and things are hectic here right now. Can I call you back, maybe later tonight?"

"Are you at the bookstore now?"

"Yes."

"And you have the kittens with you at the store?"

"Uh, yes? I didn't really have a choice. They need feeding every five hours and I can't leave them at home. They're too little and I need to check on them constantly, and I brought everything with me. I have too much to do in the next three days to not to be here. The store is heated, obviously, and I have a hot water bottle in their basket, and they have blankets. I did everything I could think of. Everything you said. I can send you photos, or you can come by and check on them." He made a humming sound. "Oh no. How do I know if I'm not doing something right?"

"It sounds like everything you're doing is great. Warm and fed is about all they need right now."

"And cuddles," he added. "I'm trying to get them used to being held and to know that they're safe with me."

That made me smile.

He offered for me to come check on them . . .

"Unless you think I should come past. My lunch break is at twelve and I have forty-five minutes."

"I don't want to be a bother," he replied.

"It's no problem. I must go help my dad with ferrets now. They bite and squirm."

"Oh, okay. Well." He made a funny noise. "Good luck with the ferrets. I'll see you after twelve. It's fine if you can't make it. If there's an emergency or something. If there's a ferret calamity. Don't worry too much; I'll understand. If I don't see you today, I'll call you later, if that's okay? Is this an office number you're calling from or your phone?"

"My phone."

"Then I have your number. If I have a kitten calamity, I'll call you."

"Yes, of course."

"Thanks again for calling. I really do appreciate it," he said. "I should go while these two little monsters are sleepy and get as much done as I can."

"Okay," I said, and ended the call.

I was still smiling when Dad came in.

"I take it by the look on your face that it went well," he said.

I nodded. "He called them little monsters. The kittens."

Dad's smile widened. "Then it sounds like they're all doing well. The felines and Winter."

"He was feeding Merry when I spoke to him."

"Merry?"

"Yes, Merry and Bright. He kept the names I gave them. And he said Bright was a bully to his brother."

Dad chuckled, and he did that thing where he moved his head into my line of sight so I'd look him in the eye. "You feel better now?"

I nodded and held his gaze for a beat before looking away. "Yes. I think my tummy ache is gone."

"Tummy ache, huh?" He found that funny for some reason, but then he nodded to the waiting room. "Good. Glad to hear it. Because we have six ferrets—"

"I told him I'd go see him during my lunch break," I said. "Winter, I mean. He's very busy and he had questions, and he wasn't sure if he was doing everything right. I told him I could go there. I have forty-five minutes, and I won't be late coming back."

Dad paused for a second, studying my face. I didn't dare catch his eye again because I wasn't sure what he'd find in mine. "Only," he said sternly, "if you bring back something sweet from the diner for me. And if you don't tell your mother. And you better get one for Courtney as well."

Courtney called out from her receptionist desk. "Yes, please."

I laughed. "Deal."

THE BOOKSTORE WAS on Short Street, off Main Street. As the name implied, it was only short and paved, with just a few stores on each side before it met the riverbank. There were trees by the river and some new tables with chairs that weren't there before. Part of the youth center, if I recalled correctly. There was talk about it at work when the center had first opened. I remembered my dad saying it'd be good for the kids in town. There were a few kids seated there now, talking and laughing among themselves, but I pretended I hadn't noticed them.

I hadn't been down here since the center opened, and the training café next door, and now the bookstore opposite.

It was a nice little corner of town, especially with the sound of the river and the overhead sun.

The bookstore was a long, narrow shop with a glass front, and I could see Winter inside. He was wearing gray pants and a blue cardigan, putting a stack of books on the counter. He had some facial hair. Not a full beard, but enough scruff to give his jaw definition.

Seeing him made my tummy feel all jittery again, but not in an anxious way. This felt different. Like nerves and excitement, maybe? It was hard to tell.

Like when I was younger, waiting for a birthday, or the first day of spring.

I knocked on the door, and he smiled as he opened it. "Deacon, please come in."

I stepped inside, trying to rein in my smile. I was excited to see him again, yes. But as soon as I saw all the books, it became something else.

"Wow," I said. "It really does look like a bookstore."

There were shelves on both walls, some lined with books, some with books stacked on them. Piles of books on the counter, and boxes and boxes of books on the floor.

Winter put his hand to his forehead. "It's getting there. We're doing inventory right now, getting things entered into the system. It's the most labor-intensive part, but we're getting there."

That was twice he'd said we, and I had to wonder to whom he was referring just as a woman came out of the backroom. She was older, had grayish curly hair to her shoulders, she wore a bright green linen dress that matched her glasses, and red lipstick. She stopped and grinned when she saw me.

"You must be Deacon," she said brightly. "I'm Rowena, Winter's aunt." She picked up a laundry basket with a blanket in it and slid it onto a stack of boxes. "Good timing for you to be here because these two just woke up."

Ah, the kittens.

The reason for my visit.

I went over to her, peering inside the jumble of soft blankets. Two little blue eyes peered back at me and let out a tiny, squeaky meow. Then Winter was beside me, standing close enough for me to feel the heat of his body but not touching.

I was grateful.

He reached in and scooped out the kitten. "This is Bright. He's a menace." But then he cradled the cat to his chest and gave it a gentle kiss on its forehead. "He's a big old meanie to his little brother. He just barrels right over him."

I found myself smiling at them, then reached in to pick up Merry. "It's normal for one to be dominant, the leader, if you will. The strongest, biggest."

"Loudest," Winter supplied. "Hungriest. Meanest." He reached over and gave Merry a gentle rub. "Poor little one."

"As long as he gains weight, he'll be fine. Is he eating okay?"

Winter gave a nod and a shrug. "He takes his bottle just fine. It's best to feed this little monster first." He gave Bright another kiss. "Then Merry can take his time and get all he needs."

"Well," I said, "it sounds as though you've got them figured out. Seeing they have different needs, even at this age, is great. But you said you had questions?"

"Yes. I made a list." He went over to the counter and collected a piece of paper. "I wrote things down as I thought of them."

Then he proceeded to ask me things about toileting frequency, increasing milk, introduction of solids, is the basket and blanket suitable or should he use something else, how often should he change the hot water bottle . . .

It was quite a list.

He'd tried googling such things but found conflicting information, and he was petrified of doing the wrong thing.

His worry for them and his affection toward them was sweet.

He heated up some of their milk and showed me how he'd been feeding them. He'd taken to it so well and was doing just fine. The kittens seemed to be doing well, and I had no doubt they'd be growing by the minute.

They were so cute, as all baby animals were, but the way he was with them—the way he held them and talked to them—made me feel warm and swoopy inside.

"You have no reason to be worried," I told him. "You're doing a great job."

"That's what I told him," his Aunt Ro said.

I'd forgotten she was there. I looked up, surprised and embarrassed as if I'd been caught doing something wrong.

She seemed to pick up on this. Or whatever the pointed look she gave Winter was about, I wasn't sure. "I'm just going to duck up to the diner," she said. "Leave you boys to talk."

That made me check my watch because I'd lost track of time. "Oh," I said, seeing it was already half past. "I must be going. My dad requested I buy him a sweet treat from the diner before I go back to work. He also requested I not tell my mother. There's a tug of war of loyalty I'm not sure is entirely fair, but I told him I would."

Winter chuckled.

"I don't normally leave during my lunch break," I admitted, not sure why. I wasn't quite sure how to end this conversation, or maybe I felt the need to delay my leaving, or something.

"Oh, well, I'm very glad you did," Winter said. "I appreciate it."

Then his aunt Ro came up to him and handed him his coat. "I have a better idea. Why don't you go to the diner with Deacon and bring us back some lunch?" she said. "I'll stay here and watch the babies and keep going with the inventory." She all but shoved him toward the door. "Save me the trip. Deacon, it was lovely to meet you. I hope to see you again soon. I'm sure I will."

She gave Winter another look I couldn't quite read. But she was right. I did need to leave.

Winter put his coat on, giving his aunt a severe stare as we went outside. I wasn't good at reading between the lines. "Did you not want to walk with me?" I asked.

Winter's eyes met mine, wide. "What? No, of course I do. She was just being a bit pushy. Please don't think she was being rude."

"I didn't."

"Good." Then he seemed to notice two men over at the youth clinic who were watching us. He gave them a wave. "Rob, Gunter."

"Afternoon," they replied.

"You know people already," I said as we began to walk.

"I do. Everyone here seems really nice."

I nodded. "Yes."

"Have you lived here long?"

"All my life," I replied as we rounded the corner onto Main Street. "I was born here. Dad's had the vet clinic for as long as I can remember."

"Nice." He gestured up the street. "It's such a pretty town. Was it fun to grow up in?"

I shrugged. "I suppose. I don't know what it would have been like to grow up anywhere else."

He smiled at that. "Fair enough."

"I like small towns," I admitted. "I went to college in Boise, and the noise and the crowds were a lot. I like the quiet here."

I felt his gaze on me but I didn't look at him. "I like it too," he said.

"I would go fishing with my dad in the summer," I said, again not entirely sure why I volunteered that. "And skiing and hiking. I tried soccer, but I was never good at that."

"Sports really aren't my forte," he said. "And as for skiing and hiking, I wouldn't be opposed as long as there's a promise of no bears."

We got to the diner, and he held the door for me. I went inside, but it was warm and there were so many sweet smells, plus it was busy and there was so much noise. I didn't like it, but I didn't want to embarrass myself by leaving. And I didn't want to stop my conversation with Winter.

I liked him.

"You okay?" he asked me quietly.

I tried to nod.

"It's a bit overwhelming, isn't it," he said, not really asking. "We can order and wait outside if you'd prefer?"

I met his eyes then, and something inside me settled.

I felt calm with him. Something I'd only ever felt with my parents or in my house, in my room. Despite the noise, the heat, the smells, I knew I'd be okay. I liked that he gave me options. I didn't want to leave him just yet, but I didn't want to stay here. "Yes, please."

So we ordered and paid. Winter seemed to know the man behind the counter. Jayden, his name was. He'd been in town long enough now, working at the diner and the B&B, for almost everyone to know who he was.

"We'll just wait outside," Winter told him.

Jayden looked at me, then back to Winter, and again they seemed to exchange information without speaking. It was about me, no doubt.

Winter held the door for me again, and as soon as I was outside, I could breathe and let the tension out of my shoulders.

"It's a busy diner," Winter said. "Gets a bit much, doesn't it?"

I nodded, having to swallow before I could speak. My mouth was dry, and licking my lips didn't seem to help much. "I don't like it," I said. "It closes in on me."

It closes in on me was something my father had taught me to say when I was going to college—if I got overwhelmed, overstimulated, and started to feel panicky, because most people understood that.

And he was right.

He always was.

Winter gave me a patient smile, looking up at me. He was close but not touching, and I wasn't sure why, but maybe I wouldn't mind his hand on my arm. A soft touch, just for a second. I wondered what, if he did, it might feel like?

But he didn't.

"I get it," he said quietly. "It's fine. It's why I like bookstores and libraries. I like quiet and calm. Being overwhelmed is an icky feeling, isn't it?"

And just like that, he made me shuck off the panicky feeling and smile. "Icky?"

He nodded. "Totally icky. It's awful."

Then the door to the diner opened and Jayden appeared, holding our bags of pastries. "Here you go," he said. "Deacon, good to see you. Say hello to your dad for me. Win, I'll come see you tomorrow around nine?"

"Perfect."

Then he was gone.

"I don't know how he knew my name," I said.

"You're the vet in town," Winter said. "Along with your dad. Pretty sure everyone knows who you are."

I wasn't sure how to feel about that.

"And you grew up here," he added.

That was true.

"He called you Win," I said. "And he'll see you tomorrow."

I really wasn't sure how I felt about that either.

"Most people call me Win," he said. "Except you."

"I like the name Winter." I shrugged. "Though it depicts cold and dormancy, and I don't think you're either of those things."

He grinned and his cheeks went pink. From the cold, surely.

"You should have worn a scarf if you're cold," I told him. "A beanie too. It gets very cold here. Do you have a beanie?"

He looked at me then, smile wide. "I do, in fact. I should wear it tomorrow. And Jayden is doing a food stall out in front of the shop on Saturday for the grand opening. That's what he'll be seeing me about."

That made sense.

I stopped walking next to the truck. It had Hartbridge Veterinarian Clinic written on the door, so I assumed he'd know it was my stop. "I'm looking forward to it, though I told Dad I'd prefer later in the afternoon when it's not so busy."

"You're coming?" he asked, eyes bright.

"Yes, of course." Now I was confused. "Why does this surprise you? I'm an avid reader, and given you sent a flyer out to everyone, I'm assuming the whole town will be there."

He made a face. "Oh, I do hope so. I'm nervous, but also excited. There's still so much work to do. It feels as if Saturday is coming too fast and I won't be ready. I mean, I'm sure I will be, but I want it to be perfect, and I don't even know if three of me could get it all done."

"There were a lot of boxes," I agreed.

He grimaced. "I know! And that's not even half of it. You should see the storeroom." He looked back toward the storefront. "I should get back there. We'll be there until midnight every night, at this rate, trying to get it all done, and having two little kittens doesn't help right now. I barely slept at all and I don't see that changing any time soon. Until they're on a better schedule and not feeding so often."

"A few weeks, at least," I said.

He deflated but then offered me a smile. "Oh well. That can't be helped. I'm sure we'll get through it."

I liked his positive attitude, and I wished there was something I could do to help.

Well . . . until I realized there *was* something I could do.

"I can help you," I said.

He blinked. "With the kittens?"

"No. Well, yes. As their veterinarian, it's my job to care for them. But I meant the book inventory. After work, I could help you. Actually, it would be after dinner, and then Dad and I watch our show together, but it's over by eight o'clock, and if you'll be there until midnight, I can help for four hours. I mean, I don't have to watch our show. Some episodes are reruns. I'm sure he won't mind. But I'm very efficient with inventory. Cataloging and order are my specialty. I do most of it for the clinic. I actually enjoy it, so it's not a chore or anything."

I don't know why I suddenly felt so nervous. As if everything hinged on his yes or no.

"Deacon," he said softly. I looked at him then, at his eyes, and some of that anxiety melted away. "I'd like that. That would be very helpful, thank you."

The force of the relief I felt almost knocked the air out of me, and yet I couldn't help but smile. "Excellent. Then I shall see you at around seven, if that suits you?"

"Did you want to watch your show first?"

I was a little torn about that, but this seemed more important. "No, it's fine. I'm sure Dad will understand that you're on a deadline."

"Well, I do appreciate that," he said. "What show is it that you watch, by the way?"

"Antiques Roadshow. We like to try and guess where each item originated, and when, and what it's worth."

"I love that show! I love the English version best."

"Same." A thrill ran through me. I couldn't believe he liked my show. "We have a lot in common."

He laughed at that. I wasn't sure why, because I hadn't meant it as a joke. But then he nodded, still smiling. "We do."

I looked at my watch, alarmed to see it was already a quarter to one. "Oh my goodness, I'm late," I said, rushing to the driver's door and opening it, almost dropping my bag of pastries. "I'm never late." Then I stopped and turned to where Winter was still standing on the sidewalk. "I have to go. Bye. I will see you at seven."

"Okay," he said, smiling, his cheeks pink again.

He really needed to wear a scarf. Perhaps I would take him one tonight.

I drove to work and hurried inside, taking in the bag of pastries. I hadn't even had time to eat and now my lunch break was already over, and I hated when my schedule was impacted, and this was my doing, which made it worse.

Dad was at the counter giving Courtney a file. "Oh, there you are," he said. "Everything okay with the kittens?"

Oh, the kittens . . .

"Yes. They're feeding well. His concerns are unfounded, as he's doing a great job. I offered to help him with inventory and cataloging tonight at the bookstore so I won't be able to watch our show. I hope you don't mind. Here's your pastry." I held out the white paper bag. "I haven't eaten yet because I didn't realize the time."

Dad took the bag and looked inside, then gave me a warm smile.

It was my favorite of all his smiles. The one that said he was happy and a little proud of me.

I wasn't sure why he was proud. "It's just a pastry," I added. "The one you asked for. The diner was very busy and loud, and I wanted to leave but Winter was with me, so we ordered and he waited outside with me."

Dad's smile got warmer, prouder.

"We've got a quiet afternoon," he said. "So come on, let's go have coffee and you can tell me all about it." He looked in one of the bags and gave it to Courtney. "For you!"

"Thank you, Deacon. This is so nice of you," she said. "Perfect timing because I just poured myself some coffee."

"Dad asked me to get it for you," I said, and she laughed.

Dad was still watching me, but he spoke to her as he ushered me toward the breakroom. "Give us thirty minutes. We have a lot to talk about."

I wasn't sure what he meant. "I just told you everything that happened," I said, as he sat me at the table. "What else is there to talk about for thirty minutes? If you're disappointed I won't be there to watch our show, I can tell

Winter I'll be there after eight. I doubt he'll mind. I told him we watch our show at seven every night, so he won't be surprised. In fact, he said after is fine, so if you'd prefer—"

Dad put two plates on the table. "You told him?"

I nodded. "Of course. Dinner at six, *Antiques Roadshow* at seven." It wasn't like I told him I showered in between.

Dad poured two cups of coffee. "And what did he say about that?"

"He said he loves that show, and he prefers the English version."

"Like you do." He put a cup in front of me and sat in his seat. "That's nice."

"I told him we have a lot in common."

"You did, huh?"

I nodded again, remembering how his cheeks had been so pink. "Do we still have any of those promotional scarves from the sales representative?"

"Ah, yes. I believe so, why?"

"I think I'd like to give one to Winter. He was cold. He said he has a scarf at home but he didn't have one with him."

"I don't know, Deac. He probably doesn't want to wear a scarf with the logo of a dog wormer on it."

I didn't see why that would matter. "Better than being cold."

"True." He put the pastries on our plates. "Eat up."

I was rather hungry. Now that I no longer had a tummy ache.

Dad's mind must have gone to the same place as mine. "Feeling better now?" he asked after a few bites.

"Much."

"It's normal to be nervous when you're excited about something but unsure of how it will go."

I nodded, but my mouth was full so I couldn't speak.

"Like before you started college. Remember how nervous you were, and that turned out just fine. And Winter waited outside the diner with you? That's nice of him."

I nodded again, sipping my coffee to wash down the food. "He said it can be overwhelming. He likes quiet places too."

Dad smiled at that. "Like a bookstore."

"Yes."

"And you offered to help him?"

I nodded. "I asked and then I felt all anxious again. I thought he might say no, but he didn't. He said he'd like that, and it made my legs feel funny."

Dad laughed. "I think that's a good feeling. How do you feel about seeing him again? Nervous and excited?"

My tummy did that twist and swoop thing again and it felt both good and bad at the same time. "Yes. Both." Then I frowned. "I don't know, Dad. I know I'm not like other guys."

"Nope, you're not. You're better than other guys."

That didn't comfort me like it probably should.

The thing was, I really wanted Winter to like me. I wanted to spend more time with him. It seemed as if I could talk to him, and he made me feel at ease. I was comfortable with him, which was a rarity for me. I knew I was different; my mind didn't work like most people's. I said things out loud most people knew not to say, and I'd been reminded far too many times that I lacked social skills. My few attempts at dating in college were disasters.

But my parents had raised me to believe that while I might have been different—when the kids in elementary school didn't want to be my friend—there was nothing wrong with me. I just walked to a different beat, that's all.

That's what my mom had said. I was intelligent, kind, and empathetic, and those were traits any person would be lucky to find in a friend or partner.

I soon learned that real life didn't always work that way, though.

"What if he doesn't get me?" I asked. "What if he doesn't understand?"

Dad gave my hand a quick pat. "Deac, from what you've told me, I reckon he already does."

I pulled my hand back and rubbed away the feeling of his touch, another impulse of mine that I wished I didn't have. I didn't like to be touched. And that was something other people struggled with. Prospective dating partners, anyway.

The quirks and lack of social grace were something they could tolerate, but no touching? I'd never even been kissed before, let alone done anything more. I didn't want to do anything more. Touching was . . . not for me.

And that was something other guys couldn't deal with.

I had no reason to believe that Winter would be any different.

Dad finished the rest of his pastry and drained his coffee. "Just take it one day at a time, Deac," he offered. "And remember, having good friends is just as important. If you and Winter turn out to be great friends, then that's awesome!"

Yes, friends.

I didn't have many of those either.

Or any, if I were being honest.

I nodded because I knew he was right. Having Winter as my friend would be very nice, and I would normally be very excited about that.

But there was a part of me that wanted more. Even though I could never have it. I would never find someone who walked to the same beat as me. Who understood me and didn't want more from me than I could give.

"Oh," Dad said. "Something else I need your help with."

I appreciated the change of subject, the distraction. "Sure."

He grinned. "We need to figure out what to get your mother for Christmas."

CHAPTER FIVE
WINTER

"SO," Rob said with a sly grin. "You and Deacon Clark were having a cozy little conversation earlier."

Rob and Gunter had been standing outside and watched us leave. Then, of course, they noticed me walk back alone. Ro and I had decided to have our pastries at one of the tables in the sunshine, and of course they took it upon themselves to come over and get their fill of gossip.

"He's cute," Gunter said. "Don't you think?"

I'm surprised he didn't nudge-nudge or wink-wink me.

They'd both acted a bit weird about little old gay me turning up in this town at the beginning of the holidays. They'd assured me it wasn't some sex-cult thing like I'd first assumed, but I still wasn't entirely convinced.

"He stopped by to check on the kittens," I explained.

"He *is* cute," Ro added, giving my foot a nudge, which of course made me blush, and Rob and Gunter both thought that was funny.

"He's . . ." I wasn't sure if I should tell them, but I figured I may as well throw myself into the fire. "He's coming back later tonight to help me with the inventory."

The three of them were intensely interested in this development.

"Ooh," Ro said. "I will make myself very scarce."

"Or you could stay and help," I added. "More hands, the more we get done."

I ignored the way the three of them were looking at me until I relented. "Yes, okay. He's very nice, very cute. He's very smart, and I do like my guys quirky. Let's be real. Give me a quirky book nerd over a gym-bro any day. But," I said, holding up a finger. "And this is the most important part. I'm not looking. I'm not interested. I'm too busy, especially now I have two kittens who demand feeds every five hours."

Rob sighed. "I said the same thing last year."

"And me three years before that," Gunter added. "And Braithe and Colson two years ago, and then there's Jayden and Cas. And Hamish and Ren." He sighed. "And I don't know how to break it to you, but you probably won't have much say in it. I mean, you can try and refuse, but there's totally a Christmas Cupid thing that goes on in this town every year, and I'm pretty sure you're it this year."

I stared at him.

"I'm sorry, what? I won't have much say in what?" I repeated. "So this is a cult thing! And you told me it wasn't. You know, for inductees, you seemed normal. Is there an initiation ceremony? Please tell me it involves cake. If it involves going into the woods for some hazing ritual, well, I can just stop you right there because I don't do the outdoors so much. So good luck with that."

They all laughed.

Which was weird because I wasn't joking. "So there is cake?"

Rob snorted. "It's not a cult. But it's totally a thing. I didn't believe it either."

"Neither did I," Gunter added.

"But here we are. New to town, some kind of shade of queer, and bam! Unsuspecting, then meet the guy of your dreams."

"That sounds ridiculous," I said, rolling my eyes.

"It's true," Rob said. "I moved in next door to Soren and went out to yell at him for starting his Harley Davidson so early. He took one look at my flamingo pajamas and it was love at first sight."

"Flamingo pajamas?" I asked.

"Harley Davidson?" Ro asked. "You mean to tell me that fireman who came to rescue the kittens rides a Harley Davidson?"

Rob grinned. "Oh, he certainly does."

"Yeah, cool," I said. "Can we get back to the flamingo pajamas for a second?"

Gunter laughed. "And I moved here, and the sexiest lumberjack I'd ever seen delivered a load of wood."

"I bet he did," Rob said.

Gunter snorted. "And he also checked my chimney."

Ro burst out laughing. "Oh, I bet he did."

I sighed. "You're all depraved."

Of course, that made them all laugh.

I settled on a sigh. "Which brings me back full circle. Your Christmas Cupid can go take aim somewhere else. I'm not looking. I'm just gonna live my very best asexual life with books and that cake you mentioned before. I don't want to disappoint another man who says he's okay with it but really isn't. I just need my cute little bookstore in this cute little town with my cute little kittens."

"And your cute little aunt," Ro added.

"Yes. Maybe the Christmas Cupid will come for you," I told her. "Maybe you're the intended recipient this year! You just moved here, you're single, and you're queerer than me."

She gasped, her hand to her heart. "It's not a competition. The Kinsey Scale has a lot of colors. I've told you that all your life."

"True," I told Rob and Gunter. "She has."

But then she shook her head and, reaching over, squeezed my hand. "And darling, while that sounds like a lot of fun, I've seen the way Deacon looks at you. That Christmas Cupid's already taken aim and fired his little arrow."

Rob and Gunter both grinned, and all I could do was sigh.

"Well, that's a lie," I said. "Because he doesn't make eye contact. Although he hasn't told me as such, I've known a lot of neurodivergent people in my life to recognize the tells. He's looked me in the eye exactly twice in all the times we've met."

"Yes, but when you're not looking," Ro said, "that's when he looks at you."

Oh.

I felt my cheeks burn.

"Oh."

"Look," Gunter said with a wince. "Just between us—and I can say this, Rob is a doctor and is bound by confidentiality, but I'm not—and this is no secret. It's well known in this town, not that it's a bad thing, just that it's common knowledge. Deacon is autistic. Everyone knows it. He was born here, grew up here, and the townsfolk were proud that he went off to college to be a vet like his dad. The Clarks are real good people." He made a face. "I don't mean to be talking out of turn, and I mean no harm, but if you're interested in him, maybe a heads up couldn't hurt. You already said you assumed he was neurodivergent, so . . ." He finished with another wince and looked at Rob for some kind of confirmation?

Rob gave me a smile. "Neurodivergence and autism are two different things. All people with ASD, autism spectrum disorder, are neurodivergent but not all neurodivergent people are autistic. There are many differences. But," he added, making a face, "what Gunter said is right. It is common knowledge here. That's a small town for you though. Everybody knows everyone else's business. So while I won't say anything about this particular person specifically, what I can say, generally speaking, is this: if you do find yourself in a relationship with a person with ASD, any person, be it simply a friendship or something more, then clear communication is key. Don't use sarcasm or innuendos, don't assume he understands what you may think is a given. He will have different experiences and reactions, and most things will be achieved or encountered on his time, not yours."

I nodded. "I understand all that, but you are right. Even as Deacon's friend—and I do want his friendship; we have a great deal in common—some research on my behalf can't hurt. Even just terminology. I'm assuming the vocabulary around ASD changes often, and I don't want to upset him."

Rob smiled at me. "I think you'll do just fine."

"He is incredibly smart," I allowed. "When I first took the kittens to him, our conversation was . . . well, I don't want to say awkward, but between his standoffishness and my tendency to overshare, it was a rollercoaster of a conversation, lemme tell you. But then when he was talking about the facts and all the medical stuff, he was very articulate."

And now, looking back, I was surprised I didn't click with autism earlier. I mean, at my last job at the bookstore, I dealt with a lot of eccentric and idiosyncratic folks on the regular. In fact, most of the staff were neurodivergent, or neurospicy as most of them called themselves. Did I clock that Deacon had some idiosyncrasies or quirks? Sure. Did I want to assume anything?

No, I didn't.

I thought it was just him.

It certainly didn't bother me. Because before I'd been told he was autistic, I was thinking he was kinda great. And my opinion of him now hadn't changed.

"I should talk to him," I decided out loud.

"It might be best if you think he's interested in you and you don't want that," Gunter said.

"Oh no," I amended quickly. "I just meant that I should talk to him."

They all stared at me.

It made me flustered. "About . . . stuff. And I should read up on ASD, and whatever . . ."

"Mm hmm," Ro murmured sarcastically. "Still trying to convince yourself you don't like him?"

I shot her a glare. "I've met him all of three times, and I'm not entirely sure the first meeting counts because I was snot-sobbing."

"And he quoted one of your favorite books to your face."

I narrowed my eyes at her. "I'm not looking for any kind of romance right now."

She pursed her lips. "How's that working out for you?"

I sighed. "Oh, shush."

Rob chuckled, but Gunter held up an imaginary bow and arrow and shot me with it.

IT WAS DARK OUTSIDE, the streetlights downtown casting an orangey glow in the chilly air. I'd stopped working to feed Merry and Bright, but Ro soldiered on, getting through another box of books.

It was a tedious process at the start. Each book needed to be scanned and entered into the system, then shelved. Setting titles up in the software took a long time, especially to organize an entire store, but it was only because we were starting from scratch. Getting orders in the future wouldn't be so tedious or time-consuming.

I watched the clock as it ticked down to seven o'clock, nervous for Deacon to arrive.

No, not just nervous.

I was excited too. The truth was, I liked him. And I didn't want to like him. I had told myself I was coming to Hartbridge to leave behind the dating disasters. I didn't want to get my hopes up only to have them trampled on again.

I was done with it.

I didn't need it. I was too busy, too distracted, and too determined. This was a fresh start for me. I wanted to focus solely on my business and just enjoy small-town life without the pressure to conform to societal expectations that, as a gay man, I needed to date and have sex and . . .

Okay, so that wasn't entirely fair.

Not *all* men assumed that. Just the ones I'd chosen to date, apparently.

And I was done with that.

I didn't want Deacon to have expectations I couldn't fulfill. Not that I assumed he had expectations. I was getting way ahead of myself. He might not even be interested in me, despite what Ro had said about the way he looked at me.

I had to tread carefully to set boundaries so as not to confuse him or possibly lead him on.

Because I *did* want him as a friend.

I did like him, and we had a lot in common. And having good friends was all I needed.

Okay, so maybe some kissing and cuddling would be nice, but in my experience, that was always construed as consent for more. Even though it wasn't. It was just better not to start something I was expected to finish.

So, platonic friends it was.

Someone to have coffee with, talk books with, that's all I needed.

"Are you done overthinking everything?" Ro asked.

I startled, looking up at her. "What?"

She pointed to her forehead. "You get that line right here when you're overthinking." I scowled at her, and she laughed. "You'll get wrinkles if you keep doing that."

I gasped. "I will not."

She chuckled. "I think little Merry is done."

I looked down at the kitten on the bundle of blankets in my lap, who was milk-drunk and now looking for bed. I wiped his mouth and put him in the basket with his brother, just as there was a knock on the door.

"Oh, the reason for the overthinking is here," Ro said.

I scowled at her over my shoulder before opening the door. Deacon was wearing jeans, a sweater and a coat, and he was holding something purple. "Deacon, come in."

He stepped inside. "It's seven o'clock."

"Yes, it is," I said. I got the feeling punctuality was important to him. "You're right on time."

"Hello, Deacon," Ro said, carrying a stack of books to the table. "It's so generous of you to help."

He looked around the store, at the books, at the still unopened boxes, and at the pile of flattened cardboard. "It's very messy."

I laughed. "It is. It's organized chaos though. We have a system." I gestured to the books on the table. "Those have been entered into the computer, and these are yet to be done," I said, gesturing to the unopened boxes.

It was then I realized I was still holding the small milk bottle. "Oh, I just finished feeding the boys. Which is good timing, actually, because we should be good until it's time to go home."

He nodded, then handed me the purple thing he was holding. "This is for you. You said you had a scarf at home, but that meant you didn't have one here."

Oh . . .

He got me a scarf?

"You didn't have to do that," I said, touched by his thoughtfulness. "That's so nice of you."

"It's just from work. We get them for free. It has a brand logo on it for a dog wormer. Dad said you might not want that, but at least you won't be cold."

Dog wormer . . .

I unfolded the scarf and sure enough, there on the purple fleece was a black, gray, and white logo on the end of it. It made me laugh again. It was the ace pride colors, and it was so utterly perfect for me.

Not that he could possibly know I was ace. It was purely coincidental but still . . .

Perfect.

"I love it," I said. "Thank you so much."

I wrapped it around my neck and grinned at him. "Do you like it?"

He nodded. "Yes."

I looked at Ro, and she was smiling so fondly at me. She was such a sap. I silently told her with my well-aimed, very-pointed glare not to say anything. She took a deep breath in and let out a sigh, going for her coat.

"I'm going to go home," she said, putting her arm through the sleeve. "I'll take Merry and Bright with me, get them settled. If you're not home by the time they want supper, I'll feed them, so don't you worry."

If I could shoot lasers out of my eyes, I would have. She had no tact.

She picked up the basket with the kittens in it and gave us both a huge smile. "You boys be good. Don't stay up all night," she said with a wink at me, before going out the back door.

I sighed and turned to Deacon. "I really do appreciate you helping me. Ro needed to leave, apparently."

"You have a lot to get done," he said, looking at the majority of still empty shelves.

"I do, and just two more days to do it in. I want it all done by tomorrow night, if I can. Then I can spend Friday doing all the final touches, adding the display to the window, ready for the grand opening on Saturday."

"Then we should stop talking and start working," he said without any trace of humor.

It made me smile though. "We should. What did you want to do? You said you stock inventory at the clinic. Computer entry or sorting products?"

"Both. I do it all."

I grinned at him. "Perfect."

As it turned out, he was very proficient at both. I only had to show him one book entry in the software, and he was a pro in no time. And at sorting books and gifts, and organizing, categorizing. When he'd said he enjoyed doing stock inventory, he wasn't joking.

We worked in a comfortable silence. Actually, it was more than comfortable. It was so damn easy. Enjoyable, and fun.

We got a lot done in such a short time, faster and more efficient than me and Ro working together. I guess because she and I stopped to chat more often, and not having the kittens here helped a lot.

I got so much more done when I wasn't stopping to check on every squeak or noise.

But Deacon worked with a military precision, and I could have worked right through the night with him if he hadn't stopped to stretch and yawn.

"Oh, look at the time," I said, checking my phone. It was after ten. "You must be so tired. You've worked all day, then came to help me."

"I like doing this," he said.

"You're very good at it. I got more done with you in three hours than I did with Ro in six hours."

"I can help you tomorrow night if you'd like," he said.

I looked around at what was left to do. "I think we'll have the inventory done by then."

He frowned. "Oh." He wore his emotions for all to see, and I liked that.

"But I'll still have the display to do, and the signage, and all the finishing touches," I said. "If you wanted to help me with that instead. I know you said you liked inventory, so it's fine if you'd rather not."

"I would," he said quickly. "I can be here at seven again."

"I'd really appreciate that," I said, and he beamed at me. "Your dad won't mind missing another one of your shows with you?"

He shook his head. "No. He said this would be good for me. I don't have many friends here, so I should help them when they need it."

Friends.

Yep, there it was.

The word I wanted to hear. Until I'd heard it.

The stab of disappointment I felt was real.

"Friends are great," I said, hoping he couldn't see through my forced smile. "And helping friends is even better. I don't have many friends here either," I said. "Given I've just moved here and all."

He nodded again, looking around the store, looking at anywhere but at me. "I like books."

"I love them."

He laughed then, and it was such a beautiful sound. His face lit up, his blue eyes sparkled like topaz, his pink lips smiling wide. "I love them too."

God, I could look at him smile like that forever.

"Tell me," I said, "how did you find the book on Japanese death poems?"

His smile died and I immediately regretted asking. "Initially, in the college library. I spent a lot of time there, and I liked the cover. It was a fascinating insight into the acceptance of fate, so I searched for more."

Oh, how I loved that.

"I spent a lot of time in the library at my university too," I said. "It was quiet there, and I wasn't very social."

He shook his head. "Me either. I did have friends there, but . . ." He shrugged.

"I get it," I said gently. "Sometimes making friends is easy. Sometimes keeping them is hard."

His eyes darted to mine for a brief moment before he looked away again, and he nodded. "Yes. Exactly." Then he made a face, uncomfortable and pained. His face went a bit red, and he began to fidget.

"Deacon," I said softly. "Are you okay?"

He shifted his weight and licked his lips. "I'd like to go home now."

"Of course," I said. "Want me to walk you to your car?"

He blinked a few times. "No, I'm fine."

He didn't seem fine.

I wanted to go to him, to put my hand on his arm, to reassure him, but we hadn't discussed boundaries yet.

"Well, I do appreciate you helping me tonight. And I'm happy you're my friend."

He smiled shyly then, giving me a quick glance before nodding. "I'm happy too."

"Will I see you tomorrow at seven?"

He gave a nod. "Yes." He put his coat on and stood at the door. "It's cold out. Don't forget to wear your scarf."

I grinned at him. "I won't."

He ducked his head and went out the door, the bell chiming in the silence. I stood there, smiling at the door for a long moment, then remembered I had Merry and Bright at home who would no doubt be wanting another feed soon. Ro had said she'd do it, but they weren't her responsibility.

I turned everything off and locked up, looked around one more time at just how much Deacon and I got done together, and smiled all the way home.

Ro was up, of course, waiting for me in the kitchen, mugs of hot chocolate steaming. The little monsters weren't meowing for me yet, but it wouldn't be long. "I just made these, so they're hot," she said. "And Merry and Bright are still asleep."

I all but fell into the seat next to her.

"So?" she asked, excited. "How did it go?"

I didn't need to ask to whom she was referring. I sighed. "I don't know, he's . . ."

She studied me for a long moment, and when I didn't continue, she prompted me. "He's what? Cute? Sweet? Thoughtful?"

I met her gaze. "Yes. He's all those things." I let my head fall back with a groan. "He used the f-word."

Her brow furrowed. "He swore? He doesn't seem the type. But just so you know, the use of profanity has been used in society for thousands of years—"

I snorted. "No. Not that f-word. He used the *bad* f-word. I don't care if he cusses, gawd. Friend. He said he wanted us to be friends."

"Oh."

Yeah. Oh.

"I thought you didn't . . ."

I looked at her.

"Oh."

I groaned. "I thought I wanted that. I thought that was all I wanted. Until he said it. Then I realized maybe it wasn't." I looked at her then. "Every reasonable and logical part of my brain says no. I don't have time for this. I don't want or need the complication. I don't want to disappoint him, and I don't want to be disappointed. I'm sick of feeling like crap for not wanting a sex life. I shouldn't feel guilty."

"You shouldn't," she said quietly, her hand sliding over mine. "Don't put that kind of pressure on yourself. And if he just wants to be friends, well, then . . ."

I waited for her to finish imparting some beacon of wisdom that would make me feel instantly better. But nope. All she could offer was a grimace and a shrug. "I'm sorry it's not what you wanted."

I sighed again, long and loud. "We got a lot of work done. It's so easy to be with him. We just click, I don't know." I ran my hand through my hair. "And I don't have time for anything else right now. Finding a friend so fast is a good thing, right? So I don't know why I feel this way."

She sighed quietly and frowned at her hot chocolate, then at me. "The heart wants what it wants." Then she smirked. "And apparently there's a Christmas Cupid in this town? What's up with that?"

I snorted, grateful for her ability to make me smile. "Weird, huh? I guess this town couldn't be too perfect."

"I don't know about that." She was quiet for a moment. "They're predicting snow."

"I'm actually looking forward to snow this year," I admitted. At my old job, at my old apartment, it meant wet and gray slush. "Being in my bookstore, all warm and cozy while it snows quietly outside the front window . . ." I sighed wistfully. "It's one hundred percent the aesthetic I'm going for."

She chuckled just as there was a small squeak from the basket by the fire. I stood up and began to get the first bottle of milk ready. "Duty calls."

CHAPTER SIX
DEACON

"HOW WAS LAST NIGHT?" Mom asked over breakfast. "You got home late."

"It was good. Winter said he got more done with me than he does with his aunt Ro." I liked that too. "I met her. She's very nice, but she left and took the kittens home. I think he gets more done with me, not because of his aunt Ro but because of the kittens."

"What about the kittens?" Dad asked as he walked into the kitchen. He poured himself a coffee. "Did you see them last night? Are they feeding okay?"

"Yes, I saw them, but not for long," I answered. "And they are feeding well. They looked brighter already."

Mom smiled at me. "Amazing what some TLC can do for someone, isn't it?"

I wasn't sure the kittens qualified as a *someone*, given they weren't a singular person, and I was going to say that but decided against it. My tendency to ruin the flow of conversation was something I tried to work on. Not always successfully either. Learning when not to speak wasn't easy.

I decided to change the topic. "I told Winter I'd help

tonight also. He still has the non-fiction to organize. He would get them all done today if he didn't have to stop so often because of Merry and Bright."

"He kept the names, huh?" Dad asked.

I nodded, smiling. "He did. He said Bright is a mean big brother, and Merry needs more time to feed. I liked that he recognized the difference and adjusted to suit them, not himself, even if it took longer. Especially given how busy he is."

Dad and Mom exchanged a look that I pretended not to see.

"Well, he sounds very nice," Mom said. "And I'm sure he appreciates you helping."

"He said he did, yes."

"Do you think he'll have the store ready for Saturday?" she asked. "I think he'll be busy, given it'll be the first of December, and Main Street is always busy then. The Hendersons will put the Christmas trees up and down the sidewalks; the Christmas lights go up. It's always so pretty. And of course, the lighting of the Christmas tree in the park." She sighed. "Oh, how I love this time of year."

Dad stood up, kissed the top of her head, and put his plate on the sink. He almost tripped over Mildred, gave her a pat and told her to be good. "Come on, Deac. We've got a busy day ahead. Gotta make a house call first to see Col Jenkins' horses before we get to the clinic."

Oh, that's right. I'd forgotten. I shoved the last of the toast into my mouth and stood up. "Thank you for breakfast, Mom."

"You're most welcome, darling," she said. "Don't forget to take your lunch today."

"I won't," I said, taking Dad's lunch as well.

A few minutes later, Dad drove the truck out on Cottonwood Road toward the Jenkins' ranch. He hadn't said much, as he knew I preferred silence, but he was happy, smiling as he drove.

"Did I miss a good episode last night?" I asked.

"Nah, it was a repeat. I still watched it though." He grinned at me. "I guessed every price correctly."

I rolled my eyes. "I think you mean *remembered* every price correctly."

He laughed, then he pointed out the windshield, up on the left. "Oh, is that Winter's car?"

There was a small, blue SUV parked at the side of a house, steam billowing out from the exhaust. "Ah," Dad said, as if something made sense. "That's the Morgan's old place. I did hear that it sold."

Hmm.

"He said he lived out on Cottonwood Road," I added as we passed the house. I couldn't see him in his car—he must be warming it up, or maybe he forgot something and ran back inside with the engine still running—but I smiled, knowing it was his car, his house. "His aunt Ro wants to do it up, apparently. He said it needs some work."

"Ahhh," he said, nodding slowly. "I bet it does, but those old farmhouses sure are beautiful."

He was quiet then, looking over at me every few seconds, as if he wanted to say something but wasn't sure how to.

"So he lives with his aunt, huh?"

"Yes."

More silence, more sidelong glances.

"Do you have something you'd like to ask?"

He laughed, embarrassed. "Well, I just wanted to know how last night went, that's all. You seemed to enjoy it, and you're helping him again tonight . . ."

"I did enjoy it. I like cataloging and doing the inventory side of it. He showed me the computer system for entering the stock items. The software has a huge database. If you enter in the ISBN, it brings up all the information, and I would put in the stock amount so he knows how many copies he has of each book, and you can order more when it gets low, or if a customer requests a particular book."

"That sounds great," Dad said. "A bit similar to ours, but with books instead of medicine and equipment."

I nodded. "He said I picked it up really fast."

Dad grinned at me followed by more silence and more sidelong glances. "So," he hedged as we slowed down to enter through the Jenkins' gate. "Is he seeing anyone? Is he single?"

I shot him a look, heat crawling up my face. "That . . . How would I know? That's not an appropriate thing to ask."

"Sure it is," he replied. "You can just ask in general conversation. Getting to know someone involves asking questions; otherwise, how are you expected to know? Like what his favorite book is, which movie did he like, where he lived before moving here, if he's dating anyone, that kind of thing."

I shook my head, feeling uneasy at the thought.

Because what if he is seeing someone? What if he does have a boyfriend, or a girlfriend?

And more importantly, why didn't I think of that before?

He very likely would have a boyfriend or girlfriend. Of course he would.

"Oh." I wiped my hands on my thighs, and my tummy ache was back.

Dad pulled the truck up to a stop at the side of the Jenkins' house, just as Col Jenkins came outside.

"No time to dwell on those things now," Dad said. "We've got work to do."

❄

BEING BUSY HELPED—AND we were busy all day, which I'm sure Dad did on purpose—but every so often my mind would drift back to Winter and asking him if he was single, and my tummy would feel all blah again.

I didn't like that feeling.

But not having a minute's break all day gave me less time to think, and overthink, and get myself into a state. Making me focus on other things was the only way to stop me from focusing on Winter. Usually the more I tried to not think about something, the more my brain latched onto it. So Dad kept me busy with full lists of things to do all day long—appointments, rechecking stock numbers, ordering, and cleaning—right up until it was past closing time.

We were late for dinner and basically walked inside and sat at the dining table with Dad still recounting his day and asking my opinion on each case, not giving me a chance to think about anything else.

Until it was time to leave.

Mom fixed my coat at the door. "You have fun," she said.

"I think Dad's tired himself out today by trying to keep me occupied," I whispered. "He'll be asleep in his chair soon."

Mom laughed and handed me my beanie. "I think so too."

"I should be home around ten," I said. "Please leave the kitchen light on."

"Okay, love. Drive carefully."

"Always do."

And wow, the temperature had dropped a lot. I parked on Main Street and began walking down Short Street. I quickly pulled my gloves on, wondering if Winter had gloves with him. That was something I could ask him. Another thing in my ever-growing list of things I should ask.

Small talk made me uncomfortable, but Dad was right. It was part of the getting-to-know-someone stage, and of course friends asked friends questions. Otherwise how would we know if we were even friends?

What if he liked things I couldn't stand?

What if he believed in things that didn't sit well with me? Like, what if he cared about money more than people? Although he seemed very kind to me, and he was caring by nature. I'd seen that with how he adopted Merry and Bright and cared for them.

What if he hated things that I loved?

Well, I already knew he loved the same book as me. And our TV show.

But what if he didn't like Tolkien or Tolstoy?

What if he didn't like pancakes?

What if he wasn't single?

What if he had a girlfriend or a boyfriend? What if he was straight? That would be fine. I knew a lot of straight people, and I liked them just fine. But what if he didn't like gay people? What if he . . . ? Oh god, what if he laughed at me or sneered at me in disgust? What if he asked me to leave and never see him again?

What if he . . . ?

I was at the door to the bookstore but I couldn't bring myself to knock. Maybe I should go home. Going home would be good. Maybe I should—

The door opened, and Winter stood there, smiling at me. "Hey," he said. Then he frowned. "What's wrong? Deacon? Are you okay? Come inside out of the dreadful cold."

He ushered me inside where it was nice and warm and closed the door behind me. Then he stood in front of me, his eyes wide and full of concern. "Did something happen? Are you okay?"

I shook my head, then squinted my eyes shut, seeing if everything was better when I opened them again. Winter was still looking at me, still standing very close, not touching me, but his hand was out as if he'd like to. "I just . . ." I licked my lips and started again. "I have questions and I've been trying not to think of them all day, but on the drive here, I thought of so many I should ask you and it overloaded my brain. Some of them not good. I'm sorry. I should go home."

I expected him to look at me as if I was the weirdest person he'd ever met—it wouldn't be the first time people looked at me like that—but no, there was only kindness and understanding.

"I was just making hot chocolate," he said. "Would you like some?"

He was offering me hot chocolate? That wasn't what I expected, but the change of direction was good for me.

And I really liked hot chocolate.

"Then afterwards if you still want to go home, you can," he said. "Come through to the storeroom. It actually looks like a storeroom now, not a warehouse for cardboard boxes."

I noticed then that most of the boxes were gone, most of the shelves were full, and it now resembled an actual bookstore.

It made me feel better. Somehow. *He* made me feel better.

"You got a lot done today," I said.

"Well, most of it was with you last night. Today was mostly organizing and tidying, which helped. We only have those boxes to go through tonight," he said, nodding to the boxes on and under the table. There seemed to be more signage on the shelves and stands on the service counter with bookmarks and fun trinkets.

"Is that *Howl's Moving Castle*?" I asked, going over to the small boxes of collectible characters.

"Yes, do you like it?" he asked from inside the storeroom.

"The movie, yes."

He came out holding a mug of hot chocolate. "You haven't read the book?"

I shook my head. "No. I did know it was a book but I haven't read it."

He handed me the mug. It was warm to hold, but not hot. "Oh, you must read it. I have a copy at home. I'll let you borrow it."

I thought about that. "That doesn't seem like a good attitude for your business," I said. "You should tell me to buy it."

He laughed. "Well, yes, but it's okay for friends to lend books, right? As long as you be kind to the book and don't dog-ear the pages, it'll be fine."

My eyes went wide. "I would never."

He grinned, his hand to his chest. "Oh, I'm so relieved to hear that. Not sure I could be friends with someone who does." Then he winked as if to tell me he might be joking.

But he'd called me a friend.

I liked that. It felt nice. Even though I might want to like him more than a friend, being friends was still good.

He came back out with his mug of hot chocolate. "Ro took Merry and Bright home. You just missed her. She said to say hello."

I nodded, but something he'd said caught my attention. "You call her by her first name?"

"I do. She is my aunt. My mother's sister. But I'm closer to her than I am to my mother. She's been on my side since I was very little, and she's younger than my mom. She said me calling her *Aunt* Ro made her feel old. Plus, she's more like a best friend or an older sister than my aunt."

I nodded again, processing that. "I have two aunts," I supplied. "On my dad's side. And two uncles on my mom's side."

"Nice," he said like he meant it. "How's your hot chocolate?"

I forgot I was holding it, so I sipped it. It was warm and sweet. "Good," I said. "It's very good. And sweet."

His eyes met mine. "I love sweet things."

It made me feel all tingly and swoopy. Like a bellyache, but a pleasant one.

He took a sip of his own. "I love hot chocolate at night," he said. "Coffee in the morning, though."

"Same."

I realized then that, along with the good feeling, I also felt at ease; all my worries from before were gone. I also realized that he was giving me information, details about himself, without me asking questions.

"I'm not very good at conversation," I said. "My dad said I should ask you questions if I wanted to know something."

"I'll let you in on a secret of mine," he said. "I'm not very good at conversations either."

I looked at him then, and it made me laugh, because he was smiling at me. "It's not a secret because it's not true," I said. "You're very good at conversations. You make me feel at ease. I'm not anxious like I was before. I almost went home, and now I don't want to."

He grinned at me. "I'm glad to hear that. Being anxious is not a nice feeling. And I think you're good at conversations. Look at us talking right now."

I laughed and sipped my hot chocolate.

"Did you still have any questions you wanted to ask

me?" He looked at me curiously. Kindly. "You can ask me anything you want to know. I won't mind."

Hmm.

I made a face because now I wasn't sure. In the end, I shook my head. I didn't want to ruin anything.

"That's okay," he offered, as if he wasn't bothered at all. "Just know that it's okay. You can ask me anything when you're ready."

I nodded and drank some more. "Do you value money over people?"

He stared at me, his mug stopping halfway to his mouth. He blinked and then he chuckled. "Okay, so I thought you were going to ask me what my favorite color is."

"Oh." I grimaced. "Well, yes. Favorite color too, I guess. It occurred to me earlier that if we are friends, then I should know important things because I don't think I can be friends with someone who doesn't value the same things I do. But I also think someone who is kind and thoughtful wouldn't be a bad person. And I think you're kind and you care for Merry and Bright, even though you're busy."

His smile widened and he sighed. "I think being a good person is very important. I think we should be the kindness we want to see in the world, and I would always value people the most. I also don't think I could be friends with someone who doesn't share my values, so we have that in common too."

I was so relieved. I'd assumed as much, but it was still good to hear him say it.

"And orange," he added. "My favorite color is orange."

I found myself grinning, so very happy. My tummy was jittery again but in a good way. "I like green," I said. "Phthalo green, specifically. Though all greens are good."

He nodded thoughtfully. "That is an *excellent* choice."

"Phthalo is short for phthalocyanine, which are a family

of blue and green synthetic organic pigments based on variants of copper phthalocyanine, a deep blue compound produced by the reaction of phthalic anhydride, urea, copper, and ammonia."

"I didn't know that."

Not many people did. Probably.

"Do you like animals?"

He brightened. "I love animals." Then he stopped and made a face. "Okay, so I'm not a fan of frogs. I'll just have you know that if I encounter an unexpected frog, they may hear my screams on the International Space Station. So, animals in general, yes. Frogs are a no."

I chuckled. "Frogs are cute."

He shuddered. "Frogs are slimy and unpredictable. Their legs are absurd and they stick to things with their little suction cupped feet."

He made me laugh.

"Do you have any pets? As a vet, I'd imagine you'd have a menagerie."

"We have a dog. Her name is Mildred. She was surrendered to the clinic for euthanasia but Dad said we'd take her."

Winter put his hand to his heart. "Oh my heart."

"We don't have a menagerie," I added. "We had a cat but he died two years ago. We'll wait until we get another surrendered animal, probably."

"Or like me, when you orphan two kittens," he said, grimacing. "But you treat animals of all kinds? You mentioned ferrets the other day."

"Yes. All kinds. Mostly cats and dogs, and livestock, of course. Some alpacas. But there are rabbits, gerbils, ferrets, birds."

"Hmm," he said. "Okay, so I like birds as long as they don't come near me. I'm not good with the flappy wings."

I was still smiling at him, still surprised by how comfortable I was with him. "It sounds to me like you just don't like unpredictability. Frogs, birds tend to move erratically."

He stared at me, then began to nod slowly. "I think you're right. I've never really thought of it like that."

My tummy swooped again, and that nice jittery feeling flittered through me. I couldn't look at him though. It was too honest, too exposing, and it made the pleasant feeling turn sour.

"Well, we should get started," he said brightly. He nodded to my cup. "Are you done? Or not yet?"

I looked at the hot chocolate, seeing I still had some left, but I didn't want to risk drinking it. My tummy was too sensitive. "I've had enough," I said, handing him the cup.

I hated that I was nervous again. It was a yo-yo of feelings, relaxed to nervous every other minute. And I knew why. I needed to ask him that question. The question I couldn't stop thinking about, even though the answer scared me more than not knowing.

Once I'd started thinking about it, I couldn't stop. It was all I could think about, and I knew it would come out eventually.

It always did.

"You okay?" Winter asked, concerned. "You're nervous again."

I grimaced. "Yes. See, once I get something in my head, it has to come out. The less I try to think about it, the more I can't stop thinking about it."

"Okay," he said with a patient smile. "Is it the questions you wanted to ask me?"

"Yes." My hands were fists, my nails biting into my palms. I opened and closed them a few times and it helped. "I wish I wasn't like this."

He made a sad face and came to stand in front of me,

looking into my eyes. I tried to look anywhere else, but then he reached out and put his hand on my arm. "Deacon."

I pulled back. "No."

His eyes went wide and he took a step back, his hands up, palms forward, as if I was like Mr. Jenkins' skittish horse. "I'm sorry. I should have asked permission."

"I don't like it," I said quickly. "Being touched."

"I'm sorry," he said again. "I didn't mean to upset you. I should have asked first, and if I'd known, I certainly wouldn't have."

I tried to lock down the urge to run away, and I took in a deep breath. I'd been in this situation a hundred times—people were so touchy-feely without a second thought. A hand on the arm, the shoulder, a handshake.

I shuddered as I remembered my time at college when Marcus Hardwick had kissed me without warning.

It hadn't ended well.

At all.

"It's okay," I tried. I didn't want Winter to feel bad. He hadn't done anything wrong. Not really.

"No, it's not okay," he said. "I should have asked first. Maybe we could ask each other what we like and what we don't like. What makes us uncomfortable, so we know not to do that. Would that help?"

It took a second for me to repeat in my mind what he said. I nodded. "Yes. That would help."

"Okay, I'll go first," he said. "I don't like loud noise I can't control. If it's my music, that's okay, because I can have it as loud as I like. But if it's someone else's loud music, I don't like that. I can't control their noise, and I get agitated."

"Like when you're on the bus and someone listens to music without headphones."

"Yes!" he said, smiling. "Exactly."

"I don't like that either."

"Okay, your turn," he said, smiling as if this was a game.

It somehow made it easier.

"I don't like being touched," I said, which he already knew. "But it's okay if I do it or if I expect it. Like if Dad pats my shoulder, that's okay."

He smiled. "If you can control it," he said. "Like the noise. And if you trust that person not to overstep."

I hadn't really thought of it like that, but yes.

"It's not easy for me," I said. "And people don't understand. I make them uncomfortable."

He frowned now. "Sounds to me like they weren't the right people for you. Real friends would understand."

I shook my head. "People at college made fun of me."

"Oh, Deacon, I'm so sorry."

"In my first year, I went to a party. My first real party. But the music was too loud, and the room was too crowded and hot. Most people were drunk, and I made myself stay because I wanted people to like me and to have friends, but Marcus Hardwick kissed me and I freaked out so bad, Lacey and Jessica had to take me home."

Winter's face was one of shock. "Oh, Deacon, I'm so sorry. He shouldn't have done that. That's not acceptable behavior."

"He said later he just thought I was shy. He didn't know I was . . ." My tummy ache was back. "He thought I liked him, so he was . . ." I made a face. "There were a lot of people kissing at that party and he thought that's what I was there for."

"I remember those college parties," he said gently. "I only went to one. I left early and never went to another one."

"I did like him, but not after that," I admitted. My face felt like it was burning. "I do like guys. I'm gay. But I . . . I have never . . ."

He smiled and chased my gaze until I looked at him. "I like guys too. I'm gay as well. But I'm asexual. I don't want—"

"Asexual?" I asked, stunned. I looked him up and down, so confused. "How?"

He wasn't smiling now, and I knew I'd said the wrong thing. Like I often did. But I was still so stunned. How was it possible?

"What do you mean how?" he asked. He took a step back, his face sad. "I thought you'd understand. I'm sorry if you think there's something wrong with that."

Wrong with it?

"It's not wrong," I replied. I'd hurt his feelings, I could see that, and it was the last thing I'd wanted to do. I quickly clarified. "It's just not that common in the animal kingdom, and certainly not common in vertebrates. Well, there are Komodo dragons, of course, and certain sharks. I've read about it in my studies. The ability to reproduce through parthenogenesis—"

"Wait, what?" He stared at me, eyes wide. Then he realized something and waved his hands and let out a laugh. "Oh. Oh. Not that kind of asexual. Not asexual reproduction or biology. That's not . . . that's not what I meant. I forgot you're a vet. Of course your mind would go there."

Well, now I was just straight up confused. "What?"

"Asexual, as in doesn't experience sexual attraction or sexual feelings. That's what I meant. I've never experienced sexual desire."

I stared at him, my cheeks burning. "Oh. I'm . . . I'm not familiar with that . . ."

But he was smiling again, thank goodness. "That's okay. It just means that while I feel a romantic attraction to guys, I have no desire to have sex with them. I've never looked at anyone and thought, 'Gee, I'd like to have sex with them.'"

Oh.

Oh my . . .

I thought my face might actually catch fire. "Sex." I shook my head. "That's . . . That's . . ."

I was so mortified, I couldn't even get a sentence out.

Winter chuckled. "It's okay, Deacon. Does that embarrass you? I'm sorry."

I was so conflicted. I needed this conversation to end, but I didn't want to leave. Tonight had been a roller coaster, but it also felt as if I'd taken a big step forward.

I looked at the boxes still yet to be unpacked. "We have more cataloging to do. We should do that." I checked my watch. "We've already wasted a lot of time."

Winter nodded, but he was smiling as if me not running out of there made him happy. "Good idea."

I tried to relax, the cataloging, the inventory, the repetitiveness was methodical for me. Yet I kept thinking about what he'd said.

He was asexual, but not in the biological sense. I'd definitely have to read up on that so I could better understand.

He said it meant he didn't feel sexual attraction.

I wasn't entirely sure what that was either. I knew what the textbook definition would say, but had I ever experienced that? I wasn't sure.

I didn't want to have sex with anyone.

I didn't want them to touch me.

I knew sex was supposed to feel good. I knew when I touched myself, it felt good. I could do that well enough. Not that I did that often.

Did I want to do that with Winter? Did I want him to touch me like that?

The idea was . . . overwhelming. Too overwhelming.

I could picture that in my head, and it made those jittery feelings sink lower than my belly.

Oh.

I stood up and away from the computer. "I need to go now," I blurted out.

Winter turned to me, books in hand, his eyes wide. "Oh, sure. Is everything okay?"

I blinked, trying not to think about how my body felt so wrong. Wrong size, wrong shape, and wrong temperature. Too hot. "I need to go home now," I said, taking my coat from where it was slung over the counter. I checked my watch. It was 9:42 p.m., almost time to leave anyway, and we were almost done with the last box of books.

"Deacon, are you okay?" he asked, coming over to me.

I put my hand up, stopping him from coming closer. "Yes. I'm . . . fine. I just . . ." I shook my head. There was no way I was telling him what was actually wrong. I pulled on my coat and opened the front door; the cold air cleared my head a little. The shock of it felt nice.

A relief.

I spared a glance at Winter before I left. He seemed confused and concerned, but he lifted his hand as if to wave me off. Then, remembering something from earlier, I took my gloves from my coat pocket and put them on the closest shelf. "You should have these," I said. "I meant to ask. One of my questions . . ."

That I never got around to asking.

I couldn't look at him though. So I ducked my head and ran to my truck.

CHAPTER SEVEN

WINTER

Winter

"WHAT DO you mean he freaked out?" Ro asked.

I was doing the six a.m. kitten feed after nowhere near enough sleep.

I shrugged, helping Bright take the bottle. "If you'd calm down, you'd be drinking by now," I told him. "Goodness me."

"He might be ready for some solid food," Ro suggested.

Hmm, maybe. I'd have to ask . . .

I sighed. "I could ask Deacon, but after last night, I don't know." Then I remembered she'd asked me a question. "When he arrived, he was a bit panicky. I made him hot chocolate, which worked to calm him down a bit, and he admitted to overthinking."

"Oh, if only you could relate," she deadpanned.

I rolled my eyes. "I expect he's got me beat in the overthinking department. Anyway," I said, getting back to the story. "And he'd said he had questions for me, but he gets something in his head and can't let it go until he's either asked the question or found the answer. I don't know." I took a deep breath in. "He told me he likes guys. That he's gay."

She wiggled in her seat. "Oooh."

It was far too early for that. "And I told him I was too. And that I was asexual, which he assumed I meant biologically, that I could reproduce with myself."

She pressed her lips together so as not to smile.

I snorted. "That's okay. It was funny. After I realized what he'd assumed. He mentioned Komodo dragons, and I was like, what the heck?"

She chuckled, her hand to her mouth. "Oh, how I wish I'd been there."

I gave her a look that said, *Uhhh, no you don't.* "Then he shared a story from college where a guy had kissed him without permission and how greatly it had upset him."

She quickly frowned. "Oh, that's terrible."

"And then I went ahead and touched his arm, also without permission." I sighed, still mad at myself about that. "He doesn't like to be touched. Not without warning, at least."

"Oh." Ro shrugged. "That's fair enough. No one should touch anyone else without permission."

"I know," I said, defeated. "I was just trying to reassure him. I don't know. It was stupid."

Bright finished all his bottle, so I wiped his cute little mouth, put him carefully back into the basket, and fixed Merry's bottle. "Anyway," I continued. "After we cleared the air on that, by me deciding to play a little game of let's tell each other what we do and don't like, he was relaxed again."

"Until the asexual conversation."

I nodded, picked up little Merry, and sat back in my seat as he took his bottle. "Yes. Until then. He was fine, I thought. He did go a bit red when I mentioned sex, or the lack thereof, being asexual and all. But then he declared we should get work done, which we did. Then when we were almost finished, he shot up, flustered and panicky, and he bolted. Not before stopping long enough to leave his gloves with me in case I didn't have any."

"Aww." She gave me a sad smile. "Do you think the mention of sex was the trigger?"

I'd replayed the entire conversation in my head a hundred times instead of sleeping. "I think so, yeah. But that's just the point. I don't want that."

"But he probably sat there thinking about everything you'd said, thinking about sex, and . . ." She gave me a pointed look. "Maybe he thought about sex."

I groaned out a sigh. "It's such a mess. Maybe I'm not the one he should befriend. I don't want to upset or confuse him. It's just . . . he's so smart; he can pull facts and random tidbits of information out of nowhere. And he loves peace and quiet, and he loves books. I'll see him skimming pages and he likes to touch the pages. It's so adorable."

"You like him," she said.

"I do. But . . ." I sighed again. "It's complicated. He's complicated. And I'm so busy right now. It's got disaster written all over it. And I worry that he'll get hurt."

She studied me for a few long seconds. "I don't think he's that complicated. I think once you figure out his ebb and flow, you'll be fine."

"His ebb and flow?"

She gave me that patient smile that I knew prefixed some pearl of wisdom. "You know the Māori people of New Zealand have a word for autism. Takiwātanga. It means *in their own time and space.* I think that's beautiful." She patted my shoulder before putting her cup on the sink.

"You'll figure each other out, Win. In your own time and space."

I GOT TO THE STORE, still thinking about Ro's words, still thinking about Deacon, still thinking . . .

The problem was, I did like him.

I liked the quietness about him, the restraint. He was unassuming and unpretentious. There was no ego, no subterfuge. I doubt he'd ever told a lie in his life, and there was much to be said about that.

So yeah, I liked him.

And I could tell myself that a friendship with him would be great—and it would be—I'd be lying to myself if I said I didn't want more with him.

I wanted to sit somewhere cozy and read in blissful silence together. I wanted to cuddle on the couch with him and watch *Pride and Prejudice*. I wanted to hold his hand when he got overwhelmed with the world . . .

And that there was the problem.

That was very likely more than he could offer.

Which was fine. More than fine, actually. Because I certainly had limitations too. It'd be grossly hypocritical of me to blame Deacon for his boundaries in physical expressions of affection when I expected other men to respect mine.

So friendship it was.

And friendship was great. Not to be underestimated or taken for granted. I valued friendship first and foremost. I always had.

My very reasonable brain understood this.

My heart was just a little confused.

"Oh wow," Ro said, scaring the shit out of me. She was standing in the store, holding two cups of coffee to go, looking around at all the floor space that used to be boxes, looking at all the full shelves and signs. I hadn't heard her come in.

"Jesus," I breathed, hand to my thumping heart. "Make a noise or something next time."

"I called out," she said, handing me one of the cups. "You were too distracted."

Ugh. "Yeah, sorry."

"You got busy in here. Looks great."

"That's mostly Deacon's doing," I said. Given the inventory machine he was.

Her eyes softened, and I needed to not fall down that rabbit hole of misery, so I gestured to the one remaining, rather large box on the table. "Just the Christmas decorations to go. And there should be another delivery today, I think. Well, I hope. We can do another final test run of the point-of-sale system to triple check we're ready for our first day tomorrow, but it should be an early finish today." I shrugged. "I hope."

She gave my arm a reassuring squeeze. "You're more than ready."

It wasn't lost on me that such a simple gesture as touching my arm was what upset Deacon last night. Well, one of the things . . .

"It should be a more relaxed day, anyway," I said. Because I was ready. I was soooo ready for the store to be open.

I sipped my coffee and sighed at how good it was. "Did they sell out of the lemon scones already? Just wondering why you didn't buy any."

She snorted. "No, there was a whole cabinet of amazingness at the diner, but I thought we could close at lunchtime and have some downtime at the diner. It'll be the last time we get to do that for a while."

She was right, and I felt bad for not realizing that. "I'd love that."

Some rather loud and persistent meows came from the basket. "Oh, Bright," I said, not even having to see which of the kittens was yelling for a feed. Sure enough, he was trying to climb out. "Listen here, little mister," I said, scooping him up.

He was so stinking cute.

"They're growing like weeds," Ro said, giving him a little pat. "Oh, don't forget to ask Deacon about introducing some solid food."

My eyes met hers and I sighed. Right, yes. I had to speak to him.

"You have to speak to him at some point," she said gently. "He's their vet. And the longer you leave talking and clearing the air, the harder it will be."

I narrowed my eyes at her. "Do you have to work at being right all the time, or does it come naturally?"

She laughed at that. "Oh, darling. Rhetorical questions and sarcasm this early in the day wouldn't bode well. I should have ordered you a triple-shot latte."

Yes, yes she should have.

Being this tired before the store opened probably wouldn't bode well either.

As if she could read my mind, she put her coffee down and pulled the box of Christmas decorations over. "Okay, so for you to have an hour lunch break *and* an early night tonight, we need to get cracking. You feed the boys, and I'll start on this."

And so that's what we did.

Ro hummed happily as she took everything out and began to assemble the Christmas stands, and I gave Bright his much-demanded milk. When it was Merry's turn to be fed, I took out my phone and, assuming Deacon would be busy at work, I decided a text would be less intrusive and he could reply when he had time.

When he was ready.

> Hi, it's Winter. I have a question about introducing solid food. Mostly for Bright. I think he's ready but the internet has conflicting information. I wanted to ask you. When you have a moment to reply, that'd be great.

I sent it and let out a slow breath.

Then, realizing far too late, I hadn't mentioned anything about last night or even conveyed any niceties at all.

I should have said something.

Would he think I didn't care? Would he prefer I didn't mention it at all? Would he rather I never mention it at all, or would he want me to acknowledge it so he could get it off his mind without having to be the one to bring it up?

Ugh.

Why was this so hard?

Why was I overthinking every little thing?

Because you like him. Because you want to fix it. Because you like him.

Goddammit.

I quickly thumbed out another text.

> I hope you're okay after last night. If you want to talk about it, I'm here. If I did or said anything that upset you, please tell me so I don't do it again.

I hit Send before I could second-guess myself.

Gawd. Should I give him an out? I probably should . . . take the pressure off him.

> It's also okay if you'd rather not talk about it. I just worried that I'd done something wrong, but maybe it's not about me? Anyway, feel free to text me back or call. Either is fine.

I pressed Send again, hoping it sounded better.

Until I re-read it and realized I'd probably made it worse.

"Ugh," I grumbled. "This is ridiculous."

I thumbed out one quick and final text.

> I also never got a chance to say thank you for helping me last night. You're a good friend.

Send.

You're a good friend.

Cripes.

I couldn't believe I'd just texted him that.

"Why would I say that?" I mumbled, beginning to text again.

> Hey, so this is now getting embarrassing—

And Ro appeared beside me and took my phone out of my hand. "Just stop," she said gently.

"I didn't hit Send," I said, trying to peer at the screen.

She held the backspace button, deleting that last line. "You can thank me later."

I sagged with an agonized groan, giving little Merry a cuddle against my neck. "Why am I like this?"

She patted my shoulder. "The list is long."

I snorted out a laugh. "Thanks."

"He'll get back to you when he can," she said. "Now, put that little button back to bed and help me with this. We have less than five hours to get this done before their next feed, which will bring us up to a late but acceptable lunchtime."

I whined but did as she asked.

The Christmas display for the front window had cost me a small fortune, but it was going to look amazing. There was a fine line between not overcapitalizing and over-spending before the store had even opened and getting the presentation on point.

I wanted it to look amazing so customers could see the effort, and so they loved coming into the store. It was all about the aesthetic, the feel of the store. And this Christmas decoration was the cherry on top of the cake.

It was a miniature living room scene, complete with furniture and a rug on the floor, a Christmas tree with lights, a glowing fireplace, and books, of course.

The store window would be adorned with fake snow and garlands, and I wanted people to feel as if they were looking into a fairytale house where it was warm and cozy, where they were welcome.

But that also meant there was a bit of assembly required and making sure all the small lights worked and that every-thing was perfectly positioned.

I had to go outside a few times and direct Ro to move things half an inch here and there to ensure things were perfectly positioned. On the third time of me going out, Gunter came out across the street.

"Morning," he said brightly. When he got close, he looked at the display, then got a proper look inside, just as Ro turned all the little lights on. "Oh wow. That looks amazing."

I smiled proudly at the display. "It does, doesn't it?"

He peered in at the rest of the store. "It all looks great. Big opening day tomorrow, right?"

I nodded. "Yep. December first."

"Oh, that reminds me," he said. "Did you know about the lighting of the Christmas tree tomorrow?"

"No. What's that?"

"Oh, every December first they light the Christmas tree in the park by the river. The mayor welcomes everyone to the holidays and they light up the tree. It's kinda fun. The whole town comes along."

"But tomorrow is my opening day," I said. How could I not have known about this?

"Oh no, they light it up around seven at night. You might catch it after you lock up for the day." Then he shrugged. "We all go. Our group of friends." Then he leaned in and, with his hand hiding his mouth, said, "All us queer folk, that is. The whole gang. You've met a few of us but I can introduce you to everyone."

Oh.

That actually sounded nice.

"Sometimes we go to the diner or the pizzeria afterwards. Not sure what's happening tomorrow night though. It's fun, low-key."

Fun, low-key?

He must have noticed my picking up of his choice of vocabulary. He had to be close to fifty . . .

"I've been hanging out with the kids too much," he said with a laugh. "It doesn't make me feel old at all."

I'd seen kids coming and going, and when I looked over at the café, there were some faces peeking at us through the glass front. "I think we have an audience."

Gunter turned around and his face broke out in a smile. "They're very excited about your store," he said before he waved them over. "Come on, let's get this over with." Then he spoke out of the corner of his mouth. "Don't let them smell your fear."

Three teenagers burst out of the door, trying not to smile too big. You know, to appear cool and whatever. There was one guy and two girls. The first girl, who had blue hair and a nose ring, shoved her hands in her back pockets of her corduroy pants. "Hey," she said.

Gunter made quick introductions. "Evie, Holly, and Max."

"Hey guys," I replied. "My name's Winter. This is my store."

"Winter," Evie repeated, nodding approvingly. "Cool name."

"I have thirteen years of school-yard trauma that would disagree, but thanks."

Gunter chuckled, but then he gestured to the front window display. "What do you guys think of this?"

They all went to the window, and from the noises they made, I think they approved.

Aunt Ro stuck her head out the door, smiling brightly at them. "Hello!"

Now, everyone loved Ro. She wore bright colors, had cool gray curly hair, bright heavy rimmed glasses and lipstick, and her entire vibe was approachable and fun. These three teens were no exception.

"Hi," they chorused, more enthusiastically than they'd greeted me.

"Who wants to see something really cool?" Ro asked, then produced the laundry basket.

They stared at her.

But then the blankets rustled and Bright stuck his head out and gave the cutest little meow ever.

The three kids squealed and swarmed Ro. "Come in out of the cold," she said, and they all disappeared inside.

"Ah, the little rescues," Gunter said. "How are they doing?"

"Yeah, growing like weeds, or so Ro said."

"You're keeping them?"

"Yep. I did feel obligated because, you know." I grimaced. "I was the one to orphan them. But they've grown on me. I could do without the lack of sleep though."

He laughed. "I bet. They got names?"

"Merry and Bright."

He grinned. "Very festive."

"Deacon named them. It was written on the box I took them to the vet in. If it were up to me, I'd have probably called them Mr. Darcy and Heathcliff or something else just as literarily insufferable and conceited. Merry and Bright suits them."

His eyes met mine, and he nodded slowly, smiling. "And how are things with Deacon?"

I groaned. "Ugh. I don't know. I would have said going well, but then last night I think I upset him. I'm not entirely sure what that was. Well, there were a few things, which I won't bore you with, but anyway, he left rather abruptly, and I may have sent a barrage of apologetic texts this morning until Ro confiscated my phone." I patted down my pockets, finding nothing but keys. "I should check to see if he replied."

"Ah, I see. So things aren't going that well."

I sighed and shrugged with as much disappointment and pity as I could muster. "I wouldn't think so, no."

"Okay, well, crap," he mumbled, seeing a man walking toward us. Gunter turned to block him from my view. "Because here comes his father."

Then he turned and greeted him, and yes, I could see

now that it was, in fact, Deacon's father. They looked a lot alike. Gunter held out his hand with a bright smile. "Wayne," he said. "Good to see you again."

"Yes, same," he replied to him before eyeing me nervously.

"Do you know Winter?" Gunter asked.

"Yes, we've met," Wayne said. "At the clinic."

"Oh, of course," Gunter said. "The kittens."

"Hi," I said, feeling suddenly very nervous and possibly nauseous.

"Can we have a little chat?" Wayne asked. "I know you're busy, but I won't take much of your time. A few minutes, that's all."

"Oh." I tried to swallow. "Is . . . is everything okay?"

He smiled. "It is. Nothing bad. I didn't mean to scare you or anything."

I made a face. Well, more of a face than I was already making. "Am I that obvious?"

Gunter snorted and clapped my shoulder. "I'll go wrangle these kids," he said, opening the door to my store. "Come on, guys, we have a café to open."

There were a few protests, most of which I think was actually Ro, but the three kids soon filed out and went back across the road with Gunter.

I gestured to the door. "Should we go inside?"

He nodded, and I held the door open for him and followed him inside. There were very quick introductions to Ro, and with a big, somewhat-fake smile, she bundled up Merry and Bright in their blankets, picked up the basket, and carried it to the door. "I'll just be over with the kids," she said, and was gone.

I watched as she headed straight over to the youth clinic, and when I plucked up enough courage to actually look at the man beside me, he appeared to be just as nervous as me.

"Mr. Clark," I began.

"Please, call me Wayne."

"Wayne," I amended. "I can guess why you're here. And I'm really sorry. I don't know what I did or what I said, but Deacon left here last night in a hurry, and I think he was upset—"

He put his hand up and smiled. "It's okay. He was agitated when he got home, yes. But he didn't want to talk about it, so that was that. There's no point in pushing because it just upsets him. Then this morning he said some things . . ." He paused and his eyes met mine. "Uh, I probably should have started this conversation at the beginning. You are aware Deacon has autism, yes?"

I nodded.

He sighed out a chuckle. "Phew. Thought for a minute I had to back up the info dump some more. He's a great kid —" He made a face. "Well, he's not a kid. He's a grown man. But I just wanted to come down and have a chat. If Deac knew I was here, he'd be royally pissed."

He clearly loved his son very much, and it made me smile. "I won't tell him."

His eyes met mine. "He likes you." Then he put his hands up. "Now, I don't need to know your personal business."

"I'm gay," I said, letting him off the hook. "Just putting it out there."

"Oh," he said. "Good. I mean, that's good. Because he is too. Not that it was ever anything he came out and told us. He was never interested in anyone for a long time, not like that anyway, but as he got older, he always got flustered around the boys and never the girls, so we kinda assumed . . ." Then he sighed. "Then he went to college and there was an incident with another guy that, well, it more than upset him. He almost quit school."

"He told me," I said. "Some guy kissed him without asking."

He seemed surprised that I knew, but he nodded. "We've always taught him about the importance of consent, because sometimes people can give mixed signals, which is very confusing for him, so asking is always important. And anyway, long story short, after we talked about it, it was clear that he had liked that boy, and then he told us, yes, he does like guys. That was never an issue for us." He looked me dead in the eye as if he needed me to see his sincerity. "I need you to know that. We don't care who he likes."

Oh god. Was this about to be a conversation about the birds and the bees?

Well, just the birds. Or just the bees. I never really understood that analogy. One was the pollinator, so—

"Anyway," he said, getting my attention.

"Yes, sorry. I am listening."

"You look a little horrified," he said. "I'm sorry if this is embarrassing."

"No, no. Uh, you said Deacon said something this morning? About what upset him last night?"

He sighed, grateful, I think, that I was helping to move the conversation along. "Yes. He said you talked about sex."

"Oh, dear god, no."

"But then he mentioned Komodo dragons and starfish. Not entirely sure what that was about."

I buried my face in my hands. "Oh, dear heavens."

"Yeah, I was a bit lost on that too."

I looked at him then and put my hand on his arm. "I'm asexual. That's what that is. When you said we were talking about sex, we were talking about not having sex. How I don't feel sexual attraction, so whatever horrifying scenarios you were envisaging, it was the opposite of that."

He stared. "Oh."

"When I said asexual, he automatically assumed asexual reproduction."

Wayne stared some more, then barked out a laugh, his hand to his mouth. "Oh my god, I'm so sorry." Then he laughed some more, pure relief, if I had to guess.

I couldn't help it. I laughed too. I mean, it was kinda funny. Now.

It wasn't funny last night.

He nodded. "Oh, well, that explains the . . ."

"Komodo dragons and starfish." I nodded too. "Yep. So for a few horrifying seconds there, he thought I had the ability to reproduce with myself."

He laughed again. "Shoot, I'm sorry."

I waved his apology off. "It's fine. We cleared the air. On that matter anyway." I sighed then. "But I did touch his arm, just like this." I showed him how I'd done it. Hell, I'd touched his arm a few seconds ago. "And that upset him. That was before the asexual conversation though, and I thought we got past that."

"Yeah, he doesn't deal with touch very well."

"I learned that, yeah."

He let out a sigh. "Look, Winter, I'm going to be very frank with you and I don't know how you feel about him, but he likes you. As in, he *likes* you. So if you're not on the same page as that, or don't think you ever could be, we'll need to be clear about what we tell him. I don't expect you to answer right away. I mean, you've just met him, just moved here, been super busy getting the store ready." He looked around. "Looks great, by the way."

"Thanks."

"I guess I wanted to come see you and, one, ask about what happened last night, and two, just see . . . well, I didn't know what else, to be honest. I just wanted to let you know where he's at. He's not like most other guys, so even as his friend, I wanted to catch you up, I guess. He might take some patience, that's all."

"I do like him," I said, then scrubbed a hand over my face, feeling the heat in my cheeks. "I do like him. He's smart and funny, and he quoted one of my favorite books to me the very first time we'd met. I mean," I shrugged. "Kinda sealed the deal right from the get-go."

He smiled, a real smile if the creases at the corners of his eyes were anything to go by. "He is smart and funny," he repeated. "Not many people take the time to get to know him, so thank you for saying that."

"Well, they're missing out on knowing a great guy." I shrugged. "But I have to say, I *am* busy. Grand opening is tomorrow, and I'm hoping December will be a super busy time for me. Plus, I now have two kittens . . ." That reminded me. "Oh, I texted Deacon earlier and asked about introducing solids because I think Bright is ready. Not sure about Merry, but Bright, definitely. And—"

"I know you texted him," he said. "He was smiling at his phone for a good hour. I'm running out of stock and inventory tasks at work to keep him distracted. Keep him busy and he's a workhorse, but let him get all up in his head, and it can spiral pretty quickly."

I chuckled at that and put my hand up. "Also guilty." Then I looked around for my phone. "Aunt Ro took my phone away from me before I could send him another text, because apparently ten in a row was too many, and I don't know where she put it."

"Well, if you wanted to come around this afternoon, to

the clinic, I'm sure he'll be happy to see you," Wayne said. "I mean, you have both kittens with you, yes?"

I nodded to the youth center across the way. "I believe the town's teenagers are spoiling them rotten as we speak."

He smiled as he nodded, then he chewed on his bottom lip, nervous for what he was clearly about to say.

Oh god.

"I should let you get back to it," he said. "And they're probably wondering where I am. I was only going to the post office."

Well, that wasn't bad . . .

"Look," he said quietly, grimacing. "Please don't think too much about me coming to see you. I don't want you to feel pressured at all, because there is no pressure. None whatsoever. And I'm not being a weird parent, honestly. I just . . . I just didn't want you to think any less of Deacon after he left last night; I thought I might have to explain the situation, so I'm glad you understand." He shrugged. "I just want him to be happy."

Gawd.

"If only all gay kids had a dad like you," I said. I certainly didn't. Not a mother, either. But I did have Ro.

Maybe it was the lighting, I wasn't sure, but his eyes seemed a little glassy. "Thank you," he said. Then he let out a breath and headed for the door. "Thanks again, and good luck with the grand opening tomorrow. We'll be down in the afternoon." Then he stopped and held my gaze. "If you're going to the Christmas tree lighting tomorrow night, we'll see you there."

I nodded. "I'd like to. Gunter mentioned it. I hear it's quite the event."

He smiled as he looked up the street. "It's a great little town. I hope you like it here."

He left after that, and I stood there for a moment, trying to process what I felt.

Happy, grateful. Respect.

Confused.

About how I felt about Deacon. About what I should do.

With a heavy sigh, I went in search of my phone, finding it in the storeroom. There were messages from Deacon.

> Hello.

> I'm sorry I left early. Did you get the last boxes done last night? I can help again tonight if you need. Please let me know.

> Yes or no is fine.

> Tomorrow is the big grand opening day. I would like a copy of Never Let Me Go by Sir Kazuo Ishiguro and I know you have two. Please don't sell both before I get there.

That made me smile.

> Texting is sometimes easier for me.

> Regarding introducing solid foods to Bright, I'm sure he's ready however if you'd prefer me to check the emergence of his premolars, I'm happy to do that and I can also monitor his intake and ability to chew and swallow effectively.

> I have some samples at the clinic and I'm more than happy to discuss options for him. Any time which suits you is also fine.

> Also Merry too. He may be more ready than you think.

I look forward to your reply.

Thank you for messaging me first.

I was still standing there, smiling at my phone, when Ro came back in. "So," she said smugly. "I take it that went well."

It took me a moment to realize she didn't have the kittens. "Where are the boys?"

"Calm down, Dad," she said, rolling her eyes. "Evie has them well taken care of. We're leaving them with her while we go and have some lunch."

I opened my mouth to protest but she put her hand up. "Relax," she said. "Evie's own cat has had two litters and she's very adept at caring for them. Plus, it's good practice for tomorrow."

I stared at her. "What's happening tomorrow?"

"She's minding the boys tomorrow, all day." She ignored the look of horror on my face. "We're going to be far too busy and will not have the time to stop every time they make a sound."

Well, that was aimed directly at me. "I don't fuss over them every time they make a sound." She deadass looked at me until I revoked that claim. "Okay, so maybe I do. But they're so little and helpless, and it's only been a handful of days and I already cannot imagine my life without them."

She chuckled and collected her scarf. "Okay, let's go to the diner for lunch and you can tell me everything that you and Deacon's father talked about."

I FELT MUCH BETTER after a long lunch with Ro. She listened to me, nodded, and smiled patiently as I told her everything, and I was ever so grateful. She'd never once been anything but supportive, much like Deacon's father was with him. It made me appreciate Ro even more.

I couldn't imagine where I'd be without her.

"I should totally cook us dinner tonight," I said. "Given it'll be the last chance I get for a week or so, at least. Or until I get a routine at the store." I fully expected some late nights, particularly in this first week.

Well, I hoped I would.

I needed to be busy. I needed this to be a success.

"Orrr," Ro said. "And hear me out on this, we could totally order pizza, grab some wine, and have a totally chill night before your life changes forever."

"My life won't change forever," I countered.

"Win, you'll be a fully-fledged bookstore owner, small business owner, marketing manager, cleaner, accounts manager, social media manager, public relations—"

"Okay, okay," I relented with a laugh. "Pizza it is."

"Plus," she added, "you won't have time because you need to take the boys to the vet clinic on the way home so Daddy Deacon can look at them."

"What we're not going to do is call him that," I said flatly, because dear god. "Ever again."

"I thought it was fun. Pairs nicely with Papa Win."

I stared at her. "I will pay you actual money to never say that again."

"Just kidding," she said with a laugh. "You can pay for lunch though."

"Deal."

She pulled on her coat, then collected her purse and scarf. "Did you need to see Jayden about tomorrow?"

"Nope. It's all organized."

We waved to Jayden as we were leaving. "See ya tomorrow," he called out.

We turned for the door and literally ran into Hamish from the hardware store as he was coming in. "Hello again," I said, giving him some room.

"Oh, hi," he said, brightly, giving us a killer-watt grin. "Looking forward to tomorrow. We'll be there, don't you worry. Oh, and you must come to the lighting of the Christmas tree tomorrow night. I know you'll have had a crazy day, but it's a great way to meet everyone."

"I will," I said. "Given you're the third person to ask me, I think that's a sign that I should go."

He beamed at that, then he turned to Ro. He grabbed her hand but looked at me. "You never mentioned a gorgeous sister."

"Aunt," I corrected.

"Oh my goodness, I love you already," she said, her grin matching his, and it suddenly felt like I was in a Colgate commercial.

"Oh, good, I'll never hear the end of that," I mumbled, and Ro shushed me. Someone else tried to come through the door—a man wearing a deputy uniform who Hamish called Colson—so I took that as an escape route. "We should get going. It was good to see you again, Hamish."

"We'll see you tomorrow," he replied, already talking to Colson about something else.

As we made it to the sidewalk, Ro slid her arm in mine. "Is everyone in this town gay?" she asked.

"Statistically, I'd say that's unlikely."

She hummed. "But still. Statistically speaking, of course, I love that for us."

I laughed, both of us smiling all the way back to the store.

CHAPTER EIGHT
WINTER

I BUNDLED the boys and their basket into the vet clinic just after four. I hadn't made an official appointment, but both Deacon and Wayne had said to just turn up, so that's what I did.

Courtney, the receptionist, seemed very confused, but when Deacon came out and saw me, his smile damn near stole my breath. Courtney seemed to notice too, because she did a little wiggle in her seat when Deacon ushered me into the examination room.

Pretty sure Deacon didn't notice, but I did.

He was wearing his cute vet uniform and a huge smile, with flushed cheeks. "Is everything okay?" he asked.

"Yes, I'm fine, thanks."

He looked at the basket I was still holding. "I was talking about Merry and Bright."

"Oh." I snorted, because of course he was. "Yes. They're doing great! But I worry that Bright isn't getting enough to eat, and I was wondering about introducing solids."

"Your text messages," he said quietly.

"Yes. Sorry, I kept pressing Send and then I worried

that what I'd said could be taken a dozen different ways and—"

"You didn't reply to me."

I stopped. "Oh. I'm sorry. I got so busy. Well, first of all, Ro confiscated my phone for a while. We had to test the point-of-sale system again and the accounts program. It's all integrated, as you know. Of course you know; you've seen it. Anyway, I had some invoices to pay. I wanted to get them out of the way before I open tomorrow, and the accounting software should be automated but it wasn't automating. Anyway, I found the reason. It was totally my fault, which is not surprising in the least. God, I'll stop talking now."

He was staring past me, in that way that he does, his eyes darting to mine for a second before going back to the basket. He reached in, found Bright in his little warm hidey hole in the blankets.

"He looks bigger already," he said, and thus began the actual vet appointment. He weighed them both, checked them both over, asked all the questions about feeding and toileting. He was very happy with their progress. Even sweet little Merry passed with flying colors.

Deacon produced some samples of kitten food and showed me how to put a small amount on my finger and see if Bright was interested.

Oh boy, was he interested.

He made the cutest little savage noise as he munched on my finger. "Ow. Well, those little teeth sure work fine," I said, looking to see if he actually drew blood.

He hadn't, thankfully.

Deacon laughed as Bright went a bit feral looking for more of my tasty finger. "Oh yes, he's ready."

Then it was Merry's turn.

I put some on my finger. Merry's little eyes went wide and he licked at first, but then greedily gobbled it down, making the cutest little noises ever. "Ooh, gremlin mode activated," I said. "But he's still the sweet one. Bright's permanently in gremlin mode."

Deacon's smile was everything.

The way he held Bright made my heart so freaking happy.

He then showed me how to introduce more and more solid food over the next week, and noted that within two weeks they should be off the milk formula for good.

I was excited to hear that, even if it meant they were growing up so fast.

"I ordered one of those kiddie playpen things," I said. "Because they can't stay in the basket forever, and a bunch of different toys that simulate learning." I'd probably spent far too much money on them, but whatever. "It will fit in the storeroom at work if need be. Just while they're so little, it might have to be bring-your-kids-to-work days."

Deacon made sure they were both back in their blankets with the hot water bottle. "You're doing a great job with them."

"Thanks."

His cheeks went pink again. "You're wearing the scarf I gave you."

I patted the purple polar fleece. "I love it." Then I pulled the ends of it out of my sweater. "Even if the logo is a worming medication, the text is black, gray, and white, and those are the asexual flag colors. So you literally couldn't have picked a better scarf for me."

He ducked his head, his expression happy and shy. "I did some research on that."

"So I'm not like a Komodo dragon or a starfish anymore?"

He chuckled and shook his head. "No." Then he shrugged. "Unless you want to be."

"Uh, not particularly."

"I understand it better now."

"I'm glad. But if you have any questions, you can always just ask. I'm an open book."

The blush on his cheeks ran down his neck. "I like books."

Oh, damn.

"Me too." Wanting to leave on a good note, I picked up the basket. "I better get going. I'm having a chill evening with Ro before the big opening day tomorrow. It'll be an early start."

He held the exam room door for me. "I'll see you tomorrow."

"Oh, yes," I said, stopping at the reception desk. "The book you wanted. *Never Let Me Go* by Kazuo Ishiguro—"

"Sir. Sir Kazuo Ishiguro."

"Sorry, yes. Sir." I didn't even mind that he corrected me. "I'll be sure not to sell both copies. It's a great book, by the way."

He gave a nod. "It is. Perhaps you could order in a copy of *Howl's Moving Castle*. That way I won't need to borrow yours."

I grinned at him. "Perfect."

He gave a nod and stood there while I paid for my appointment and the stack of new kitten food I'd just bought. While I had my phone out, I found his text messages and thumbed out a quick reply.

Thank you for seeing me today

His phone beeped behind me, and when I got to the door, I turned to see him reading it, grinning at his screen.

It made my heart squeeze and thrum in the very best of ways. I was still grinning like a loon when I got home.

"Oh, someone looks very happy," Ro said as she took the basket from me.

I sighed dreamily. "I am."

"Things went well, I take it?"

"Yep. And you know what?" I put the pile of kitten food cans on the kitchen counter. "I think I've cracked the code."

"What code?"

"The Deacon Clark code."

She snorted. "I didn't realize he was some code that needed cracking but do go on."

"Not him," I amended. "He's not the code, but the code to maybe dating him."

She gasped. "Dating? Uh, hold up. Stop the phone and hold the press."

"Pretty sure that's not how that goes."

"What do you mean dating? You want to *date* him now? What happened to 'I'm not looking' and 'I'm not interested' and 'I don't have time' and 'I've sworn off men for all eternity'?"

I sighed. "Well, those things still apply. Kind of. And I did say 'maybe dating him,' not *actually* dating him."

"But you are," she said. "Considering dating him because you said you cracked the code."

"Well, maybe. I don't know." I turned and looked at her. "I like him. I do. He's cute as hell, and you should have seen him in his cute little vet uniform, and he blushed so hard. It was the most adorable thing ever. And the way he is with the boys. Oh my god."

"Okay, so I think we can safely assume we're well past the maybe-wanting-to-date-him stage, because Win, my dear, you are down bad already."

I chuckled. "And yet, less than twenty-four hours ago, I was sure there was no way."

"What changed?"

"I think I figured out where I went wrong."

"Ah, the dating-Deacon code. Do tell."

"That's just it. I think we need to actually date and not just hang out."

She stared at me for a good long while before she blinked. "Huh?"

"Courting. I'm going to court him, and maybe he'll court me back."

"You've read *Pride and Prejudice* too many times."

I laughed. "Never. But think about it. We can exchange pleasantries, small exchanges, nothing too big or overwhelming." Then I decided to go full Jane Austen. "We can take walks two feet apart at all times, hands behind our backs. The yearning will be masterful."

"Yes," Ro cried. "With an escort at all times. And should you be so bold to show some ankle, you'll be forced to walk the streets with a red *A* painted on your chest while the townsfolk throw mud and insults at you."

I laughed. "Not showing the ankle! Oh, the horror." I looked down at my socked feet. "Actually, if I ever show any part of my disturbingly pale legs in public willingly, please see it for the sign of duress that it is."

Ro chuckled but waited for me to continue, to explain.

"I don't know . . . I just think maybe we tried too hard in the beginning," I said. "We were trying so hard to be friends, but given we're both so awkward, it was a disaster. I think we need to grow closer organically. And become friends by getting to know each other in small amounts first. Does that make sense?"

Her eyes locked with mine and she nodded. "Totally."

"So maybe a coffee date first. I'm not sure. No, maybe not. More like a lunch break date. Short and sweet and simple." I shrugged, realizing that maybe it all sounded better in my head. "We exchanged a few texts today; that was fun. Then at the clinic, I saw him for all of ten minutes, and it was all sweet and shy. I think I learned more about him in those shorter interactions."

Ro made a face, and I knew she was about to impart something I didn't really want to hear.

"You learned about him in the longer interactions too," she said gently. "Where he panicked and left, or when there was a misunderstanding. That's also him. And there's nothing wrong with that, but try not to romanticize the shorter, sweet stuff. You will have to spend longer bouts of time with him if you want to date him."

"I know," I relented. And I did know what she was saying was true. "But if we have shorter mini-dates to begin with, I think we'll understand each other better, and he'll trust me more."

"I think he trusts you already."

"Maybe. But I want him to trust me to the point that if he does have questions, instead of overthinking and getting to a panicked state, he could talk to me. Ask me questions instead of being too shy, that kind of thing."

Ro afforded me a patient smile. "I can see that you do like him. Perhaps taking small steps is the right approach."

I let my head fall back with a groan. "I know the timing is bad. But Ro, if you could have seen him at the store last night. The way he stops and reads the blurbs on the back cover of a book, and how he smiles when it's something he likes. Or today, when I texted him back as I was leaving the vet clinic. His smile, my god, it just lights him up."

Just then, Bright crash-tackled Merry in their basket and they rumbled for a little while, just cute as hell. Merry even gave him as good as he got. "You show him, Merry," I said. "Don't let him bully you."

I looked to Ro to see if she was watching the cuteness,

but she was watching me. Her smile was softer now, more genuine. "You know what I think?"

I braced myself for more of her wisdom. "What do you think?"

"I think we need pizza and wine."

"Oh my god, yes. Great idea."

I WAS at the store early. I'd given the boys their breakfast, packed up their bag so Ro didn't have to worry about that when she brought them down later, and decided coffee from the diner was in order to get me through what I hoped would be a fantastically busy day.

My first day as a bookstore owner.

Hartbridge's very own Fox and Fables Bookstore.

I was dressed in my sensible and comfortable brown pants, with my sensible and comfortable loafers, a fawn-colored button-down, and my umber colored sweater vest that was mostly hidden by my big brown coat.

If fall colors were a person, it'd be me. Odd, given my name was Winter.

I was going to wear a bowtie but thought that might be overkill. I was nervous but oh so excited as I walked up the road and turned onto Main Street, my breath steamy plumes, and I stopped.

With snow on the ground and beams of sunlight cutting through the clean, crisp air as it came over the mountains, and all the cute storefronts and heritage awnings, it stopped me in my tracks.

It was so beautiful.

And I took it as a sign. There was no way today could be anything but amazing.

Jayden wasn't at the diner when I walked in, but

Crystal served me. "Morning," she said brightly. "Big day for you, huh?"

"Yes. I'm really excited," I said. "But mostly relieved that the wait is over."

"I bet. Everyone in town is excited. It's all they've been talking about."

That made me so freaking happy to hear. "Oh, thank you. I sure hope so anyway."

"What can I get for you?" she asked. "Your usual coffee order? Is your aunt Ro with you, or just the one?"

"Just the one for now. She'll be down later." Then I made the mistake of looking in the cabinet. "And I'd better have one of those bear claws."

She nodded sagely. "Wise choice. You'll need the sugar today."

"And a treadmill if I keep this up," I added, because oh lord, there were so many good things in this town.

She slid my order onto the counter and rang me up. "Don't forget they're lighting the Christmas tree tonight," she said. "And it's December first. Main Street gets all prettied up today."

"I just stopped out there before because of how pretty it was, with the snow and the sunbeams over the mountains. Like, how is this place even real?"

She laughed. "You haven't seen anything yet. Just you wait, when you close the store this evening, do yourself a favor and take a look at Main Street. You'll see what I mean. Christmas is coming to town. Santa will be here before we know it."

And I was so looking forward to it.

Christmas had always been a weird time for me. I would normally go see my mother for lunch, give her a gift, sometimes get one in return, and exchange pleasantries neither of us truly meant, before I'd then go spend the afternoon and dinner with Ro. She'd usually make some joke about how she should smudge me with burning sage, then we'd laugh and have a wonderful dinner together.

Just us.

And we'd done that for years. The first time had been when I was twelve and my mother had taken herself on a cruise over the holidays, leaving me with Ro. Ro had made sure it was the best Christmas ever—and it was—and every year thereafter, we'd made it our tradition.

But this year it was different.

We weren't in Boise anymore. We had no obligation to deal with the wicked witch of the west—as Ro had every right to call her sister—and we could enjoy the whole day together, just the two of us. The way it should be. Ro was the only motherly figure in my life, and I adored her with every fiber of my being.

I made a mental note on my way back to the store to begin a list of food that I could order to make for Ro's Christmas lunch.

She deserved something special this year.

Well, every year, but extra special this year. And a gift . . . *I need to think of a gift.*

A thought I put out of my mind as I readied the till, re-perfected the table display, made sure the mood music was at the perfect volume, and that the storeroom was tidy and the stock of all the super popular fiction books I'd been posting about on the store's website were easy to grab.

And the two copies I had of *Never Let Me Go* were still there. Was it likely I'd sell both copies today? No. Was it possible? Maybe.

At least, I reasoned, it'd be amazing if I did.

With that in mind, I took one copy and popped it behind the counter, wrote his name on a holding card, and slipped it inside at the top.

Ro arrived just after eight-thirty, coming in through the back door with the basket of two very bright-eyed little white-and-ginger monsters trying to escape from their blankets, and not ten seconds later, Evie knocked on the back door. "I saw you come in," she said. "I'm so excited to babysit today."

I noticed then she had a baby-carry-pouch thing strapped to her body under her coat. She saw me notice it and grinned. "I used this for my dolls when I was young," she explained. Then she lined it with one blanket, shoved both kittens in it and tucked them in so their little faces were peering out, picked up the bag with all the kitten stuff in it, and waved us goodbye. "I'll be across at the center all day. I'll bring them over so you can see them, so you don't miss them too much. If it slows down for you, that is. It's looking pretty busy out there already."

"It is?" I said, looking out the front. I'd noticed people but not any more than usual.

"Yes, Win," Ro said. "They're lined up on the sidewalk toward Main Street."

"They are?" I went to the window and tried to peer up the road instead of out across to the youth center and café. Oh, they were right! There were people. Actual people.

Oh, and Jayden was setting up his stall.

It was busy out there, and they were waiting for me to open.

I turned to Ro, a little teary-eyed. So relieved and excited, but mostly relieved. "We still have twenty minutes, but there are people!"

She came over, gave me a quick hug, then pulled back and put her hands on my shoulders. "You can do this, Win. Open early. Don't keep your customers waiting."

So with a deep breath, and putting all the hard work

behind us, I made my dream a reality. I unlocked the door, and Fox and Fables was officially open for business.

IT WAS NON-STOP FOR HOURS. The first time I even looked up, it was after two. I hadn't stopped, not even once. There was a steady stream of customers, excited and asking questions, loving all the bookish merch, games and puzzles, and putting in requests for books I didn't have but was more than happy to order.

It was better than I expected.

Jayden came in with a grin. "We are sold out and packing up," he said, personally delivering two cups of tomato soup and two cheesy bread rolls. "For you guys." He nodded to the youth center's café across the way. "Those guys had a steady stream as well. The kids are doing great over there."

"Giving the kids job experience is a great initiative," I said.

"It is. Gunter's a great guy." He looked around my store. "Have you got any books left?" he asked with a laugh. "You've been flat-out all day!"

"I'll definitely need to put an order in later," I said. "It's been great. Better than I expected, honestly."

Someone came to the counter with two books in hand, and Jayden took that as his cue. "Enjoy the rest of your day. We'll see you tonight down at the tree lighting."

"Thanks for the soup!"

He waved as he walked out, and I focused on the customer. "Ah, great series," I said, nodding to her selection.

"Ooh, you've read this? I read the first book and loved it so much."

"I sure have. I basically read anything I can get my

hands on. But book four in this series will be out in March, I believe."

This pleased her immensely and we chatted about these books, then other books, and then another customer lined up behind her, and she frowned. "Oh, sorry to keep you. I could talk about books all day long."

"Me too," I said, handing over her paper bag of books. "Maybe we should have monthly book club meetings."

Her face lit up and she gasped. "I would so be here. Please say you'll do that."

I'd kinda said it as a throwaway comment, but the more I thought about it . . .

The next customer put his books on the counter and Ro stepped in to ring him up. "I'd come along," he said. He was an older gent, and his books were popular political spy reads. "Hartbridge needs something like that for us readers who don't go out much."

"Oh, do I get that," I said, agreeing wholeheartedly.

The other woman nodded. "Absolutely."

When they left, Ro handed me the cup of tomato soup Jayden had left for me. "Have something quick to eat. It's delicious," she said. "Monthly book club meetings is an amazing idea, and a great way to get folks into the store regularly. Sounds like you've found a little niche community group already," she said with a proud smile.

Another customer came up to the counter with a question about a certain edition, and Ro commandeered me out of the way. "I can help you with that," she said, and I took a moment to have a bathroom break, then to have my soup.

It really was amazing.

This whole day had been amazing. So far, anyway. I couldn't have asked for a better opening day.

More customers came in, even though it slowed down a little by mid-afternoon. There was a steady stream of browsers and buyers, and between Ro and me, we were either serving customers or restocking, or tidying shelves and displays.

Non-stop.

Busy enough that I didn't always get a chance to greet customers every time the bell chimed over the front door. So while I noticed that three people came into the store, I was busy serving a customer and didn't really pay them much attention.

Until a familiar face came up to the counter. "Hello," Wayne Clark said. He was with a woman who was clearly Deacon's mother because of how much they looked alike. And I'd thought he looked like his dad . . .

"Oh, hello," I said.

"Winter, this is my wife, Vicky," Wayne said.

She smiled fondly at me. "So nice to meet you."

"Likewise. This is my aunt, Ro," I said, introducing her because she'd magically appeared like a genie.

"So nice to meet you," Ro said.

But I looked around the store for Deacon and found him at the shelves, searching for something. He was shaking his head, and I knew he couldn't find what he was looking for. "Deacon," I called out.

He turned to face me, his expression a mix of sad and disbelieving. "*Never Let Me Go.* You sold them."

"I sold one," I said. Then I held up the copy I'd put aside for him. "I kept one just for you. See?" I pointed to the little slip of paper. "It has your name on it."

His smile . . . his smile was everything. Like it lit him up from the inside.

Hell, like it lit *me* up from the inside.

He came over to the counter, his gaze going from the book to my eyes and not leaving. Full eye contact, unwavering, unbroken. "You kept it for me," he said quietly.

I wasn't really prepared for how intense an effect his gaze would have on me. It made my heart stutter, butterflies tickled my belly, and I was lost to it in that moment. Like the world fell away. Until Ro's hand on my back broke the spell and I realized they were all waiting for me to speak. "Of course I kept one for you," I managed.

Great.

Just great.

Deacon and I just had a moment. In front of his parents, in front of Ro.

Embarrassed, cheeks burning red, and ignoring the way Ro and Vicky were smiling at each other, and most definitely ignoring how Wayne was smiling at me, I patted my hair down and cleared my throat.

"Deacon," I said. "Would you like me to ring this up for you now, or are you happy to browse a little longer?"

Vicky took Wayne's arm. "Oh, we're happy to browse. Take your time."

"And I was going to go check on Merry and Bright," Ro said, pulling on her coat. "See how they managed with lunch. Be right back." She grinned at Vicky and Wayne as she raced out the door.

And that left me with Deacon. He was still staring at me, smiling at me, still making my heart thump absurdly out of rhythm. "I like you," he said quietly.

Oh.

Did he mean to say that out loud?

Pretty sure he hadn't meant to. But he had. He had said that. To my face. And those butterflies that were fluttering in my belly were now a flood, and my heart . . .

Well, my heart went and said the quiet part out loud. "I like you too."

CHAPTER NINE
DEACON

I SLID the book onto my nightstand, carefully opening the pages to where the small slip of paper was. Winter had written my name on it. He'd set the book aside for me, and the book was great.

But this little slip of paper meant so much more.

My name in his handwriting.

I'd told him I liked him. Probably shouldn't have just said it like that, but usually if I thought it, I said it. There was no taking it back now, and I wouldn't even if I could.

Because he'd said he liked me too.

Those words shot through me like a bolt of lightning, a pinball of excitement.

I hadn't wanted to leave. I wanted to stay there and help him in his store, but he was so busy and it was his first day, so when Mom and Dad said it was time to go, I went with them.

I wished I hadn't, though.

Mom had asked him if he'd be going to the Christmas tree lighting tonight and he'd said yes. Then she'd told him we might see him there.

So now I had to wait until it was time to go to that.

Thinking about seeing him again made me nervous, but in a good way. Not a tummy ache this time. More jittery. Exciting.

I liked him.

And he liked me.

Just knowing that made me feel . . . well, I felt everything all at once. But it made me feel that we'd be okay. That we'd established that first step, and now we could see what was next.

I'd read up on everything I could find on asexuality. I wanted to better understand him and what he meant when he'd said he'd never felt sexual attraction.

It was almost a relief, to be honest.

Had I thought of sex? Yes. Did I want to have sex?

I couldn't imagine I ever would want that.

I wasn't comfortable with touch, or intimacy, or scrutiny.

Did I touch myself? Yes. Not often, though. Did it feel good? Sure. Could I ever imagine doing that to someone else? Or having it done to me by someone else?

Undecided, leaning heavily toward a no.

Knowing Winter didn't want that, knowing he wouldn't pressure me into that, was such a relief. Considering I couldn't even imagine holding his hand, anything more than that seemed foolish to worry about.

Even holding hands and kissing seemed so far out of my comfort zone that I couldn't even imagine it.

Maybe one day. But also maybe not ever. And either was fine with me.

Only maybe if I was okay with it. If I'd worked up to that. And as of right now, my answer would be no, but I couldn't logically say that might change in the future.

According to everything I'd found online about asexuality, some people still liked to kiss and hold hands and cuddle and hug. They just never felt any need for anything more. Some didn't even want to do that. They wanted nothing physical; just to hang out, have deep and meaningful conversations, have dinner and watch movies and read books. They wanted to feel connected to a special person who understood them, valued them as a person without any physical aspect to their relationship; a purely platonic relationship.

I liked the sound of that very much.

I had to wonder what Winter wanted. If he wanted anything.

I would need to ask him.

Now that we'd established that we liked each other.

A jittery thrill ran through me every time I remembered him saying that. And as I sat there on my bed, holding that tiny slip of paper, touching the ink, my name, I couldn't ever remember feeling like this.

"Deacon," Mom called out. "Dinner's ready."

"Okay," I replied. I went to my bookcase, to the small tray where I kept my special things, my snippets of things I'd collected over the years and wanted to keep forever, and placed Winter's note right in the center.

Dinner was quiet, though Dad kept smiling at me. He obviously felt no need to distract me or keep the conversation away from certain topics. I always knew when he did that, trying to shield me from the mental gymnastics I often put myself through. But he didn't do that tonight.

Mom, on the other hand . . .

"The bookstore was lovely," she said. "I'm grateful Hartbridge now has one. It'll save me a trip to Mossley every so often."

"We bought eight books," Dad said. "I think we're good for a while."

"Eight books *and* a jigsaw puzzle," I corrected. The truth was eight books between three avid readers wasn't a great deal.

"Oh, the puzzles were a nice surprise," Mom said. "I didn't know he would have so much fun stuff. I think Christmas will be much easier this year. The store has such a cozy feel. And his aunt Ro seemed so nice."

"She is," I said before taking a sip of water. "She's more a friend or older sister to him than an aunt. He and his mother aren't close."

Both Mom and Dad frowned. "Oh, that's a shame," Dad said. "Then I'm glad he has her."

"If you'd like to invite him over for dinner one night," Mom said, "that's fine with me. You just let me know, and I'll make extra."

Oh.

I wasn't—

"Pretty sure they might prefer going to the diner or the pizzeria," Dad said, patting her hand. "Where the parents aren't listening in on every word."

"Uh," I said, uncertain. "I haven't thought about that. I don't know what food he likes to eat. And what if he wants to eat food I don't like?"

Before I could let that whole new source of worry derail me, Mom gave my hand a quick pat. "You just have to ask him, sweetheart. Asking someone their favorite foods or their most disliked foods is a good way to get to know them. Favorite food, favorite movie, favorite song."

Dad shook his head. "Nah. You wanna know a guy, ask him what his favorite dinosaur is."

"Not sure if Winter's the dinosaur-loving type," Mom said. "Maybe ask about books."

"I already have asked about books," I said. "He has many favorite books, most of which align with mine. I quoted his favorite poem the day we met. And," I added, "I think he *is* a dinosaur-loving type."

"Most guys have a favorite dinosaur," Dad said. "Mine's the Pachycephalosaurus. It was super-fast and had a built-in helmet."

"Ankylosaurus," I said. "But also the Kosmoceratops."

Mom sighed. "Fine, then ask him about dinosaurs. But try and think of some other fun things to ask about. Get to know him. Dating is when you find out if you're compatible, but it's also supposed to be fun."

Dating?

"Dating?" I blinked, and blinked again, my cheeks beginning to burn. "I don't . . . I don't think that's what we are."

Was it?

No, definitely not. We'd spent some time together when I was helping at his store, and he'd been to the clinic twice. But those weren't dates. A date, by definition, was a social or romantic appointment, and while me helping at his store was a planned appointment, as such, it wasn't a date.

"The word date was never used or agreed upon," I explained.

"Then," Dad said, "if it's what you want, you need to ask him."

I stared at him, certain the horror I felt was clearly visible on my face. "Ask him on a date? I thought I was asking him what his favorite food was. Or dinosaur."

Mom gave me a patient smile. "It doesn't need to be complicated, darling. Just ask him when you can see him again. He'll be busy with the store, no doubt. So if he's short on time, ask if you can bring him lunch one day. Or coffee. That's all. It doesn't need to be any grand gesture. Just so he knows you're thinking of him and being considerate of his time."

Dad nodded as if that was all good and well, but then he shrugged. "I'd just ask him about the dinosaur."

I laughed. "I can't believe I'm getting advice about this."

Dad pointed to the clock. "Well, you're about to see him, so we gotta be prepared, right?"

"See him?" I looked at the offending clock.

"The lighting of the Christmas tree."

Oh. I'd already forgotten about that . . .

"We better get moving and grooving," Dad said. "Don't forget your beanie. It's cold out there tonight. The weatherman said it'll be snowing tonight."

I DID ALWAYS ENJOY the Christmas tree lighting night. As a kid, it signaled the beginning of Christmas. I didn't even mind the crowd because it was dark and everyone stood facing the tree, and there was order and quiet until the mayor said his piece and flipped the switch. The tree would come to life, pretty Christmas lights in the biggest Christmas tree ever. Everyone said, *ooooooh*, then they clapped and everyone was happy, wishing Mom and Dad a merry Christmas and shaking hands while I stood back and nodded and smiled and returned the greeting with my hands firmly shoved in my jacket pockets or behind my back, lest someone try to shake my hand.

That was how it went every year.

Most people in town knew my dad, and my mom had always been involved in community things, volunteering whenever she could. But they knew me now, and they knew not to touch me. They respected my personal space.

Especially since that episode many years ago when one of Dad's older clients thought giving a five-year-old a rough shoulder-shake was an appropriate thing to do, and I'd had a very public, very epic meltdown.

He'd said he didn't know, wasn't aware I was *like that* and was most apologetic, but anyway, most of the town learned about my no-touching rule that day.

Then I'd began school and the kids in my class knew, my teachers knew. It was just my thing. I was mostly normal —whatever that was supposed to mean. I just had a few quirks.

But it did make meeting new people uncharted territory, and I never really knew what to expect. Which, of course, was the hardest part for me. The not knowing how people will react and usually bracing myself for rejection or ridicule.

I was, unfortunately, very used to that.

Which was why it threw me out of sorts when we'd arrived at the tree lighting and Winter was standing with a group of men. I hadn't expected him to be surrounded by guys. I knew most of them, by name, mostly. I knew Hamish and Ren because their dog Chutney was on my roster. I knew Jayden from the diner. I knew Clay Henderson from the sawmill. Plus, he'd grown up here. I knew Deputy Price, and Doctor Rob, of course, because he was my doctor, and I knew Gunter because he'd opened the youth center.

But I didn't *know* them.

And there were a lot of them, all standing around. It was a large group, a circle of friends that I was not part of and therefore was an outsider to, and meeting that many people at once was not a good thing for me.

Winter was supposed to be meeting me, not them. Wasn't that the assumed thing? Did I misread his intent? He was wearing the scarf I gave him, and he did smile at me when he spotted me, and Gunter gave Winter a nudge—I wasn't sure what to make of that.

Why would he nudge him like that? And why was Winter's coat so puffy at the front? He looked pregnant and he kept rubbing his front, as I'd seen pregnant folk do.

What was that about?

Disappointed and sad that things weren't going as I'd expected, I faced the tree, waiting for it to be all over, wishing I'd stayed at home.

"Did you want to go over and say hello?" Mom asked me.

I shook my head. "No."

She gave me one of her sad smiles but then brightened when she looked over my shoulder. "No need. He's coming over."

I turned around to see Winter walking toward me, his orange beanie pulled low, his smile wide. "Hello again," he said brightly.

"Hello," Mom said. "Glad you could make it."

"Hey, Winter," Dad said. "How was your first day at the store?"

"Amazing," he said, grinning now.

I liked his smile so much.

"Couldn't have asked for a better opening day." Winter's eyes met mine. "This is a great turnout, huh?"

Small talk was never my strong suit. Especially when I couldn't stop noticing his gloved hand rubbing over his protruding tummy. "You look pregnant."

He laughed and slowly unzipped his coat a little, and a tiny white-and-ginger kitten poked his head out, then another. I couldn't help but laugh. "Oh."

"I have the boys with me," he said. "Evie babysat them all day for me and she had the baby carrier pouch thing. Turns out they love it, so she insisted I borrow it. I think Merry loves it because he's warm and cuddly, but Bright loves it because he can see everything and has a better vantage point for mischief."

Bright meowed his agreement.

It made people turn around and they smiled too when they saw him.

I gave Bright a little scratch on the head and Merry popped his little face out. "Hello to you too," I said.

Winter was smiling at me, and it made me all swoopy inside, but I couldn't look at him. "Yes, the turnout is always good for this."

He nodded back to the group of guys he'd been standing with. "I met all the crowd tonight. Such a great group of friends," he said. "They wanted to meet you, but I said maybe another time and maybe not all at once."

I looked at him then.

He was still smiling. "They understood. There's a lot of them and it's kind of overwhelming. Hamish said you care for his dog?"

"Chutney." I nodded. "They have a coat and matching shoes. And yes, maybe another time and not all at once. I wasn't expecting you to be with all of them, and I don't do well with unexpected things."

"Me either," he said. "I need fair warning. Especially when it involves a lot of people. I've seen just about all the people today that I can handle, and I'm honestly hoping tomorrow is a bit quieter."

That made me chuckle. "Probably not a good business plan."

He laughed. "Probably not. But I'll be very glad to go home where it's quiet. Except for these two," he said, and the bulge under his coat shifted. "They've certainly entered their gremlin mode."

"Is your aunt Ro not here with you?" I asked.

He gestured to the crowd. "Oh, yes, she is. Probably off

talking to anyone and everyone. She, unlike me, is a social butterfly."

I was smiling at him. "Unlike me, too."

Then the mayor took to the microphone and did his spiel of good wishes and happy holidays before announcing it the official Hartbridge holiday season, and after a dramatic pause, the tree lights flickered on.

Bright blues and reds and greens shone against the dark night, and everyone cheered. And then, like it was all part of the show, it began to snow.

People laughed and clapped, some folks began to sing "Silent Night," and I was very pleased that Winter did not.

He looked at me though, grinning, then he looked up at the sky in wonder. "How is this even real?"

I knew a rhetorical question when I heard one, even though I almost itched with the need to tell him about barometric pressure and precipitation.

I was saved by his aunt Ro. She came up behind him and, putting one arm around his shoulder, gave him a hug. "Isn't it magical?" she asked.

"It really is," he replied.

Then she was talking to my mom and Winter was still smiling at me. "I should get these little ones home where it's nice and warm," he murmured. "I left my car behind the store. Want to walk with me?"

Yes, I did. But . . . "Oh." I paused. "My mom and dad—"

"That's fine," Dad said, interrupting us. "We can wait."

"I can drop him home," Winter suggested. "It's not far. Well, I assume it's not far. This is Hartbridge. Nothing is too far."

Dad faced me. "Deacon, are you okay with that? It's okay if you're not. Pretty sure your mom will be chatting a while."

I appreciated my dad asking because this was not planned, but . . .

I wanted to.

"I'm okay with it," I said. Then I turned to Winter, his eyes on mine. "You can drive me home?"

"Of course," he said.

"Okay, have fun," Dad said, then implanted himself into Mom's conversation, leaving me and Winter.

He nodded up the hill. "Should we go . . . ?"

The flurries of snow were heavier already. "Yes."

Winter waved goodbye to his group of friends, and they all waved back. Pretty sure they'd been watching us, if their smiles were anything to go by. I pretended that was fine and fell into step beside Winter as we headed up toward Short Street.

"A good opening day means more inventory," I said. "Though I'm sure you're aware."

He grinned at me. "I am, yes. I've already placed another order. It's incredible. This town is incredible, and the people, of course." He stopped walking as we crossed the street and waved his gloved hand at Main Street. "Have you ever seen anything so pretty?"

I looked around, wary and concerned, uneasy. I wanted to grab his arm and urge him to safety but stopped myself. "It's not sensible to stop on the street. This isn't a pedestrian crossing and there are too many parked vehicles, which further impede visibility. The dark and snow make it even more dangerous."

"Oh, yes," he said, hurrying to the sidewalk. "You are quite correct. I shouldn't stop in the middle of the street." I thought he might have been annoyed by my little lecture on street safety, but he just smiled at me as if I'd done him a favor. Which I had, but probably not as patiently as I could have. "I was just so distracted by how picturesque

Main Street is," he said, looking again up the street. "I was told the town goes all out on the Christmas decorations, and I thought I was prepared, but it stopped me in my tracks when I walked down here tonight. The little Christmas trees, the decorations. It's just . . . it's just so lovely."

"It is," I agreed. "Guess I'm just used to it."

One of the kittens inside his coat moved and meowed, and he rubbed them gently. "Okay, okay. We're going." He began to walk again, slowly though, as though he wanted to prolong his time with me.

That's what I liked to believe anyway.

He even seemed content to walk in companionable silence, or perhaps he thought that was what I wanted?

It made me nervous; trying to fill the void with small talk was not one of my strengths. "Have Bright and Merry taken to their new diet?" I asked.

"Oh yes," he replied, his smile wide. "Very much. And they're playing more now. They're just so cute. Bright is still bigger and more adventurous, but Merry's not far behind him. I think he's just quieter by nature."

"You're still keeping their names, I take it."

He laughed. "Yes! They suit them now; like they're growing into them. It was a great suggestion."

I don't know why it made me so happy that he liked the names. "I've never named someone else's pets before," I said. "It's a first for me."

He grinned at me. "Well, I'm honored."

We turned into the short road where his store was. It was all dark, save lights strung up in a zigzag between the roofs of the buildings.

"Ahh," Winter said, putting his arms out and doing a spin. Then he put his hands to his face and looked at me. "It's even prettier now. Look at it!"

It *was* pretty. The soft glow of the lights overhead, the falling snowflakes. Him.

Mostly him.

Definitely him.

His cuteness, his excitement, made me smile and feel a little embarrassed, but mostly I just felt . . . excited and happy. Maybe a touch nauseous, but that was just the giddiness. It was a good-tummy feeling, not a bad one.

"It is quite remarkable," I said. If he took my comment to mean the lights were remarkable or that *he* was remarkable, I wasn't going to clarify.

I meant both.

Why on earth I felt so brazen tonight, I wasn't sure. Maybe because he'd told me he liked me, because he wanted to walk with me, spend extra time with me, and drive me home.

These were all positive signs, right?

I was painfully aware my ability to read cues wasn't great, but I wasn't stupid.

Far from it.

Intelligence I had in spades. Social skills, not so much.

"You okay?" he asked. "You look worried."

I shook my head and focused. "Sorry. I . . . get in my head."

"Hey," he said. "If overthinking was a contest, I'd have you beat."

That made me smile. "Highly unlikely, but I'll concede defeat if it would make you feel better."

He laughed. "Yes. Yes, it would." Then he brushed snow off his beanie. "Come on, I need to get these boys home and into their bed by the heater. And it's dinnertime for me."

"You haven't eaten yet?" Then I realized, of course he wouldn't have. He was at work until just now.

"We knew we'd be home late tonight, so Ro made some stew in the slow cooker earlier," he said as we neared his car. "Or there's leftover pizza. I'm so hungry I could eat both."

Hmm. I didn't like that he was so hungry.

He unlocked his vehicle, and we got in. He started the car and cranked up the heat. "Are you comfortable?" he asked.

I wasn't entirely sure what he meant, but I wasn't uncomfortable in any way. "Yes."

He chuckled, then unzipped his jacket a little. "You boys comfortable?"

One of them squeaked out a meow in response, and Winter laughed and did the zip back up. He looked at me, a picture of happiness. "I know I should probably take them out when I drive, but it's cold and they're still so little." He carefully buckled up his seatbelt. "Okay, so which way is home for you?"

I gave him directions and was very relieved that he was such a careful driver. I was more than comfortable to be in a car with him, to be around him.

I liked him more tonight than I did even earlier today.

We didn't speak in the car, apart from my giving directions, and while I rather liked the silence, I knew a lot of people didn't. It made things awkward for them.

"Are you comfortable?" I asked him.

He looked from the road to me, still smiling. "Yes. Why do you ask?"

"Because you asked me. I thought I should perhaps return the question. I wasn't sure if you were referring to the seat, or the temperature inside your car, or if I was comfortable with you."

His smile became a grin. "Well, all three, I guess." Then his smile faded. "Does it change your answer?"

"No, not at all."

The grin was back. "Well, good."

"I'm not very good at small talk," I admitted.

"Me either. Small talk, meeting new people, that kind of thing."

"Some people can't deal with silence. I happen to like it."

"Oh my god, me too," he said. "And I have peopled so hard today. I've had my quota, well and truly. I shall be going home, eating all the food, and relishing in the peace and quiet. Decompress, ready to do it all again tomorrow."

"You're very good with people though," I said. "Meeting them, being polite. Conversation, that kind of thing."

"I've worked in retail since I was fifteen," he explained. "So yes, while I can deal with people all day, I do find it taxing."

"This is our gate coming up on your right," I explained, and he slowed down carefully before applying the turn signal and turning into our driveway. "You should perhaps take food with you to work tomorrow so you can eat."

"I should, yes. I was just so busy today. Maybe tomorrow it won't be so hectic so I can sneak a few bites."

"I can bring you something if you'd prefer," I offered.

"Oh no, you don't have to do that. I'll be fine." He grinned at me. "I do appreciate the offer though."

I wanted to ask him if he'd like to come for dinner one evening, as Mom had suggested, but I was too nervous to ask.

He pulled up in front of the house. Dad's truck was in the garage and the porch light was on, as were lights inside, and I knew I had to get out of his car even though I wanted to stay with him for as long as possible.

"Thank you for the lift," I said.

"You're very welcome. I'm glad we had a chance to talk."

Oh boy.

I was going to do this . . .

"I, uh . . ." I held my breath, my fists closed on my lap. "I would like to see you again. My mom said I should ask you over for dinner, because it is an appropriate thing to ask."

I couldn't believe I'd managed to say that . . .

"I'd like that," he said. I looked at him then, just quickly, to find him smiling at me. "I'm very busy this week though, so I don't know when that will be possible. Maybe for a few minutes on your lunch break, or if you're on Main Street for anything, come and say hi. I'm just not sure I'll have time to leave the store, being my first week and all. And then I have these two little gremlins in the evenings," he said, rubbing his jacket. "I can't expect Ro to look after them. She already does enough."

I nodded, because that was a totally reasonable reply. Even if it felt like a rejection.

"I think it will all start to settle down soon though, and I'll have a better routine," he added. "Tell your mom I said thank you for the dinner invitation. Maybe next weekend? Or one night early next week when I have a quieter day and can finish at five."

"So it's not a no?"

"No," he said with a laugh. "Definitely not. It's a yes, but I'm not sure when. I don't want to commit and then have to cancel because I'm caught up at the store." Then his face softened a little. "I won't ever be dishonest with you, Deacon. If I didn't want to see you again, I'd say no. If I didn't want to have dinner, I'd say no. If I didn't want to talk to you or spend a few extra minutes with you, I wouldn't have suggested I drive you home."

I met his eyes then, felt my cheeks heat, and I nodded. "Thank you. I won't ever be dishonest with you, either."

"So we'll text this week," he said quietly. "And I'm fine

with phone calls if you want. In the evenings. If you want to call. Totally fine if that's not your thing. Sometimes it's easier just to call than all that extra thumb work." He grinned. "Totally up to you."

The idea of texts and phone calls with Winter made my insides all jittery. "I'd like that."

"Okay then. That sounds good." He nodded to the house. "You should probably get inside before your parents worry that I'm holding you hostage out here."

I laughed because that was ridiculous.

"I'll text you," I said. "Maybe I'll call you if my thumbs aren't up for all that extra work."

His eyes went wide and he laughed. "Did you just mock me?" Then he pretended to text on an invisible phone. "It's a lot of work and my thumbs get tired and repetitive strain injury is a common problem with Gen Z."

His laughter made me genuinely happy, as if the sound struck a chord inside me. I wanted to hear it every day.

"Goodnight, Winter," I said, my hand on the door handle. "Thank you again for driving me home."

One of the kittens meowed from inside his jacket.

"Get them home and inside where it's warm," I said, still so reluctant to say goodbye.

"Pretty sure that was a call for supper," he said. "But yes, I should get them home. Have a good night."

I got out then, stepping into flurries of snow, and watched Winter drive back down the driveway, his brake lights and blinker transforming the falling snow into neon red and orange.

"Deacon," Mom called out. I turned to find her at the front door. "Everything okay?"

I came up the porch, unable to keep from smiling. "Yes. Everything's fine."

She hurried me inside and helped me take my coat off,

careful not to dump snow on the floor. "Boots off," she said. "Your dad's making hot chocolate."

She gave me a smile as she disappeared into the kitchen. I knew they'd have questions, so I was prepared. I just had to stop smiling first.

WHILE I really wanted to text Winter that night, I didn't. I told myself one text the following day would be sufficient. I didn't want to overdo it, or annoy him while he was at work, so I left it until the afternoon.

> I hope your second day is as busy as the first.

He replied fourteen minutes later.

> Very busy but great. I'll be here a while yet. How was your day?

> My day was good. We had clinic rounds in the morning to check on the animals staying overnight, but Sundays are generally quiet. I do a lot of cleaning on Sundays. Mom and I decorated the Christmas tree this afternoon.

His next reply came through twelve minutes later.

> Yay for the Christmas tree. That sounds delightful. But boo to all that cleaning

I smiled at the little frowny face.

> Hope you remembered food today?

His reply didn't come through for twenty-two minutes so I knew he must be busy.

> I did, thank you. I learned my hungry lesson LOL

But then I had nothing else to specifically ask him, and no idea what to contribute, so after grimacing at my phone for a full three minutes, I settled for a closing statement.

> "There is a certain slant of light, Winter afternoons"

I waited and waited for his reply but after twenty minutes, I assumed he was either super busy or perhaps he didn't like the quote. And watching my phone and waiting, imagining scenarios where he thought I was too much or not enough, or not right for him, did nothing but upset my tummy. I was almost queasy and having trouble sitting still when my phone rang.

Not a text, but a phone call.

Winter's name flashed on the screen, and I was so excited I almost dropped my phone.

"Hello?" I said. "This is Deacon Clark speaking."

"Hello Deacon Clark, this is Winter Atkins," he said cheerfully.

My heart rate took off and the butterflies in my tummy soared. "Hello. You said you'd text, not call."

"Well, yes, but then you quoted Emily Dickinson and that warranted a phone call."

"It did?"

"Oh yes. Very much. You see, if you quote poetry to me, then I will squeal, and Ro will shove me into the storeroom so I don't scare the customers."

He made me laugh. "Is that what happened?"

"Well, I'm calling you right now from the storeroom, so

yes. It very much did." He sighed. "That's twice now, just so you know."

"Twice you were shoved into the storeroom?"

He snorted. "No. Twice you've quoted poetry to me. I have to say, Deacon, if your intention was to impress me, you have done exactly that."

"I actually didn't do it with that intention. I was otherwise unsure of what to say. And your name is Winter, so I thought it was fitting."

"When in doubt, poetry is your answer. Especially when you're talking to me."

"You liked it," I said, smiling.

"Uh, loved it. So thank you. You made my very busy, very great day even better."

"Very busy, very great day."

"Yes. Apparently half the town who couldn't make it to the grand opening yesterday decided today was the day. It's been incredible."

"I'm very glad to hear that."

He sighed. "I should get back out there. But I'd like to see you," he said quietly. "Later this week, if that suits you? I'm sure I can steal five or ten minutes of my day, perhaps at the same time as your lunch break one day?"

A rush of jitters bloomed in my chest; a new feeling, and one that I liked very much. "I'd like that."

"Good. Let me know which day suits you and I'll make sure Ro is here to hold the fort if I duck out to the diner or the café, or if you wanted to call into the store, that'd be fine too. My evenings run late, and then I have Merry and Bright . . ."

"It's not so much if I want to, because I do want to, but this week is particularly busy. Tomorrow we have clinic rounds in the morning and livestock inspections in the afternoon," I explained. "Tuesday and Wednesday will be much the same."

"Livestock," he said. "And there I was thinking you looked after dogs, cats, and ferrets."

"And horses and alpacas, goats and pigs," I added. "Birds, lizards, hermit crabs."

He gasped. "Hermit crabs? How do you treat a sick hermit crab?"

"Depends. They can present with a multitude of symptoms. Usually from an inadequate environment, but not always. Lethargy, dry skin—"

"Dry skin?" He made a gagging noise, and then kind of yelled, "How do you even know when a crab has dry skin?"

I heard what sounded like Ro intervene in the background, as if she was admonishing him for yelling that out in the store.

"Uh, Deacon, I have to go," he said quickly. "I'll text you later, but we'll aim for Thursday lunch, or coffee if work allows. Otherwise, I can possibly do dinner on Sunday night? If your mom's offer still stands, that is."

I was smiling again. "I'm sure it does."

"Good. I'll text you before then though, and you can text me. Just so you know, poetry quotes will *not* go unnoticed."

My insides were being all jittery again. "Noted."

His voice was soft and warm in my ear. "Bye, Deacon."

"Goodnight, Winter."

I went out to the living room to find Mom and Dad on the sofas watching some movie from the '80s. "Oh, hey sweetheart," Mom said. "Everything okay?"

I sat in my usual spot and tried to hold in some excitement, when what I wanted to do was scream into a cushion. "Yes, very. You offered for Winter to join us for dinner, so I asked him and he said yes. Next Sunday would suit, if that's okay?"

They both watched me and Dad sat up straight, the movie forgotten. "A date?"

"Unclear on the technicalities, but I would believe so." I licked my lips, still trying to rein in my excitement. "And also possibly Thursday lunchtime, though that needs to be confirmed. It depends on work, both his and mine."

Dad's eyes went wide and he grinned. "Two dates?"

I cleared my throat. "I quoted Emily Dickinson. The fact he knew who that was without having to google anything was quite surprising. But yes, technicalities aside, we discussed meeting twice this week."

"Reciting poetry would have won me over too," Mom said fondly. "Do you want to know where your father took me on our first date?"

"Where?"

"To watch a foal being born."

"Emergency births are hardly planned that way," Dad said. Then he smiled at Mom. "Anyway, it worked like a charm, did it not?"

She gave his hand a squeeze. "Yes, it did."

"Well, I hope there are no emergencies next Sunday," I said, making a face.

Oh good.

I had seven days to wait. Seven days to think up a hundred different equally awful scenarios.

Seven days of overthinking, seven days of anticipation and a belly full of butterflies.

I had to come up with something to distract myself . . . and I thought I knew of the perfect way.

CHAPTER TEN
WINTER

THE NEXT WEEK began in a bit of a blur.

I had deliveries of stock, which meant more inventory, customers almost every minute of every day, late evenings, and two gremlin kittens who were growing like weeds taking up every spare moment of my day.

I got a text every morning at eight o'clock sharp from Deacon. Not just any kind of mundane text. Oh no . . . these were quotes, simply one line from a poem and nothing else.

It made every part of me happy.

Monday morning: *Hope Is the Thing with Feathers* by Emily Dickinson.

Tuesday morning: *I Wandered Lonely as A Cloud* by William Wordsworth.

Wednesday: *Joy And Woe* by William Blake. If he knew how much I adored his work.

I'd replied to each one with a gif of epic swooning because no words could so adequately describe how it made me feel.

I was positively on cloud nine.

I did text him every night when I was finally at home, in bed, done with the world for the day. Not with anything as profound as he sent me, but just small snippets of thought.

> Crazy busy day today. Ordered more Studio Ghibli fun stuff

> Did you know that Emily Dickinson's father was a US senator?

> Yes I knew that.

Of course he knew that.

I sent him a photo of Bright and Merry curled up asleep together in their blankets.

And a photo of the page of *Howl's Moving Castle* as I re-read it for the nth time.

> "Doors are very powerful things."

> Remind me to bring you this to read.

He'd replied with a photo from his book, the one I'd kept aside for him at the store.

These small snippets of him, the gestures of poetry every morning, his thoughtfulness, his reaching out to me because I'd told him it wouldn't go unnoticed, made my heart sing.

He made me happy.

And I knew it was different than spending actual time with him. This was easier for both of us, clearly. And I liked him. As in, *really* liked him.

Any man who sent me poetry was always going to win.

❄

THURSDAY MORNING, Ro and I were already at the store. I had a delivery coming in first thing and I wanted to run through some stock numbers.

I was watching my phone as it neared eight o'clock when it beeped with a message. I'd sent him a photo of Merry and Bright in their new play pen with the caption *It makes them look so tiny.*

Right at eight o'clock came his reply.

I gasped at my phone.

"What is it?" Ro asked.

"Oh, he's good," I mumbled. Then I showed her the screen.

> "Sometimes the smallest things take up the most room in your heart" by A.A. Milne.

Ro's excited gaze went from my phone screen to my eyes. "Oh my. He *is* good. And he's playing to win," she said.

I sighed happily. "And he's not even trying. It's just him. Okay, well, this one may have been prompted. He sent me two unprompted poetry quotes and I told him all future poetry quotes would not go unnoticed, so perhaps he took that as a challenge. I mean, he knows I love them, so . . ."

"You know what I think?" she asked. "I think for someone who struggles to express himself, what he's thinking or how he's feeling, he's found a way of doing that with you."

"Aww." *My heart.*

"It's super sweet, Win."

I held my phone to my chest. "I know."

"Takiwātanga," she said gently. "His time and space, Win."

"I'm seeing him today," I said quietly. Excitement and

anticipation were wreaking havoc on my nervous system. "Well, hopefully. He's had a busy week as well. Something to do with livestock."

We both grimaced.

"Better than a hermit crab with dry skin," I added, still unable to stop thinking about that. I grimaced harder. "We'll probably just do a quick cup of coffee or something," I went on. "But then dinner with his parents on Sunday."

Her facial expressions did a whole performance, but she settled on a twisted pout that was mostly telling me she had opinions.

"Just say it."

"Well, that's a big step," she said. "Dinner with the parents is a big milestone. You were still set on doing the micro-dates so he doesn't get too overwhelmed or pressured, and the texting seems to be good for both of you, but then you're having dinner with his parents. That's not micro, Win. That's macro."

"Macro-dates are not a thing," I said. "And if it were anyone else, I'd probably agree. But Deacon's . . . I don't want to say different because that implies negative things and that's not what I mean. He's not like other guys." That was a better way to say it. "He's very close with his parents, they're a very big part of his life, and I'm guessing their opinion and approval of me would be a deciding factor for him."

Ro frowned. "Win, darling."

"It's not a bad thing. I've met them before a few times. I don't *need* them to like me. It's more that maybe they need to see I have good intentions with him. I'm sure there'd be assholes out there who would want to take advantage of him, or who'd be generally horrible to him. I can't blame Deacon's parents for that." I sighed. "He had that incident in college with a guy that upset him to the point where he wanted to quit school. It was a whole thing. I don't blame his parents for being cautious."

"I know." She frowned. "That really must have been awful."

I nodded. "And this is just dinner. Even if nothing further ever eventuates between Deacon and me, romantically, I'd still like to be friends with him." I held up my phone. "He quotes poetry to me, Ro. Po-et-tree. Do you know how amazing that is? How utterly perfect that is?"

Just then, a tiny white and orange blur ran out of the stockroom. I gasped and ran to collect Bright before he disappeared under the shelves. "Hey, little mister," I said, holding him to my chest. "How did you get out?"

I had their play pen set up in the corner; the heater was on. They had food and their bed with blankets and toys, and small litter tray. I had the baby carrier in case they needed cuddles.

I was prepared!

I was not prepared for Bright climbing out and escaping.

"We're not doing this, little wannabee Steve MacQueen," I told him. He meowed back at me, angry and defiant.

Well, as angry and defiant as a one-pound fluffball could be.

"You have been fed," I replied. "You have food, and a warm bed. What else could you possibly need?"

Then Merry meowed from the pen. With a big sigh, I scooped him up too and held them both. They were so much happier being held. I wasn't sure if it was a comfort thing, a body heat thing, or if they thought I'd left them.

"I thought I'd at least get something done today before we had to do this," I griped as I put them into the baby carrier and clipped us all into it.

Ro laughed. "You're a sucker."

"No. I'm a softy and a wonderful cat dad." I walked over so she could peek down into the baby carrier. "Look at how cute they are."

Two sets of little eyes peered back at us. Merry meowed.

Then the delivery lady appeared at the door with boxes of books and whatnot, and we got busy with that, and before we knew it, it was time to open the doors.

Gunter gave me a wave and came over, his breath steamy plumes. "Morning," he said cheerfully. "How has your first week been? There's been a steady stream of customers every day, and your opening weekend was huge."

"Oh, it was wonderful," I said. "Better than anything we could have hoped for. And I do expect it to quiet down now. Some slow and steady normalcy would be great."

Then Bright poked his head up to say hello.

"Oh," Gunter said with a laugh. "Why, hello there." He gave him a gentle pat, then grinned at me. "I see you've adopted Evie's baby carrier idea."

"Well, this little tyrant escaped his playpen today," I explained, then of course Bright decided he was climbing out and up my sweater to my neck. "Stop stepping on your brother—" I looked at Gunter. "It's going to be a long day."

He laughed. "He's cute though."

"I need to gremlin-proof their playpen."

He smiled at that. "So, how are things with Deacon? We saw you walking off together the other night."

Oh, at the Christmas light thing.

"Things are going well," I said, trying to play it cool. I didn't want to give too much away and feed into his Christmas Cupid theory. "Things are going slow and steady, which is good for us. He's . . . he's such a great guy."

"He sends him poetry quotes," Ro said, piping up out of nowhere. "There is much swooning."

"I don't swoon," I replied, even though I absolutely did swoon, every single time. "Well, maybe a little bit. Anyway, it's worthy of swooning. Swooning is merited."

Ro grinned. "It's just the cutest thing."

I rolled my eyes. "Anyway, yes, things are going well. Slow but well."

Gunter grinned at me. "I'm glad to hear that. So, a few of us guys are gonna get together for a pizza one night next week, probably Tuesday or Wednesday. Just at the pizzeria, nothing fancy. And not too late because we're all kinda busy these days, but we try to make the effort to catch up. You're more than welcome to join us. Deacon too, if you want?"

Oh.

"Oh, that's . . . that's lovely, thank you! I'm not sure about Deacon, though I can ask him. We're both short on time this week, between his work and mine here at the store, plus I have these two little monsters," I said, trying to put Bright back in the pouch.

"I can look after them," Ro said.

"I can't expect you to," I told her. "You already do enough for me."

"Nonsense," she said with a wave of her hand. "You need this, Win. Ask Deacon to go with you. Stop trying to limit yourself so considerably. You like him. He likes you. I know you're worried about overwhelming him, but sometimes you just have to jump in with both feet. Have a little faith in the universe."

"The universe?"

She sighed as if she was all out of patience and I knew a truth bomb was about to drop. "If you're already trying to censor yourself and what you want—like having dinner with friends—because of a guy, then he's not the one for you. It's okay if he doesn't want to join you, that's perfectly fine. But it's also perfectly fine for you to go without him and not feel bad about it. You're still at the getting-to-know-him stage which means he needs to learn what to expect from you, too. All this walking around on eggshells and overthinking everything when it comes to him isn't fair to either of you. Be honest with him and ask him; his answer might surprise you. *He* might surprise you. He's a grown man. He can make his own decisions."

Right, then.

I looked at Gunter. He was trying not to smile. "So there you have it," I said. "Reality check 101. I'm seeing Deacon today, hopefully. I'll ask him then."

Gunter clapped my shoulder. "Good. I'll let you know details. It won't be all of us. Maybe six or so? It could be a good icebreaker for Deacon." Just then, customers came in, and Gunter gave me a nod. "I better let you go. Have a good day."

"Same to you," I said, and he went on his way. I turned my attention to the customers, to the store, to the inventory, to the ringing phone, to more customers who were all absolutely besotted with my baby carrier and the world's two cutest kittens.

It was a good distraction. It kept me focused and busy. Pretty much for the rest of the morning, it kept my mind off Deacon.

Ro was right. She always was.

My idea of micro-dating until Deacon was more comfortable might have been well-intended, but perhaps entirely misguided. Because what if I wanted more than that? What if he did?

In my attempt to be over-considerate toward him, I hadn't considered him at all.

The truth was, if things with Deacon and me were

heading in the direction I hoped they were, then we needed to talk about expectations and boundaries.

Yep. We needed to talk.

TIME GOT AWAY FROM ME, as it did when busy, but I was stopped in my tracks when the bell above the door chimed at 11:50 a.m., and when I turned to greet the customer, I saw who it was.

Deacon, holding two white paper bags and a takeout tray with two cups. He was wearing jeans and a winter coat and beanie, his cheeks and nose pink in the cutest way ever. He was smiling and a little breathless.

"Oh hi," I said, my voice quieter and breathier than I'd intended.

"Hello. I'm early. I was, according to my father, insufferable and not entirely useful this morning, so he sent me on my lunch break early." He swallowed hard, his gaze lasered to mine, intense, and it made my heart stutter. "If that's okay . . . I should have messaged beforehand."

"No, it's fine," I said, walking over to him. I put my hand out, wanting so badly to touch him, but stopped myself, pulling back just shy of contact. "Come in. Are you warm? It's cold out today."

"I'm okay. I walked fast from the diner. I bought you a toasted sandwich and a hot chocolate. I took a guess. I should have asked. But I ordered a ham and cheese, and a chicken and cheese. I'll have whichever one you don't want." He licked his lips, frowning. "Or I can go back and get you something else."

"I eat either of those," I said, smiling at just how stinking cute he was. "Thank you so much. It's very thoughtful."

He gave a nod, his cheeks pinker now. So, not from the cold?

Ro came over holding my jacket and gloves. "Go, have lunch. The boys are asleep. I'll hold the fort here." She shooed me off. "Go on. Go." Then she looked at Deacon. "Thank you for looking after him."

He gave her a nod and looked away nervously. "It's my pleasure," he mumbled.

Oh my god.

His manners. So freaking polite. I just wanted to squeeze him. Which, of course, I couldn't.

Ro gave me a look that told me she thought he was adorable, and I wanted to let out a squeeeeeee but didn't do that either. I'd totally freak out with her later . . .

I pulled on my coat and gloves and held the door for Deacon. I gave Ro a parting smile but she was already serving a customer, so I closed the door to keep the chill out.

Deacon stood there, waiting.

I nodded toward the river at the end of the short road. "Shall we go this way?" He fell into step beside me. "I've never really seen the river," I said. "I mean, I know it's there. I can hear it, and I park my car behind the store, so I've technically seen it. But I've never taken much notice."

"In summer, it's good for fishing. And swimming, but further south. Not so much here. They used to swim down along Ponderosa Road, but it was too dangerous."

"Dangerous?"

He nodded. "A boy fell in a few Christmases ago. At the Christmas festival. They close off the street and there's food and craft stalls and a mini train ride for the kids. The firetruck comes down. It's one of my favorite nights of the year. The whole town comes to it, and two Christmases ago, a small boy fell in. Deputy Price jumped in and saved him."

"Oh my goodness. Were they okay?"

"Yes."

We got to the edge of the river. There were trees and a path where I'd seen people walking dogs that ran adjacent to Main Street behind the shops. But the incline down was almost a gorge, the steep rocky sides looked dark and dangerous, the water deep and freezing. Ice and snow clung to the edges, the water moving fast.

I pointed down to it, horrified. "He fell in there?"

Deacon pointed further down. "Down near the big Christmas tree. It's not as steep." He held the cup tray out. "Hot chocolate?"

"Oh yes, please." I took one, and between the two of us, we divided the sandwiches. I bit into mine, warm and gooey and delicious. "So, your dad said you were distracted at work today?"

"Yes. But insufferable and not entirely useful were the words he used," he said, and I couldn't help but chuckle.

"Distracted sounds better."

He sipped his hot chocolate. "I was nervous and excited about seeing you today, and I kept watching the clock. I couldn't concentrate very well. He normally keeps me busy because he knows I get like this." He winced. "Sorry."

"Don't apologize."

"If I know I have something coming up, I fixate . . ." He made a face that was sorry and sad. "And I know saying things like that out loud makes some people uncomfortable."

"Not me," I said, giving him a smile. "If you feel it, you can tell me. I like that you talk about it. It's better than hiding it. Some guys never talk about feelings and that's way worse."

He glanced at me but quickly looked back to the river. "Do you talk to other guys . . . about this stuff?"

I bit into my sandwich and shook my head as I swallowed. "Nope. I have dated other guys back in my hometown. But they never lasted very long. And they never talked about how they felt until it wasn't worth talking about."

"Because you're asexual?"

"Yes. In a nutshell, that's what it always came down to." I sighed but smiled when he looked at me. "I am who I am, and I'm comfortable with that. If they don't like that, then I'm not the person for them."

He smiled at the river as he ate the last of his sandwich, his nose and cheeks the color of cherry blossoms. "I am who I am too. I know what people say about me. My dad says my brain is just wired different from other people, but that doesn't mean I'm any less of a person."

"You're absolutely not any less a person, Deacon. I happen to like you exactly the way you are."

His blush deepened. "I like you too." His eyes met mine then, and the intensity was a fire burning into me. "I feel all jittery when I think about you and I can't concentrate, like my synapses aren't firing. I've been sending you quotes of poetry because you said you like them and I don't really know how else to tell you without getting it wrong, or overwhelming . . . it's a lot, inside my head . . ."

I couldn't help but smile, even though he looked about ready to bolt. I lifted my hand slowly, and not touching him exactly, I held the front of his coat. "Hey," I whispered. He kept his eyes cast downward and to the side, but he didn't pull away. "I feel all jittery when I think of you too. And your poetry every morning at eight o'clock sharp has been the absolute highlight of my day."

His eyes met mine then. "It has?"

I nodded. "Absolutely. And it's funny that you said you've been trying not to overwhelm me because I've been trying not to overwhelm you either. I thought maybe if we only saw each other for short periods of time, like a lunch break, that we'd get used to each other in small steps, you know?"

He nodded quickly.

"And our jobs have kept us busy this week, so it worked out well."

"Yes."

"But I realized that I was setting these boundaries without asking what you wanted. If you're happy with a lunch break during the week and maybe a dinner once a week. Or if you want to see me more often than that? Or less?" I still had hold of his coat, just holding it lightly, gently, but not wanting to let go. "What do you want to do, Deacon?"

"More. I want to see you more, if that's what you want. I know I'm different—"

"You're not different," I said. "You're perfectly you."

"I don't . . . I don't know what . . . I-I don't know what I can do . . . what I can do—" He cringed and said nothing more.

"You don't know what you can do about what?" I asked, concerned at his sudden spike in anxiety.

He cheeks went dark red and his eyelids fluttered. "I can't . . . touching or kissing. I can't even hold your hand. I want to. I want to do that but I—" He shook his head. "If you want that, I can't . . . then I'm not the one for you."

"I don't need that," I said. I could see the storm in his eyes. "Deacon, look at me." His eyes fluttered before he held my gaze. "I don't need that. I don't expect that from you. At all."

"You don't?"

"No." Then I remembered what he'd said. "You said you *want* to hold my hand but you're not ready. So if it's something you want to work up to, I'm okay with that. I'm happy to wait until whenever you're ready. We can work up to that if you want, or not at all. Okay? All I need from you is honesty. Nothing more. And I think once we've learned to trust each other, the rest will be easy."

His eyes searched mine before he blinked a few times. We were standing close, I was still holding his jacket, and I don't know if he was even aware, but I let it go.

"I am honest," he said.

"I know you are. It's why I like you. And the fact that you love to read, and you send me poems."

His smile was shy, those cherry blossom colored cheeks making my heart squeeze.

"And you're very handsome," I added.

He laughed then and shook his head. "No, I'm not. But you are."

We both stood there, smiling like a pair of Cheshire cats, and I felt so much better about everything.

"Between you and me," I said, "I think we have over-thinking and over-worrying down to a fine art."

Deacon smiled. "I get in my head a lot."

"That's okay. I do that too. But if you have any questions, about anything, we can just ask each other, right?"

"Right."

"And saying no to some things is perfectly okay. It doesn't mean we don't like each other."

He nodded again.

I inhaled the crisp, cold air and let out a relieved sigh. "I'm glad we talked."

"Me too."

"And I will be honest with you too, just so you know."

He nodded and ducked his head. "Thank you."

"Thank you for bringing me lunch today."

"You're welcome."

"Do I need to bring anything on Sunday for dinner?"

He shook his head. "No, of course not."

"So, in light of the whole honesty and transparency thing," I said, "Gunter invited us for pizza on Tuesday or Wednesday night next week. He said there'd probably be six or so people there. I said I'd probably go, though I wasn't sure what you were doing so I told him I'd ask. It's totally up to you if you wanted to come or not."

He blinked. "Uh . . ."

"You can think about it," I said, playing it down. "No pressure at all."

He was quiet for a moment, his nose pink from the cold. "I will," he said. "Think about it, that is. Social scenarios are not my forte."

"Nor mine, to be honest," I said. "But they're a little queer group and I love that they're all such good friends. They've been very welcoming, which has been great, especially in a town as small as Hartbridge, so I figured I should make the effort to join in. If you did want to go, we could tell them it'd be a quick visit because we had somewhere else to be afterward. Like we're dipping our toes in to test the water."

"Like an escape plan."

I laughed. "Exactly."

He smiled but didn't say anything else about it. Now that I'd mentioned it, maybe he could take his time to mull it over and get used to the idea. I know I certainly appreciated fair warning for social outings.

"Oh, that reminds me," I said, just remembering. "On opening day, I had some customers suggest starting up a little book club where we could meet once a month, maybe serve some coffee and cake, and talk about all the great books we've been reading. Isn't that the greatest idea? It would get them back into the store every month. Maybe I could do book club discounts to entice people to join. I could get some chairs from somewhere and we could just sit around all the books and chat. What do you think?"

His brow furrowed and he gave a nod. "I think . . . I think that sounds like a good idea. Return customers are important. Though I'd be concerned about having cake in the store, especially if they're touching books."

I grinned at him. "That's a very valid point. I didn't think of that."

He smiled, happy that he'd been the one to point it out, I think. "You could do a bite-sized treat with a toothpick in each one so they held that instead of the greasy or sticky part."

I gasped. "That's brilliant, yes!" I nudged his arm with the back of my hand. "So glad I asked you."

Only then did I realize what I'd done.

Without thinking.

I'd touched him . . .

I pulled my hands back. "Shoot, sorry. I didn't mean that. I was just excited and didn't think—"

He surprised me by grinning. "It's fine, Winter. That's actually the third time you've touched me without even realizing." His cheeks flushed dark pink. "I think I know to expect it now."

"Third time?" Well, that was horrifying. Because I didn't know. I wasn't even aware. "I don't mean to. Actually, I'm not even aware I do it."

"I know. I think that's why it doesn't bother me as much. It's always a quick, gentle touch, never a grab or a push." His eyes met mine in that intense burning way. "You get excited and it's habit for you. Plus, I'm wearing three layers." He held out his arm. "And you're wearing gloves. I barely even felt it."

I must have turned a dozen shades of horrified. "Oh god, I'm so sorry. Three times?"

He nodded, still smiling, still blushing. "I've been counting."

Well, that was kinda cute that he'd been keeping count. But not really that he had to.

"Well, I am sorry. Maybe I should shove my hands in my pockets." I did exactly that. "See? Now I can't do it."

Deacon laughed. "It's okay. I'd rather you didn't censor yourself. You get animated and excited when you talk about something you like, and it makes me happy when you do that, so I don't mind. Like I said, I think I'm used to it now."

I wasn't sure what to say to that. It was very sweet and cute, and oh boy, if it didn't make my heart swell.

He checked his watch. "I need to go back to work now."

"Okay. Same, probably." We headed back toward the store, and just as we were at the door, a customer came out, a sales bag in hand.

Deacon grabbed the door for them. "Oh, hello, Deacon," the customer said cheerfully. "Thank you so much."

"You're welcome, Mrs. Hadlow," he replied.

"You have a merry Christmas," she said. "Tell your parents I said the same to them."

"I will. Merry Christmas to you too."

She gave me a bright smile before going on her way, and then Deacon held the door for me. I stepped inside, giving him a polite nod. "Why, thank you, kind sir." He grinned and my heart skipped a beat. "I'll call you later tonight," I added.

"Okay." He closed the door and disappeared down the sidewalk, and I turned around, leaning against the door with a dreamy sigh.

Ro was standing behind the service counter, watching me with a smirk. "I take it that went well."

I did a little excited wiggle. "Swoony, dreamy, happy—"

"Okay, Snow White," she said, waving me in. "You're blocking the door."

I laughed as I walked over. "Oh, Ro. I really like him."

She patted my hand. "I know you do."

I pulled off my coat and gloves and went to hang them up in the storeroom. Merry and Bright were still sleeping soundly, so I tiptoed outta there and closed the door and got back to work. "Okay, now where was I up to . . ."

SUNDAY COULDN'T COME FAST ENOUGH.

Yes, work was super busy and I had a whole bunch of admin to take care of and teething problems to adjust to.

And speaking of teething problems, Bright had definitely found his chompers. Little rascal of a thing would try and attack anything that moved, chomping anything he could get his mouth around. Both kittens were growing so well and becoming more active and playful. Which, of course, meant cuter and funnier.

I loved them with my whole entire heart.

They weren't at all what I'd expected to occupy my time with. When we'd moved here, I had no intention of getting a cat, or any pet for that matter, let alone two very young kittens.

And even though the timing wasn't great with the new store, and they were an inconvenience at work, I couldn't imagine my life without them.

Except for the biting and whenever Bright went into gremlin mode.

It was, however, a great excuse to text Deacon.

> How do I get a kitten to stop trying to murder me?

I assume you're referring to Bright.

Correct. He's a menace.

A cute menace, and a menace I adore, but a menace all the same.

He'll grow out of it.

Grow out of it? How long must we endure this gremlin mode?

A year, perhaps.

A YEAR???? Noooooooooo

You can get him toys and activities to focus on

Okay, great idea. Will google ideas. Thank youuu!

And sending Deacon pictures of Merry and Bright was also a great excuse to text as well. When they were being extra cute. And short videos of when they were playing and being funny.

He'd reply with pics of their dog, Mildred.

It was fun and sweet. There was no pressure, no stress. Just cute animals and smiles.

What was not to like about that?

I had called him on Friday night when I got home. We'd ended up talking for a long while, about books and movies. He loved *The Wizard of Oz*, even though the wicked witch and her flying monkeys had scared him as a boy. He never did understand old Elvis movies, even though his mom loved them. He loved DC comics and Marvel movies, and even though he loved history books and documentaries, he hated war movies—refused to watch them—even though his dad enjoyed them.

I told him I was a sucker for black-and-white romance movies, circa the 1940s with Humphrey Bogart, Rita Hayworth, Cary Grant, and Katharine Hepburn.

He preferred chocolate cake over vanilla, and his favorite candy was peanut M&Ms.

He wore polar fleece sweaters and not the knitted kind because knits clung to him and the texture was wrong, and he couldn't stand how they felt on his skin.

I told him that was one hundred percent relatable, and then we discussed the woes of ill-fitting socks.

"I don't know why people think he's a bit weird," I told Ro. "Because I totally understand what he means."

We were standing in my bedroom and I was up to sweater number four in the outfit check.

She hummed.

"What's that supposed to mean? There's nothing worse when your clothes feel weird. What do you think of this one?" I fixed the collar. "I think the blue's a better choice. Blue is a safe, calm color. If I want his parents to like me . . . You know they've done studies on how the color of clothing affects your perception of that person, especially with first impressions. Politicians and the color of their neckties, for example."

"Well, I kinda liked the pink," she said. "But you're right. The blue is good. Very passive and smart."

I pulled at the collar again. "It feels kinda scratchy. Did the detergent people change their recipe?" Then the sleeve felt weird, and I needed to take it off.

Immediately.

I tossed it onto the pile and pulled the gray sweater out from the bottom. It had been sweater number one in today's fit check, but I wasn't sold on it at first, because I wasn't sure monochrome was the look I was going for. But once I had it on again, it felt so much better.

"Okay, this is it." I looked into the mirror, readjusted the sweater around my arms and had to pull at it a bit . . . "No. Nope." I pulled it off and tossed it onto the pile. "What the hell?"

Ro handed me the pink one. I pulled it on and checked myself in the mirror, and doing an all-over torso check, there wasn't anything bothering me. As per usual, she was right. It possibly was the better choice.

"So, Win," she said, using that tone again. The one where she was about to drop another truth bomb.

"Just say it."

"Well, do you think there's a reason why you and Deacon click?"

I turned to face her. "What?"

"And a reason why some clothes feel weird, and why you'll have a meltdown and have to pull your shoe off, regardless of where we are, if your sock feels weird? And why you don't like loud crowded spaces, or why you need to decompress in silence after a busy day, or—"

"Is there a point to this character assassination or are we doing this for fun?"

She chuckled and tilted her head. "Darling, you know I love you."

"Oh god. What is it? What's wrong? I thought you liked the pink."

"I do. The pink sweater is the correct choice. I'm just saying that you and Deacon have a lot in common, and you know, birds of a feather and all that."

I stared at her. "Are you trying to say you think I'm neurodivergent?"

"No," she said quickly. "But neurodivergence is a broad spectrum."

"You think I'm neurodivergent," I said. It wasn't a question, because that was one hundred percent what she was implying.

"Well, yes. Maybe. And that's not a bad thing," she added quickly. "Goodness, no. It's not a bad thing at all. It just explains some things, don't you think?"

I blinked. "Uh . . . well, jeez, I dunno. I don't know what to think because you just dropped this on me and I've had no time to process—"

She raised an eyebrow and smiled as if I was almost connecting the dots. "Processing, overthinking, overanalyzing, meticulous organization, hyperfocus."

"Those are . . . those are positive personality traits," I replied. "And great for business management, I'll have you know."

She chuckled again. "They are. And I wouldn't change one thing about you, Winter. Not one thing. I'm just saying this to help you realize that you and Deacon have more in common than you might think. So instead of trying to analyze every single thing he does or doesn't do, just relax."

"Oh, relax and don't overthink," I said flatly. "Why didn't I think of doing that earlier? Could have saved me a lifetime of unnecessary stress."

Ro sighed. "Don't be mad. I'm just trying to help."

"By telling me you think I have undiagnosed neurodivergence."

She shrugged. "Well, me thinking that isn't new. You've been like this forever."

"Gee, thanks."

"Remember that time when you were in kindergarten and you had to make clouds on paper with cotton balls?"

I made a gagging noise and shuddered at the memory. I had to wipe my hands on my pants to remove the memory of cotton balls. "Dear god. Why would you—"

"Or the slime at the science fair."

I narrowed my eyes at her. "That was a traumatic experience. I can still feel—"

"Or how many fidget spinners you've lost."

I put my hand up. "Okay, I think you've made your point."

She began putting all the incorrect sweaters back on their hangers for me. "Um, that's back to front," I mumbled. "It will face the wrong way in the wardrobe. They all face the front . . ."

She smiled as she fixed it. "Okay."

I sighed. "So this has been fun for me."

"You should get going. You don't want to be late," she said. "They won't notice the sweater if you miss dinner."

I gasped and checked the time. "Oh jeez." I grabbed my scarf and pulled on my boots and coat at the door. "I'll be home by ten, maybe? I don't even know. The boys have been fed—"

"Yes, yes," she said, shoving me toward the door. "Go, Winter. Oh, here, don't forget this."

She shoved the box of Christmas cookies into my hand, which I had brought to take as a thank you gift for dinner, because it was rude not to take something, which I had forgotten all about. I'd be so lost without her.

"Oh, thank you."

"Drive safe."

"Always do."

I hurried to my car to get out of the cold. Now, coming from Boise, I was used to the cold and snow. But Hartbridge was in-the-mountains level of cold.

And to think Merry and Bright could have been out in this on their own if I hadn't taken them in. Well, if I hadn't sent their poor momma cat to kitty-heaven. But still . . . they wouldn't have lasted long in this weather.

I drove to Deacon's, trying not to think about what Ro had suggested, about me having neurodivergent traits. It didn't bother or upset me any, it just . . . I wasn't sure. I'd always had idiosyncrasies. Who the heck didn't? I'd always found myself in the company of other quirky people. It was just who I felt most comfortable with.

Hmm.

Was Ro wrong?

Undecided.

I had enough self-awareness to see she may have some valid points. Objectively, I couldn't disagree with her. It wasn't a flat-out no.

So, maybe?

Did it change anything?

Not at all.

Did it explain a lot of things?

Possibly.

Did it change anything between Deacon and me?

Not one bit.

So maybe she had a point, maybe she didn't.

I arrived at Deacon's, taking the box of cookies, suddenly wishing I'd worn the blue sweater, and rang the doorbell.

I could hear shuffling and what was possibly claws on floorboards, then a deep, raspy bark. "Mildred," a familiar voice said before the door opened. Deacon grinned at me, bathed in warm light. At his feet was the cutest freaking dog I'd ever seen. Mildred was an English bulldog, and looked remarkably as if she was created in Minecraft. And no other name but Mildred that would have suited her. "Hello," Deacon said. "Please come in. Don't mind Mildred. She normally has manners."

I stepped in, my boots and legs being sniffed and snuf-fled by an excited Mildred. I handed Deacon the box of cookies. "For you and your parents." I gave Mildred a pat, which made her snuffle and wiggle in the cutest way. "Oh my goodness, she's adorable."

I pulled off my boots and Deacon hung my coat and scarf by the door. "She is."

I noticed then, the most amazing aroma. "Something smells wonderful."

"Dinner," he said, as I followed him through their house. There was wood paneling, tiled floors, timber trims. The whole house was a palette of warm greens and browns, and I immediately felt at ease here. It definitely had the feeling of a home.

In the kitchen, Deacon's mom was at the fridge, and his dad was cutting a slab of meat.

"Mom, Dad," Deacon said. "Winter's here."

They each smiled at me, fond and genuine. "Oh, hello again," his mom said. "Please call me Vicky."

His dad put down the carving utensils and quickly wiped his hand before offering me a handshake, completely pretending he hadn't come to see me at the store to talk to me about Deacon. "Hello, thanks for coming. Call me Wayne."

"Thank you for having me," I said.

Deacon held up the box of cookies. "Winter brought these."

"I couldn't turn up empty-handed," I said, a little embarrassed at being the focus of attention.

His dad peered in through the clear lid. "Oooh, Christmas cookies! My favorite."

Deacon laughed. "Any cookie is his favorite."

"Correct."

Vicky took the box. "Thank you, Winter. It wasn't necessary but I do appreciate it."

"Yes, it was necessary, thank you," Wayne said, opening

the box and plucking a cookie from the top. He shoved it into his mouth before Vicky could stop him.

"Oh, Wayne," she admonished, with nothing but love in her eyes. "You'll spoil your dinner."

He grinned at her around his mouthful, and as they went back and forth, I was struck by how affectionate they were, how much warmth there was between them. Deacon had grown up in a home so full of love, it was . . . something special.

Something I could only envy.

Deacon laughed at them, and then his mom turned to us. "Dinner will be ten minutes."

Deacon took the sleeve of my sweater at my wrist and pulled me out of the room, down a hall, and through a door. He closed it behind us, and we both stood there. He was grinning, and damn, he was handsome.

He still had a hold of my sleeve, right at the wrist. Not touching me, exactly, but he was touching a part of me. My sweater, and by extension, me.

I looked at his hand, then up at his face, and smiled at him.

His eyes met mine, and he dropped his hand. "Sorry."

"No, don't apologize. I like it."

In fact, I'd loved it.

It was somehow better, sweeter, than if he'd taken my hand.

"You can take my sleeve anytime."

He blushed deep pink and took a step back, his eyes cast down to the floor. He blinked a few times. "This is my room."

His room was large, as far as bedrooms went. There was a bed in the corner with a bedside table. His bed covers were a dark blue, his bed impeccably made. There was a rug on the floor, a desk in the other corner with a model of a plane on it, and a large bookcase by the door.

Of course I was drawn to it.

I scanned the shelves, reading all the titles. He had an eclectic selection, ranging from *The Lord of the Rings* to manga, some non-fiction animal veterinary journals, and Japanese poetry, of course. "Great books," I said. "We have a lot of the same titles. Your shelves look very similar to mine."

He was standing close, still not touching, but perhaps closer than was strictly necessary. "You have subscriptions to the *Journal of Animal Science* and *Veterinary and Animal Science*?"

I chuckled. "Except those."

Then I noticed the long, narrow wooden tray on the second top shelf. Well, more to the point, what was in the tray. There was a small anime figurine, an old plane ticket stub, a bottle cap, a small rock, among other random things, but one thing in particular caught my eye.

It was the slip of paper I'd written his name on when I'd put that book aside for him on the store's opening day.

I reached up, almost touching it, but stopped just short. I didn't think he'd like anyone touching his things. "That looks familiar."

He smiled, his cheeks pink. "Yes."

"You kept it."

"Yes." He kept his eyes on the tray, at all his little treasures. "I like to keep things that mean a lot to me."

Oh my.

"My little note means a lot to you?"

He nodded, blushing a deeper, beautiful pink. "Yes. Because it came from you. Because you wrote it, but also because you were considerate enough to put the book aside for me."

Oh my heart. It could have just about burst.

"I love that you kept it," I said. I looked at the other things in the tray. "Will you tell me what the other things are? What they mean to you?"

He smiled in a way I hadn't really seen before. Excitement, determination, and animation. He pointed as he went. "Yuri figurine. My dormmate at college gave it to me. She was in the room next to mine, and she told me to watch *Yuri on Ice*. I hadn't heard of it and, well, it was very new to me."

I chuckled. "I can see why you liked it."

"I'd never read or watched anything that had two male protagonists before. Lucy and I became friends. I would go with her to the bookstore and the library, or out for coffee, and we would discuss the books we were reading."

I loved this so much. "Oh, she sounds amazing."

"She's now at a veterinarian clinic in Boise. I haven't seen her for a while, though we do email occasionally. She gave me the little Yuri figure as a farewell when we graduated."

"Aww, that's so cool." Then I caught up to what he said. "Wait. Which bookstore in Boise did you go to?"

"Pages. It was close to—"

"No way!" I cried. "That was my store! I was one of the managers there. Are you saying we could have totally crossed paths before?"

He blinked a few times, his brow furrowed, and his eyes met mine briefly before they went back to the bookshelf. "I don't remember seeing you."

"There were a lot of people," I said, not wanting him to feel bad. "Isn't it funny that we were in the same place though? Crazy to think we could have walked past each other without knowing it."

He nodded. "Yes."

I pointed to the plane ticket stub. "What's this?"

"My first time on a plane. When I was little, I was very into planes. I loved them. I studied them, drew them, watched endless documentaries."

"The plane on your desk," I said.

He nodded. "The Lockheed Martin F-35 Lightning II. It's an American family of single-seat, single-engine, all-weather stealth multirole combat aircraft . . ." He trailed off with a shrug. "I had many more, all kinds, but they're in a storage box now. I keep that one out because it was the first one I bought with my own money. But I kind of lost interest after a few years."

"That happens."

He nodded again. "The plane ticket was my first time on a plane. I was six. We flew to Seattle."

"You must have been so excited."

"I was, yes. But it was loud and there were a lot of people. It was overwhelming. I appreciated it more when it was over."

"I can totally understand that."

He went back to the tray. "The soda cap was from my first day at high school." He shrugged. "The rock I found at a science excursion in fifth grade." He picked it up. "See the white vein of calcite. It runs right through it, perfectly symmetrical. It fascinated me to think what significant geological event must have happened to produce such a thing."

I held my hand out and he gently placed it on my palm. I could see the line of white calcite. It was kinda cool. "Like a volcano eruption? Is that what did this?"

His eyes met mine and he smiled. "Possibly. A seismic shift, perhaps."

"That's so cool. Isn't it fascinating that they can tell what happened however many millions of years ago by looking at the geological formations? And fossils. Like how crazy is it to think that whole animals were preserved in sediment or whatever, and humans find them sixty-five million years later. It's like a snapshot of history."

His eyes met mine then, that intense burning stare that pinned me in place, making my heart rate spike and butter-flies flood my belly.

"Yes," he murmured.

"Okay, boys," his mom called out. "Dinner!"

Only then did he look away and I could suddenly breathe again.

Wowzers.

What a rush.

My heart was still hammering when he ducked his head and went to his door. He paused before opening it, glancing at me again, his smile shy, cheeks pink, as if he wanted to burn the image of me standing by his bookcase into his memory.

Then he opened the door and nodded to the hall. "Dinner is ready."

"Okay," I said, carefully putting the rock back in its place, and followed him out.

Dinner was lovely. I had been nervous, obviously, but Wayne and Vicky were just the nicest people. Wayne had an endless well of dad jokes, apparently, which Deacon found funny, if not a little embarrassing. Vicky had a sort of quiet patience and a gentle maternal air about her that I found comforting. So very much the opposite of my own mother, and Ro had always been like an older sister/best friend more than a mother figure. Ro and I weren't entirely conventional, but we were family; she was my family.

And as I looked at Deacon, then at his parents, it was so obvious that they loved him unconditionally. I envied him for that. That security, that knowing in your bones that you are accepted exactly as you are.

"So Winter," Wayne said, and I had to wonder if I'd spaced out. "How are you finding Hartbridge?"

"Oh, I love it. It's a wonderful little town. Everyone has been so welcoming, and it's so picturesque. Like something out of a movie."

"It is," Vicky said. "And your store? How are you finding it?"

"Busy," I replied. "I expect it to slow down after the holidays, of course. But as far as my dream of having my own cozy, small-town bookstore, it's perfect."

"He wants to start a book club," Deacon said. "Meeting once a month to have cake and coffee and to talk about books."

"That's a great idea," Wayne said.

I nodded. "Yes, several people are interested already."

"I told him cake wasn't a good idea," Deacon added, "because of crumbs and greasy fingers on the merchandise."

"Oh." Vicky gave me a sorry a look.

I chuckled. "No, it's fine. He was quite right. Cake wouldn't be suitable. So perhaps something else. Themed cookies like the Christmas ones I bought from the diner? Or fun little cake pops. Something without cream frosting, anyway." I smiled at Deacon. "Now if only I knew someone who was really good at organizing things to help me arrange it all."

Deacon put his fork down and smiled. "You mean me?"

I grinned, nodding. "Yes, I do."

I noticed then that Wayne was looking between us, and he studied me for a few beats, and I suddenly felt a little too scrutinized. "Sooo," he began, "I've been meaning to ask you something."

Oh god.

I cleared my throat, trying not to fidget. "Yes?"

He stared at me, very seriously, and both Deacon and Vicky were watching him.

One second.

Two seconds.

"It's very important," Wayne said.

I tried to smile, but pretty sure it didn't work. "Okay."

"What's your favorite dinosaur?"

I blinked.

Deacon snorted and Vicky sighed.

"Favorite dinosaur?" I asked. That was *not* what I'd been expecting.

Wayne nodded. "I think it says a lot about a person."

"Dad was surprised I hadn't asked you yet," Deacon murmured.

"You don't have to answer," Vicky added with a defeated sigh, as if this conversation was one they'd had often. "Not everyone has a favorite dinosaur."

"Ankylosaurus," I said. "My favorite dinosaur is the ankylosaurus. It has full body armor and a mace for a tail, and that's so cool."

Both Wayne and Vicky glanced at Deacon, and Deacon smiled at his plate before looking at his dad.

"What?" I said, trying not to panic. "Is that the wrong answer? What does it say about me if a favorite dinosaur says a lot about a person?"

Full body armor and a built-in weapon-tail didn't mean I was defensive, did it? Or that I wished I was immune to scrutiny or insults . . . Surely that didn't say anything about me . . .

Wayne put his hand up and shook his head. "No, no, it's not that. It's just . . ." His gaze went to Deacon. "The anky-losaurus is Deacon's favorite dinosaur."

I turned to Deacon. "It is?"

He was not doing a very good job at trying not to smile, and he gave a nod. "Yes."

"They are so cool," I said. "Low to the ground, full body armor, and a mace-tail. It's a complete weapon. Like the most Pokémon dinosaur ever."

Deacon's eyes met mine then, his smile softening. "Exactly." His cheeks went pink and he quickly looked away. "The Kosmoceratops is my second favorite."

I nodded. "A commendable choice. I do like the Kosmoceratops also. I mean, what's not to like about fifteen spiky horns? If I had to choose a second one—" I stopped talking when I realized then that Wayne and Vicky were still watching us. "Sorry."

"Nothing to be sorry for," Wayne said.

Vicky stood up and began to clear plates, and I immediately tried to help. "I'll take care of it," she said, stopping me, before nodding to the living room. "You boys want to go in. Your show's about to start."

Our show?

Deacon stood up. "Thank you for dinner, Mom."

I stood up next to him. "Yes, thank you so much. It was delicious. All of it."

She waved us off, though her smile told me she appreciated the compliment. "You go along now. Wayne, you're washing up."

He protested. "But our show—" She gave him a look that promptly shut him up. "I will be the fastest dishwasher ever," he mumbled.

Deacon laughed, and taking my sleeve again, he led me toward the living room and what I saw took my breath away. There was a dark green velvet three-seater sofa and two mismatched single chairs which, with my very limited knowledge of furniture, looked like antique designer pieces: tan leather, well-loved. There was a lovely fireplace, a smallish television by today's standards, a gorgeous Christmas tree that smelled wonderful, and . . .

Oh my.

One entire wall was a bookcase, stacked full of, well, everything. All genres, all kinds—paperbacks, hardcovers, new, old, fiction, non-fiction, magazines, journals, encyclopedias—all neatly arranged and oh so amazing.

"Do you like it?" Deacon asked quietly.

I turned to him, eyes as wide as my smile. "Oh, I could live in this room. Everything in it is perfect. When you said your family were readers," I said, taking in the bookshelves. "Wow. You have more books than my store."

Deacon laughed. "Not quite."

Okay, so maybe not. But damn. Not far off . . .

"Both Mom and Dad love to read also. We always have. Even as a young boy, I don't remember a time when we didn't sit in here and read."

I put my hand to my heart. "I love that so much." I looked around the room again. Given the books, and the small TV, it was clear that watching television wasn't a priority for them, and I loved that too. And the lamps by the sofa and the chairs, for reading, of course. "This room is perfect. It feels like a reading den in a fancy castle or something."

He looked around for a moment. "Minus the stone walls, vaulted ceilings, and the general size."

I laughed at that. "Well, yes, all that. But I don't know, this is the kind of living room I want. It's giving me great decoration ideas for my room. Maybe I could decorate my bedroom like this. It's a very blank canvas at the moment. The whole house is, really. It needs some work. But everything about this room is perfect."

"You'd like to decorate like this?"

I nodded. "Yes. Like a fancy reading den in a castle or

something. Minus the stone walls, vaulted ceilings, and general size."

His eyes met mine, and seeing that I was joking, he smiled back at me.

Damn, if it didn't make my heart thump.

What was I talking about? Oh, that's right . . .

"Ro is doing some remodeling at our place. It was an old ranch cottage or something. It's super cute, don't get me wrong, and I love it. But my room is just blank, white walls. And boxes . . . I've been so busy with the store. I'm mostly unpacked, save a few last things. But I'm definitely going to need some floor-to-ceiling bookcases and an amazing chair by the window, reading lamps."

"Would you get sick of looking at books? All day at work, then in your room as well."

I looked at him as if he'd lost his mind. "Never."

He grinned. "I didn't think so."

"You'll have to come around sometime," I offered, trying to play it cool. "I'll return the dinner favor. You can see Merry and Bright and how playful they are now. They're just the cutest little demons ever."

Deacon smiled at me, his eyes on mine in that intense way he could just stare right into me.

"Has the show started?" Wayne called out from the kitchen.

Oh.

Yes, that's what we were doing.

Deacon picked up the remote control and aimed it at the TV then he sat down on the sofa. It was a three-seater so I assumed I was to join him. I gestured to the seat beside him. "Can I?"

"Yes."

There was a sponsorship break on the TV, so I was still clueless. "Uh, what show are we watching?"

"*Antiques Roadshow,*" he replied. "It's our thing. If you'd rather not watch, if you think it's silly . . ."

"Are you kidding?" I asked. "I love that you watch *Antiques Roadshow*. This sounds like so much fun."

Wayne came in just as the intro music began and he sat in the chair closest to the bookcases. "Ah, good, haven't missed anything yet."

Of course, Mildred followed him in and she came trotting over to me, snuffling loudly. I pet her head and earned myself a wag of her stumpy little tail.

"She likes you," Deacon said quietly.

Not gonna lie. It was an awesome feeling when someone's dog or cat liked you. But I totally downplayed it. "She can probably smell the kittens on me."

The TV show began and soon Vicky came in and sat in her chair, and I honestly loved the fact that this was a thing their family did. I hadn't seen *Antiques Roadshow* in years and this was the English version, which was even better.

The first item was a brooch in the shape of a bird. It had diamonds and sapphires and rubies.

"1920s," Wayne said. "French. £3,000."

"Late nineteen-hundreds," Deacon said. "English. £4,000."

I laughed because, oh my god, this was fun.

"Uh," I hedged. "1820s, Russian, £5,000. That's a lot of diamonds."

Deacon grinned at me, and when the expert announced the date and value, I was right.

"Oh my god," I said. "I guessed that correctly? I love this game!"

"Beginner's luck," Wayne said with a smile.

The next item was an embroidered box with little gold feet. It looked old as hell. Or maybe just well-used? I had no clue.

"Oooh," Wayne said. "1850s, French, £800."

"1880s," Deacon said. "Italian. £1,000."

"Hmm," Vicky said, studying the screen. "I'll say 1780s, English. £3,000."

"I have no clue," I said. "But I'll go 1910, £500."

I couldn't have been more wrong, and Wayne got it right.

The next item was a pale-yellow Chinese vase, maybe eight inches tall, that the owner had found in a thrift shop.

"Ming dynasty," Deacon said quickly. "£10,000."

"What?" I said. "That little thing?"

Wayne gave a nod. "I'll say £20,000. If it's real. If it's a replica, eighty quid."

Jeebus.

"That yellow is for the emperor," Deacon explained. "It was replicated a lot."

"Okay," I said, then totally guessed. "Fake, 1920s replica. £30."

And it was actually a Ming vase. Ming freaking dynasty. It was legit, and it was estimated to be worth £20,000.

I was stunned.

Then a painting worth a thousand pounds, then a plate worth one hundred pounds, then a signed autograph of some English cricketer I'd never heard of. I got none of them right, but it was so much fun. Wayne was leading by one and although it was all in good fun, they did take it seriously.

The next item were silver model planes, and before the expert or owner could even speak, Deacon said, "Tomcat V-F2, F22 Raptor, Supermarine Spitfire, Lockheed Martin SR-72."

Then he went on to describe each plane model, specs, and all kinds of things I couldn't understand.

I stared at him. "Objection, your honor," I said. "Unfair advantage."

The way he laughed filled me with something warm and lovely.

Wayne groaned because it meant it was now tied between them, but even I could see how much he liked seeing Deacon laugh. I also noticed how Vicky smiled at him, watching us.

"Last one is always a doozy," Wayne said.

And it was.

A painting on wood paneling from an old hotel, built in the 1400s, which was incredible to me. They'd found it when doing renovations and it was as if they'd removed the whole panel to bring it in. It was dark, grungy, and their faces were weird with gold plates behind their heads, which I assumed were supposed to be halos, or aliens . . . It could have gone either way, honestly.

"£10,000," Wayne declared.

"£35,000," Deacon said.

I'd have better luck throwing a dart at a number than guess. "Uh . . . £80,000?" They seemed to just give randomly large amounts at will on this show.

"Built in the 1400s," I mumbled, flabbergasted. "That's . . . that's two whole centuries before Shakespeare. Three hundred years before this country." All I could do was shake my head in wonder. "It's hard to imagine."

Deacon gave me a nod. "It is remarkable."

"Can you imagine who's seen it, who's touched it? What kind of life they lived?" I wondered out loud. "How fascinating."

His eyes met mine and he didn't look away. "Yes. I think the same thing. With any object of a significant age. Who made it, the hands which held it, shaped it, built it, or painted it."

"And the Ming dynasty," I said, still struggling to believe it. "And how it ended up in England all these centuries later. In a thrift shop, of all places."

Deacon made a face. "Items of significance like that should be given back to their country of origin. The experts will quite often say things like that may have been bought or traded back in the fifteenth century, but it's more likely they were stolen or looted. A vase from 1410, imperial at that, should rightly be in a museum in China."

Wow. I hadn't really thought of that . . . but he was right. "Agreed," I said. "That's so true. Culturally significant objects shouldn't be for sale."

The fact he thought like that made me like him just that little bit more. Which, at this point, was quite the feat. I was beginning to wonder if it was possible to like him more than I already did.

"I mean," I said with my hand to my heart. "If it was a first edition *Catcher in the Rye* or *Fahrenheit 451*, I could see myself wanting to keep it. Maybe. But if it was a first edition Shakespeare, it should be in a museum."

Deacon nodded, giving me a timid smile, but then a smell began to waft . . .

A pungent, sour, rotten smell.

"Oh, Mildred," Deacon said. "No."

Oh, sweet merciful gods.

Mildred had the audacity to smile at us. Deacon took my sleeve again and pulled me up off the couch, and the last thing I saw was Wayne, with his shirt pulled up over his nose, ushering Mildred to the back door.

Vicky evacuated to the kitchen with us. "Sorry about that," she said.

All I could do was laugh. And laugh.

"It's fine," I said.

"No it's not," Deacon said. "What did she eat this after-noon? Did she get into the trash again?"

Vicky laughed, and Deacon turned to me. "I'm very sorry."

I was still chuckling. "It's fine. I should get going though. I better get home and save Ro from my two little monsters." I turned to Vicky. "Thank you for having me over for dinner. I had a lovely time." Wayne was still super-vising Mildred, giving her a stern talking to. "Please tell Wayne I said thank you, and I'll brush up on my knowledge of antiques and put up a better fight next time."

"I will," she said gently. "We'll see you again."

"Yes, you will," I said surely. Then I turned to Deacon. "Walk me out?"

He gave a nod and held my coat for me while I pulled on my shoes, then he helped me into it. "You still use the scarf I gave you," he said when I pulled it out of my coat pocket.

"Of course I do. I love it." I put the scarf on and gave him a smile. "I had a lovely time tonight. Thank you for inviting me."

His cheeks went pink. "You're welcome. I'm sorry about Mildred."

I laughed again and put my hand on the door handle but didn't open it yet. "I'd love to do this again. I really enjoy spending time with you."

"I enjoy spending time with you too," he whispered, his eyes more gray than blue tonight.

"Next time you can come to my place, if you want. No pressure. Or we could try the diner? Whatever you want."

His brow furrowed for a second before he nodded. "Dinner with your friends," he murmured. "This week sometime? You invited me."

"I did."

"I'd like to go with you."

I was waiting for the *but* . . . There wasn't one.

"You will?" I tried not to act so surprised, but I hadn't expected that at all. "Awesome. I'll ask Gunter if they've made any final plans and let you know."

He gave a nod. "Okay."

I lifted my hand and stopped just short of touching his arm. If it was any other date with any other person, I'd have touched his arm without thinking. Hell, if it was anyone else, I might have even given him a kiss on the cheek.

But it wasn't. It was Deacon.

I pulled my hand back. "Sorry."

He looked at my hand and swallowed hard. "You can touch my arm," he whispered.

"It's fine," I said. "Habit I'm trying to break."

"I think . . . I want you to."

He wanted me to touch his arm?

"You want me to?"

"Yes." He gave one nod, his gaze on the wall, and he kind of held his arm out as if he was steeling himself for contact.

So I very slowly, very carefully lifted my hand again, and this time I gently put my palm on his forearm. I gave the barest of squeezes before I took my hand away.

My heart was hammering, and I think I'd forgotten to breathe. "Goodnight, Deacon," I murmured.

He nodded again, blushing, staring intently at the wall. "Yes. Goodnight, Winter."

I opened the door then and rushed to my car. My insides were a jumbled ball of nerves and excitement, and I was still grinning when I got home.

Merry and Bright were snoozing in their pen by the fire, and Ro was curled up on the couch with a blanket and a book. She glanced at the clock. "Oh, you're home early."

I walked in, plonked myself down beside her on the couch, and sighed dreamily.

"I take it dinner went well," she said.

I turned my head so I could meet her gaze. "Yep."

She smiled. "You really like him, huh?"

That little ember behind my ribs, of something warm and lovely, burned a little warmer. "Yeah, I do. He held my sleeve."

"He what?"

"He held my sleeve. Here," I said, holding out my wrist and showing her how Deacon had grabbed my sleeve. "Like this. And he led me to his room. And again when Mildred gassed the room, but this. This is the sweetest, most romantic thing ever."

"Mildred gassed the what? Is that . . . is that his Grandma?"

"No, their dog."

She grimaced. "Oh."

"He led me by the sleeve to his room, Ro," I said.

She raised her eyebrow. "Okay, so anyone else and I'd be asking for details but you going to a guy's bedroom raises more questions than answers."

"He showed me his bookcase."

She snorted. "Wow. So that's like second base for you."

I ignored that. "And their bookcase in their house is one entire wall, floor to ceiling. And the house is all warm greens and browns. Imagine if Bilbo Baggins owned Belle's library."

She squinted and tilted her head as she tried to picture that. "Uhhh."

"My sleeve, Ro," I said, holding up my arm again and getting back to the important part. "His sleeve-holding is my newest favorite thing ever."

CHAPTER ELEVEN
DEACON

I STOOD and watched as Winter's car drove away, as his red brake lights disappeared into the darkness.

I'd been so nervous before tonight, but my tummy wasn't churning or aching now. Instead, there was an odd flutter in my chest and my heart felt bigger somehow, warmer too.

"Everything okay, sweetheart?" Mom said behind me.

I turned, startled, my hand still to my heart. "Oh, yes."

"Close the door. You're letting all the heat out," she said.

"Oh, yes, of course." I pulled the door shut. "I was just watching him leave."

"Dinner went well?" she hedged.

I wasn't entirely sure why that was a question. "Yes. I thought so."

"He's a lovely boy."

"He's twenty-eight."

"He's a boy to me," she said with a smile. "Now, did you want hot chocolate or tea before bed?"

"No, none for me, thank you. I'm fine." Except my heart

was still too big. "I'll go get ready for bed. I have an early start tomorrow."

"Okay, love."

"Oh," I said. "Uh, Winter said his friends are having dinner at the pizzeria one night this week, and he asked if I'd like to go. I said yes. So I won't need dinner on that night. I'm not sure which night yet but I'll let you know."

Her eyes went wide and she smiled. "That's fine. And exciting."

I made a face, trying not to think about meeting a group of people. "Well, we'll see. I might not go yet."

"Might not go where?" Dad said. "And why are we having this conversation at the front door? Did Winter go already?"

"He said to say thank you and good night," Mom said. "And Deacon was just telling me he has a date night this week."

A date night?

"A date night?" Dad asked, grinning at me. "That's great. Good for you. He's a nice boy."

"He's twenty-eight," I said. I was about to dispute the date-night claim but then I wasn't entirely sure that was wrong.

Did I have a date with Winter?

By definition, I think I did, yes.

Oh boy, I had a date with Winter.

Were we dating?

To go on a date with someone would imply dating, or was there a specific number of dates to be had before the term dating applied? I wasn't sure, and I didn't feel comfortable asking Mom or Dad that question. Maybe I could ask Google . . . no.

Maybe I needed to ask *Winter* that.

He'd said if I had questions, I should ask. Would he then think I thought we were dating?

"I'm going to bed now," I said, before taking my leave. "I have a lot of overthinking to do, and I'd rather do it in my room."

Dad chuckled. "Okay. We're leaving at six-thirty in the morning, remember."

"Of course I remember."

"So don't be overthinking too much."

I knew he was joking, but I narrowed my eyes at him before I went into my room and closed the door.

The sanctity of my room . . .

For all intents and purposes, it looked unchanged. Nothing was out of place, nothing missing. But Winter had been in here, and in my memories, I could see him standing at my bookcase, looking at all my things.

His gentle questions, his bright eyes.

Then I remembered the way he'd touched my arm when we'd stood at the door.

I could still feel the warmth of it. Even though looking at my arm now, it too appeared unchanged.

But I could feel the warmth of it in my mind.

Like I could feel the memory of him being in my room.

Like I could feel the way my heart felt too big and warm when I remembered him. His smile, his eyes.

I didn't even mind him touching my arm. He'd given me warning and he'd asked permission, and those two things were apparently all I needed.

Or maybe it was because it was him.

I trusted Winter not to overstep. He knew my boundaries, my limitations, and he respected them.

He had made me feel so at ease. We'd had a few communication issues in the beginning, but that seemed to have passed. We were on the same page now.

In my head, at least.

I wanted to ask him if his skin still burned where he'd touched me. If his heart felt too big and too warm. If thinking about me made him smile the way thinking of him made me smile.

I wanted to ask him all kinds of questions.

I wanted to know his mind, his heart.

So after a quick shower, I climbed into bed and instead of reading, I began making a list.

Questions to ask Winter.

I PAUSED work at 8:oo a.m. to send Winter a text.

> "My heart with pleasure fills, and dances with the daffodils"

I was going to text him my questions but decided to keep those as conversation starters on our date, if that's what it was. I wasn't entirely convinced and would need to ask him for clarification later. But he'd made a point of telling me how much he loved the lines of poetry.

The poem from William Wordsworth that I'd quoted was probably too much—and it hadn't been one I'd selected and written down earlier—but one I'd chosen at 5:oo a.m. when I woke up unable to stop thinking about him.

A fitting poem for him.

For how I felt.

I might not be able to say such things to his face, in person, from my own heart, but I could borrow the senti-ment from poets who say it so much better than I ever could.

His reply came through as a gif.

Bugs Bunny with heart eyes fainting to the floor and the word *swoon* in big, flashing letters.

It made me laugh.

Dad clapped his hands to get my attention. We were in a barn with twelve goats. "Work now, smile at your boyfriend later."

Embarrassed, I pocketed my phone and got back to work. We had to be back at the clinic in half an hour, so we were on a time crunch. I needed to focus.

But . . . boyfriend?

Smile at your boyfriend later, Dad had said.

My boyfriend?

That word made me feel positively giddy and jittery, and swoopy and . . .

And then a ram escaped my hold, and Dad had to grab it, and it was the jolt of reality I needed.

To focus.

Focus now, think about the word *boyfriend* later . . .

AND THINK ABOUT IT, I did. I thought about seeing Winter again. I thought about dating. I thought about the word boyfriend, And I thought about what that meant.

Overthinking, overanalyzing, over and over . . .

I barely slept. My stomach ached too much to eat breakfast, and I considered not going to work. But that would just mean I'd have the whole day to overthink and make everything worse in my head.

Because that's what I did, and I was incredibly good at it.

But I was certain of one thing.

I didn't want to meet his friends at the diner. I didn't

want a date where there would be other people. I wasn't ready for that.

I knew Hamish, that was true. But I didn't know the others, and I was sure they were all lovely, but I didn't want to put myself in a situation I wasn't ready for.

I didn't want to freak out in front of them, in front of Winter.

Once I'd made the decision not to go, I expected to feel better, relieved. But no . . . I was disappointed.

Mostly at myself.

I was grateful for work and being busy. The thing with Dad was he knew when I needed to be pushed and snapped back into focus, and then other times, he knew when *not* to push and to just let me process the mess in my head.

Like I was today.

At eight o'clock, instead of the line of poetry I had planned to send, I typed out something else.

Something I knew by heart.

> "I'd rather end up wishing I hadn't than end up wishing I had."

Then I watched as his reply bubble appeared, disappeared, then reappeared, my stomach churning.

> Quoting Tolstoy at eight o'clock in the morning. Are you okay?

I rolled my eyes at myself because, of course, he would be familiar. I typed out my reply.

> Not particularly

I expected his reply bubble to appear, but my phone rang instead. Winter's name appeared on screen.

I considered not answering but didn't want him to worry. "Hello."

"Deacon, what's wrong?" He sounded so concerned. "You said not particularly. What happened?"

"Nothing, I . . ." But I had to tell him. I'd said I'd go with him and now I couldn't and I felt bad, but I had to tell him. "I can't go with you to dinner. To the pizzeria with your friends. I know I said I would, but I've thought about it. It's all I've thought about and I'm not ready for that, and it wouldn't be a good idea."

"Oh. Okay. That's fine."

Fine?

Did he not care at all that I wouldn't go with him?

"What do you . . . why is it fine?"

"Because you said you weren't ready."

Oh.

"And not being ready is perfectly fine," he said. "I'm sorry you thought about it a lot."

"I want to see you but I . . ."

"You're not ready," he said. "Deacon, it's okay. I want to see you too but not if it makes you uncomfortable. It doesn't have to be with all those guys. We can have dinner at my house on Sunday night if you'd prefer? Or you can help me at the store on Thursday evening. I'll be open a little longer for the late-night shoppers."

That sounded much better, and the knot in my stomach loosened.

"Okay."

"Okay, yes?"

I chuckled. "Yes."

He sighed. "Good. And thank you for telling me."

"Telling you what?"

"That you weren't comfortable and that you weren't ready."

My face went all hot and I was glad he couldn't see me. "Oh."

"You can tell me these things," he added. "There's absolutely no rush, okay?"

"Are you . . . are you not sad or disappointed? Because I . . . wish I wasn't like this. I wish . . ."

"I wish you weren't any different from exactly who you are," he said. "I happen to like you exactly as you are."

I was smiling now.

Now I wished I'd thought to tell him sooner instead of tormenting myself.

"There's no rush, Deacon. We're going along at our own pace, and that's perfect for us. No pressure, okay?"

"Okay," I said, my voice a whisper. "I feel better after talking to you. My tummy hurts less."

"Oh, Deacon," he murmured. "You were so stressed. I feel better too. I was worried when I got your text. I mean, I love Tolstoy's work, but oof, it can get dark."

"I love his work too."

"I know. I've seen your bookcase."

I laughed at that, but I could hear clients in the reception area. "I should go," I said. "I have clients. Thank you for calling."

"You're welcome."

"Have a good day, Winter."

"You too. Talk soon."

I disconnected the call just as the door opened. Dad poked his head in and saw my phone in my hand. "Everything okay, Deac?"

I smiled and gave him a nod. "Yes. It is now."

He seemed to understand, the way he always did. "Glad to hear it, because the O'Connell's have their dog here to see you."

"Of course," I said. "I'll come out and meet them."

❄

SO THE ONE thing worse than actually going to the pizzeria to meet Winter and all his friends was *not* going.

I was confused by this.

Because the relief I'd felt when I'd decided not to go was now anguish about not being there.

They'd decided on Wednesday night, which was fine. Great, even. Good for them. But that meant I'd spent all Wednesday night in my room pacing, unable to sit still because I wanted to be there.

Except I didn't want to be there.

And that was what confused me.

Mom knocked on my bedroom door. It opened slowly and her cautious face appeared, peeking in. "Deacon, honey," she said. "I can hear you pacing. Do you want to talk?"

No.

I didn't.

She came in and ushered me to sit on my bed. "Why are you upset? You said you didn't want to go to the pizzeria—"

"I don't," I said. "I didn't want to go. I didn't want to meet all his friends and I didn't want to be like this in front of him and them. I can be like this here, but not there. I don't want them to see me like this, but now I wish I was there. I'm missing out on seeing him because . . . because I . . . why do I want to be there now when the very idea two days ago made me feel sick?"

So apparently I did want to talk about it.

She gave me a patient smile. "You want to see him, but not with everyone else there. That's understandable."

I made a face. "Is it though? Is him being there having a good time with his friends without me understandable? Because I'm missing out and he's there with them and not me, because I wasn't comfortable going, so now I wish I was there while at the same time I still don't know if I could . . ." I sighed. "It doesn't make sense."

"It's confusing," she offered gently. "But he can meet his friends, Deacon."

"I know." Ugh, that unease in my belly was back.

"He can have both. You and his friends. That doesn't mean he's prioritizing them over you. The two can exist together."

I knew that. I did. But still . . .

"I don't want him to have to choose."

"I know. And he knows that too. You said he was very understanding."

I nodded, squeezing my fingertips. For some reason, it made me feel better. "I wish I was there," I mumbled. "I wish I was brave enough to go with him."

Mom frowned. "It's not about bravery, darling."

"If I was braver—"

"No. It's not bravery," she said, firmer this time. "It's about knowing your boundaries and what you're comfortable with, and I'm certain Winter understands that."

"I want to try, Mom," I said, feeling the urge to cry. I hated crying. I hated how out of control it made me feel. "I want to. I want to try. I want to be braver. I want to go out with him, meet his friends, have dinner. I want to be able to do those things. I don't want to be like this." I blinked back tears and my nose burned. "I want to hold his hand. I can't even hold his hand."

Mom put her hand on my sleeve, just a soft pat. "Then you're going to have to do things that you might not be comfortable with at first. Small steps. A few little things at first."

"Such as?"

"You're seeing him tomorrow evening, yes?"

I nodded. "Yes. I'm helping him at the store for late-night shopping."

"Why don't you suggest going to the diner afterwards? Or take a walk up Main Street. I'm sure the Christmas lights will make it pretty and a little bit romantic. And work up to holding his hand, get used to it slowly."

"He touched my arm the other night. He asked if he could, just like this—" I showed her on my own arm how Winter had done it. "—and I said yes, and it was okay. Better than okay. I felt it long after he'd gone."

"That's great," Mom said. "A small step already."

"It's what he does. He touches people's arms when he talks to them. He doesn't mean anything by it. It's just who he is, and I want him to be himself, not censor himself around me. And I liked it. When he did it. I liked how it felt."

She smiled at me. "You know what I think?"

I shook my head, because how could I possibly know? "No."

"I think you're taking all these small steps without even realizing it. And I think you don't realize how far you've already come, Deacon." Her smile was warm and even a little proud. "Don't be so hard on yourself for not being at the finish line yet. You'll get there, sweetheart. I know you will. When you set your mind on something, you make it happen. So there might be a few stumbles on the way. That's no big deal. We all stumble at different times, and no one is perfect. Just remember, all journeys of a thousand miles start with a single step."

"Lao Tzu."

"He was a wise man."

I nodded and with a deep breath in and a slow exhale, I realized how much better I felt. "Thank you. I get caught up in my head."

"I know you do, darling. And you're going to wear out the floorboards if you keep pacing." She winked and gave me a smile. "Talk to Winter. He'll understand, I'm sure of it."

I'm sure he would too.

"Tomorrow," I said quietly.

"And you can always talk to me or your dad," she offered. "Don't keep things bottled up, Deacon. It doesn't do anyone any good."

"I know. I just . . ." I sighed. "I just wish I . . . I know rationally how I should proceed and what I should do, but anything to do with him and my mind doesn't work properly. When you say take small steps it makes perfect sense. I don't know why I can't realize that on my own."

She sighed and patted my arm again. "Let me tell you something. Your dad was exactly the same when he was your age."

That stopped me. "He was?"

"Absolutely. When we were first dating, he'd get all these grand ideas and want to do every single thing all at once, and I'd have to remind him to stop and focus. Otherwise I'm sure he'd never have finished veterinarian school if I didn't help him stay on track. He used to say I'd point out what may have been obvious to everyone else, but it wasn't to him."

"He did?"

"Sure."

"Like what?"

"Oh, his study schedule, work, his family and friends, and our dates, mostly. Or he'd get overwhelmed with his intern roster and assignments, and be in a complete flux, and I'd help him break it all down into smaller, more manageable parts that gave him balance. And he used to say when he saw it written out like that, he could see it made so much more sense, but on his own, he found it all overwhelming and he couldn't even start it."

This surprised me. "Dad was like that?"

Mom nodded. "Yes. He's a lot better at breaking it down on his own now. With his clinic, he has routine and structure and there's a process to everything. It wasn't always like that though. When he first started out, he would work at a few different clinics, and it was a lot to keep track of. But then when we came here, it was a lot more streamlined, and it suits him so much better. He used to stress out a lot. Make himself sick, almost. But then we had you, and he soon learned to adapt to change. Better than he ever gave himself credit for." She smiled at me then. "You're a lot alike, you two."

Dad was . . . like me?

Logically, given DNA and hereditary traits, that made sense. Of course we were alike.

But he was like me?

"He used to make himself sick?"

"Oh, yes. He'd have a tummy ache, for sure."

"But he . . . he's always . . ." I shook my head. "He never stresses out. He's calm and in control. He knows what to do. He says the right thing. He—"

Mom's gaze met mine and she gave my hand a squeeze. "And so do you, sweetheart. You know what to do, and you say the right thing as well. You are in control, too. You make the right decisions, always."

I shook my head. "It doesn't feel like it. I get lost in my head and I can't see what I'm supposed to do."

"I'm gonna let you in on a little secret about being an adult," she said. "None of us know what we're doing all the time. There are no instructions on how to be a grown-up. Being an adult is hard, making decisions is hard, and no one really knows what they're doing. Best we can do is follow our moral compass and be kind to others. Be true to ourselves and try to find happiness wherever we can. That's all."

I thought about that for a second. It seemed naïve at first, but the more I considered it, the more I realized she was right.

She usually was.

"It's a good way to look at it," I said. "I do wish there were instructions though."

Mom chuckled. "Oh boy, don't we all." Then she sighed. "You know what to do, Deacon. You have to follow your heart. It might seem scary at first. That first leap will always be the scariest. But you'll be fine, no matter what happens. Even if we get our hearts broken, we're still better off for trying, yes?"

I nodded slowly. I didn't want to get my heart broken. I didn't want Winter to not love me.

Mom had given me a lot to think about, but I felt so much better already. And I knew what I had to do.

I GOT to the bookstore at 4:58 p.m., and my tummy was a different kind of jittery. I had spoken to Winter on the phone and via text, but I hadn't seen him since Sunday. I was excited and nervous, but mostly excited.

And nervous.

But determined.

I had to take a leap of faith, as Mom had said. Not the religious kind of faith, but the faith in myself, faith in Winter, and the belief that he felt the same way about me as I did about him.

I opened the door, the bell chiming over my head announcing me as I walked in. Winter was sliding a book onto the shelf at the far wall, and he turned to greet his customer.

But then he saw it was me. His whole face changed from a polite smile to a big grin and he hurried over. His cheeks were pink, his eyes wide. "Hi," he said. "Here, let me take your coat. How was your day? I've been on cloud nine since I got your poem this morning, just so you know." He hung my coat up on the rack in the storeroom. "Bram Stoker's *Dracula* is one of my all-time favorites, though I think that every time you send me a line. I think that one's my favorite, and it is. Until I get the next one. I probably wouldn't have thought Dracula to be romantic, but 'you are one of the lights, the light of all lights.' I mean I did have to google that one, not gonna lie. I was amazed I didn't recognize it immediately, but I think that comes down to your ability to surprise me." Then he stopped talking, let out a big sigh, and settled on a smile. "Sorry. I'm excited to see you, that's all. I haven't seen you since Sunday. That feels like a lifetime ago. How was your day today?"

His words made my insides run hot and tingly. "My day was fine. Much better now though. I wasn't very useful again at work today. I was clock-watching, as my dad put it, which equates to time-wasting. I was excited to see you too."

He grinned, his fingers flinching as if he wanted to touch me but was holding himself back. "I'm so glad you're here."

"I have a lot to tell you and some questions to ask," I said, determined not to back out. "But perhaps we should get work done first because that's what I'm here for. Is there stock and inventory that needs to be done?"

He laughed and waved his hand at the stockroom. "Always. Just got another delivery this afternoon."

"I can start on that."

He watched me for a second, customers in the store

forgotten. He seemed to study my face and it made me warm all over. "Thank you. And you can ask me anything at all."

I gave a nod, not wanting to meet his eyes. The other people in the store were suddenly on my radar. "I'll just . . ." I stepped past him into the storeroom and opened the first box.

He went about serving the customers, chatting about a romance book, which Winter had clearly loved.

Maybe I should read it.

Romance books weren't my go-to. I'd read them, of course, but I preferred fantasy or poetry, mood depending.

But romance seemed like something I wanted to read suddenly, immersing myself in emotions and feelings of falling in love. It might not seem so unrealistic to me now. No, not *un*realistic.

Perhaps out of reach or unobtainable was more fitting.

I'd read romance with as much firsthand experience as I had reading a fantasy about rival kings and sword fights.

But now . . .

Now I think I understood.

The bell above the door chimed again and I'd assumed it was the customer leaving, but a girl spoke. "Hi, I'll just put their bag in the storeroom—"

"Thanks, Evie," Winter said.

Then a girl appeared. She was young and had a patch of blue in her black hair and a nose ring. She came into the storeroom and stopped. "Oh."

I stood there, holding a book on economics.

"Hi!" she said brightly. "I'm Evie. I was kitty-sitting for Winter." She proceeded to open her coat and show the baby carrier with some little ginger ears poking out the top.

"Uh, yes," I managed. "I . . . I'm Deacon. I'm, uh . . ."

"Oh, Deacon the vet. Winter told me about you." She

proceeded to pull off her coat and unclip the baby carrier. "Then you'll know exactly what to do with these two little sweetlings."

Before I knew what she was doing, she had the carrier and was strapping it to me. It was all I could do to hold my arms out and blink while she just steamrolled me, buckled me in, and stood back to admire her handiwork. "Done." Then Winter was there, standing in the door watching, smiling, somewhat apologetically. Evie collected her coat. "I have to go. Grandpa's waiting."

"Thank you, Evie," Winter said as she headed out.

"Anytime. You know I love them. Nice to meet you, Deacon." The bell above the door chimed again, and she was gone.

Winter turned back to me, trying not to smile as he came over. "I'm sorry, are you okay? Need me to take it off you?"

I blinked again, took stock of my whole body, trying to determine if I felt violated or not, and decided that I was surprisingly okay. "Uh . . . no, it's okay . . . I think . . ."

Then one of the kittens popped his head out and meowed, then the second one did the same. The first one used his little claws to climb up toward my face. Bright, I assumed. Wow, they'd really grown.

"Oh, Bright," Winter said, taking the kitten and giving him a cuddle. "You behave yourself, you little menace." He held him up to his face, giving him a dozen kisses all over his little head. "Aren't they just the cutest?"

They really were.

So was the way Winter held him, cared for him.

"Yes, they are." Merry climbed up out of the carrier then and I was quick to grab him before he decided to free-fall to the ground. "And they're growing well. Eating well, by the looks of it. Little Merry isn't so little anymore."

"No. He had to grow because his brother kept beating on him. It's like a game of survivor at this point." Winter held Bright up and gave him another kiss. "You keep picking on him, don't you. So he *had* to grow up big and strong." Winter smiled at me then. "Merry gives it back to him now. They wrestle and tumble most of the day. Evie comes over from the youth center and saves me. Well, saves Bright, because he learned how to climb out of the pen. But sometimes Ro will take them home early. Or, if she's at home all day, she keeps them and I have a stress-free day."

"Kittens are a handful," I said. "Like puppies."

"Please tell me you were exaggerating when you said the kitten-rampage stage would last a year."

I snorted. "At least."

Winter made a whining sound. "Lord." Then he sighed and made an effort to compose himself. "It's fine. It's what I signed up for, so no complaining." Then his eyes went wide as if he'd just thought of something. "We should totally take a pic." He pulled out his phone, and coming to stand next to me, we each held a kitten and he took a selfie. I didn't love having my photo taken, but then Winter showed me the picture. I didn't look at me. I looked at him, at his smile, at the two kittens, and I was glad he'd taken it. "It's cute! I'll send it to you."

He thumbed the screen, and a second later, my phone beeped.

And now, just like that, I had a photo of him.

Of us.

More customers came in and Winter greeted them, still holding Bright. It was a woman with two young teens who were quite enamored with Bright, and then they realized there was a Merry as well. One of the kids came over to me, patting Merry as I held him.

"Are they for sale?" the young girl asked.

"No, no," Winter said. "They're my babies. They're too young to be at home by themselves so we have a bring-your-kids-to-work day most days."

The mother didn't seem to mind because it allowed her to look around the store. Winter held Bright as he helped the kids find the books they were after, and I put Merry back in the baby carrier and entered the stock inventory into the computer.

I enjoyed this kind of work. It was a methodical system and I liked the process steps of completing tasks. I was surprised at how busy the bookstore was for a Thursday evening. I knew most of the customers, by face if not name. They seemed to know me, anyway. Which was fine. Helpful, even, if it gave people something to say. Conversations with a variation of "Oh, you're working here now?" to which I replied, "No, just helping" almost every time someone saw me.

I didn't mind though.

It was unsurprising that people recognized me. I'd grown up here, worked here, we had the veterinary clinic. And people were mostly nice to me. I liked that.

When Winter closed and locked the door, I was surprised that it was nine o'clock already.

The time had gone so fast.

"Oh wow, that was a long day," Winter said with a sigh. He pulled the blind down over the door and gave me a smile. "I'm so thankful you were here to help."

"It was busy," I allowed. "All the new inventory is done."

"You are a superstar." He came over and peered into the baby carrier I was still wearing. "Still asleep," he whispered.

I rubbed the carrier. "I almost forgot I was wearing it."

Winter chuckled. "I know, right? I get used to it too." Then he took out his phone again. "Let me take a photo."

"Oh." I was about to protest but he snapped a photo and showed me the screen. "You're so cute."

I stared at the photo. Of me wearing the baby carrier, with a bump. "I'm not cute. I look . . . pregnant," I mumbled. "That's not good."

He chuckled. "No, you look like the cutest cat dad ever."

"A cat dad?"

He nodded, but then his eyes met mine. "I'll delete it if you'd prefer."

Ugh. I wasn't sure . . . He thought it was cute, he thought I was cute, and he'd delete it if I asked him to. I liked that he considered my feelings, so I shook my head. "No, it's fine. Though I would insist you don't show it to anyone."

He grinned. "Absolutely no one will see this but me. But hang on," he added, thumbing the screen again, and then my phone beeped. "And you have it now too. Look over it later, and if you want me to delete it forever, I will."

"Thank you."

Then he clapped his hands together. "Okay, let me balance the register and close everything down, then we can leave."

"Okay."

I stood there, not even aware I was gently rubbing the baby carrier. Best cat dad ever . . .

That made me happy.

He made me happy.

"So," Winter said, snapping me back to here and now. He was at the register. "You said you had questions for me?"

Oh.

Right. My questions.

"Uh, yes," I said, frowning, giving myself a second to get

the words straight in my head. "Your dinner, at the pizzeria, with your friends. How was that?"

"Oh, it was nice," he said. "Such a great bunch of guys. I met Braithe. He's the kindergarten teacher at the school. He got here a couple of years ago, so he was giving me all the hints and tips about being a new local. Hamish was there, and Gunter of course. And his partner, Clay Henderson."

"From Henderson Sawmills," I said. "His family has been here for a few generations, I believe."

"Oh, he's so nice. And big. The man is huge." He smiled at me. "He and Gunter are so cute together. And Hamish is a talker. And very funny."

"Hamish is a client. He has a dog called Chutney."

Winter laughed. "He told me. He said Chutney loves you."

That was nice. But . . . "You were talking about me?"

"Oh, well," he said, his cheeks going pink. "Gunter, from the youth center, he, uh . . . How do I say this?" He made a face. "He's very invested in us."

"Us?"

"Yeah. You and me and what we have going on."

What we have going on . . .

"He's a total romantic," he added. "And he's the one who invited us both. I told him you couldn't make it. He said it was fine. Maybe next time."

I stared at him, unsure, and confused.

Winter saw this and was quick to clarify. "He saw us talking outside, remember? He was asking if we were dating. If there was romance in the air because he has this crazy notion that there's some Christmas Cupid thing in Hartbridge. Every year before Christmas, someone moves to town, meets a local, and—" He pulled back an imaginary bow and shot the imaginary arrow. "—bam, Cupid strikes again. Apparently it's happened a few Christmases in a row.

Hamish, Jayden, Gunter, Braithe, Doctor Rob." He shrugged. "They're convinced we're next."

That was a lot of information and I wasn't sure what to make of any of it; if he was joking or serious. Rational minds would dismiss it as nonsense, and I considered saying as much, but I was stuck on one thing . . .

He asked if we were dating? I'd wanted to ask the same thing, but he'd brought it up first, so despite how nervous it made me to ask, now was the perfect opportunity. "What did you tell him?"

"Well, I told him I didn't think there was any such thing as a Christmas Cupid. I love a good fiction story more than most, but I still have a solid grasp on reality, so . . ."

I chuckled, because phew . . . "No, I meant about us dating," I said. It was so easy to say it like that, almost too easy, and while I had wanted to ask that, the way his gaze shot to mine made me wish I hadn't asked at all. I tried to get a hold of the panic that bubbled in my tummy. "Oh. I just—"

"I told him we maybe were," he said, making a face, his cheeks going red. "I said we hadn't broached the subject and labels weren't something I knew you were comfortable with so I couldn't confirm, but we'd had a few instances of agreeing to meet and there had been lunch or dinner included, and by definition that probably constituted as dating but . . ." He winced. "I dunno, Deacon. What do you think? Are we . . . ? Is this . . . ?"

I blinked and swallowed, my mouth dry. But his nervousness somehow made me feel better. "Yes, I think. We have had a lunch and dinner date, and by definition, I think you're correct. I'd like it to be correct." I shrugged. "If you'd like it to be."

He grinned. "I would, yes." He let out a big sigh. "So next time someone asks if we're dating, I will say yes."

I laughed because . . . because I was happy, and laughing let out some of the energy I was buzzing with. "I will say yes, too. Actually, my dad said the word dating and then it was all I could think about, wondering if we were or not."

His eyes locked with mine and I couldn't look away. I didn't want to. "I'm glad we talked about it," he whispered.

"Me too." I swallowed hard, and reminding myself that I had to talk to him about these things, I decided now was the right time. "I was very confused," I began, "on Wednesday night when I knew you were having dinner with your friends. I wanted to be there. I wanted to be with you. Yet I still couldn't bring myself to go or even to ask. I want to do those things with you, but even thinking about actually going makes me feel all nervous, and I don't know which is worse. My mom said I needed to trust myself more, because I can handle more than I give myself credit for and that thinking about things is worse than actually doing the thing. I get myself worked up, and—"

He came over to me and did that thing where he lifts his hand as though he wants to touch me, but he stopped himself.

"Like that," I said, gesturing to his hand. "It's natural for you to touch people. Well, that sounds weird. I mean, touch their arm when you're talking to them."

He chuckled.

"It's a gesture of reassurance, I know that. And I want to get used to it. You touched my arm the other night at my front door, and I could feel it long after you'd left."

"Oh, Deacon," he whispered.

"It wasn't awful."

He burst out laughing. "I'm glad. It wasn't awful for me either."

"Normally when people touch me, it feels wrong. On

my skin. It feels all wrong, and my skin doesn't like it. But not with you." I grimaced because this was probably coming out all wrong. "You haven't touched my skin. Just my arm through my sleeve. And I know, coming from you, it will be okay. You'll be gentle and won't grab me."

"I would never." Then he made a face. "Unless it was to pull you out of the way from a runaway vehicle or something."

"Why would I be in the path of a vehicle?"

He grinned. "Let's hope we never find out."

Okay.

Conversations with Winter never went the way I'd thought they would . . .

"Anyway, what I'm trying to say is that I want to go with you," I said, licking my lips. My mouth was dry and not overly pleasant. "If you invite me again to meet your friends. I should go. I want to. Even if for just a short while. I want to try. A leap of faith, Mom called it. But not in a religious way."

He chuckled. "I get it."

"And even if it doesn't go well, at least I tried."

"Of course. We can totally do micro-dates until you get used to it."

"Micro-dates?"

"Yes. I made that up." He shrugged. "But it's funny you mentioned wanting to go next time I was invited some-where, because we were invited to another dinner."

Oh.

"Oh." I blinked. "That was very fast. I wasn't expecting that so . . . soon . . ."

He grinned at me. "It's a Christmas dinner at Hamish and Ren's place. Apparently they do it every year. It's very low-key, casual. Just a meal and a few drinks. Well, they can drink. I don't usually drink alcohol."

"Me either."

"So if you want to come with me, we don't have to stay long. Just for as long as you're comfortable."

Maybe I'd volunteered my attempting to join him too soon . . .

"When is this dinner?"

"This weekend. Sunday evening. They like to meet before Christmas before everyone has other commitments."

I grimaced. "I think I'm regretting saying I'd go next time."

Winter laughed. "You'll be fine. Small steps, Deacon."

Small steps . . .

"Mom said that too. Actually, she quoted Lao Tzu."

"Ah, so awesome quotes run in the family, huh?"

I smiled and gave him a nod. "I do feel better after talking to you."

"I'm glad. Me too. Sometimes we make mountains out of molehills in our heads when talking things out is so much better."

I nodded again.

"Was there anything else you wanted to ask me?"

Well, there was . . .

"Come on, out with it," he said. "We are on a roll tonight."

I let out a rush of breath, quelling the sudden nerves. I had to get the words right in my head first . . . It took a moment, and Winter never rushed me.

"About touching my arm," I began. "I want to get used to it. I don't want you to have to censor yourself around me. You should be yourself, and I need to push my boundaries if I want to get used to it. I need to trust myself, and you."

"Okay," he said, looking into my eyes. I could read the confusion in his eyes, but still, he never pushed for more. He let me get it out on my own time.

I held up my hand, palm upward. "I want to hold your hand," I whispered, feeling a rush of nerves and elation, and possibly nausea. "I want to know what that feels like."

He had to duck down a bit so he could look up at my face, into my eyes. He was smiling. "I want to know what holding your hand feels like too." He raised his hand to mine but stopped before contact, then held his hand, palm up, next to mine. "What about if you touch my hand first? That way you control it."

I met his gaze then. He really did understand. He didn't mock me or tell me I was being stupid. He gave me the power, the control, as he put it.

So with my index finger, I gently touched his palm. It was soft and warm, and my breath caught, my tummy did that swooping thing. I traced my finger up his index finger, skin on skin.

It was . . . exhilarating.

When I got to the tip of his finger, I pulled my hand back and met his gaze. His eyes were on me, his cheeks the pinkest I'd ever seen.

"How was that?" he asked.

"Uh . . ." I had to think . . .

"Not awful?"

"Not awful," I agreed. "I liked it."

He kept his hand up. "Try it again."

I touched his palm again, this time with my index and middle fingers. Skimming his palm and along his fingers, still the barest of touches. I pulled my hand back with a puff of breath.

"Would you like me to try your hand?" he asked.

Did I want that?

Well, I did, yes. But could I?

I turned my hand over, showing my palm. My nerves

made my skin feel all weird so it probably wasn't a good idea, but I wanted to try.

Then, like I'd done to him, he gently touched his finger to my palm and slowly up my index finger. But he didn't watch our hands. He watched my face. "How's that?"

I pulled my hand back and needed to wipe my palm on my jeans. "Tickles."

Winter laughed. "It does! But it felt nice."

I blinked, trying to regulate my breathing, my heart rate, and the jitters in my tummy. "It did."

"Small steps," Winter said with a grin. "You did great."

I nodded, feeling braver now. And happy.

I'd taken a chance. I'd stepped out of my comfort zone and it had gone well. Better than well, even. "Thank you, for letting me try, and for not making me feel foolish."

His eyes softened. "You're welcome. But can I let you in on a little secret?"

I nodded.

"The other night, you held my sleeve," he said. "And that was the cutest, most romantic thing ever. I mean, holding hands would be awesome, I'm sure. But anytime you want to hold my sleeve, you absolutely can."

I huffed out a laugh, embarrassed. "I, uh, I used to do that to my parents. When I was little."

"Ahhh." He lifted both shoulders, wiggled, and sighed. "It's the cutest thing ever. I love it. So romantic."

Romantic?

I shook my head, possibly rolled my eyes. "I don't know about that."

"I do." He beamed at me. "You send me lines of poetry and hold my sleeve. Deacon, you're the most romantic person I've ever met."

My face felt like it was on fire, and I wasn't sure where to look. "I need to go home now."

He was quiet, and when I risked a glance at him, he was smiling at me. "Same."

We packed up the kittens, locked up the store, and got them bundled into his car. I opened his driver side door for him, trying to muster some of that courage I'd felt earlier.

"Thank you," he murmured, one foot inside the car. Then he stopped to face me. His breath was puffs of steam, his beanie pulled low, his nose and cheeks pink from the cold. "I'm so glad I got to see you tonight. Thank you for your help, and thank you for telling me how you feel."

"How I feel?"

"About wanting to go on a dinner date with me. About how you want to try. About all that stuff. It's not easy to talk about, but we did great. And we're dating now." He grinned. "I'm especially glad we discussed that."

"Me too." Then, before I lost my nerve, before my over-thinking could get the better of me, I said, "And yes. I'd like to go. To the Christmas dinner. If that offer still stands."

He grinned at me. "Yes, of course it still stands. I'll tell Hamish to expect us both. And you still have to come to dinner at my place sometime. Another dinner date. Or a movie date. Or to my work for a lunch date."

"Do you like saying the word date?"

"Yes." He laughed, but then one of the kittens meowed. "Okay, okay," he said to them. "I'm getting in. We'll be home soon." Then he looked at me. "Goodnight, Deacon. I'm so happy. And I'm already looking forward to your poem in the morning."

That made me laugh. "I have a list."

He sighed. "I love lists."

Both kittens meowed at him this time. "I have to go," he said, looking at me as if he didn't want to leave just yet. But then he got in his car and I closed the door.

With a wave, he drove off and I walked to my car. The

air was bitterly cold, the night dark, but I was warmed through, happy. Happier than I'd ever been. My heart felt full to almost bursting, but in a good way. I had no tummy aches, no anxiety, no confusion about anything.

No overthinking.

Main Street was lit up, the streetlights and Christmas lights were a soft glow in the cold air, the snow on the ground made it all look so peaceful.

I took a moment to enjoy it, not something I could ever recall doing, got in the truck, and drove home.

Mom and Dad were both still up, waiting to see how my night had gone. I didn't even have to say anything, but they seemed to know just by looking at me. I felt like I was walking on air.

I felt . . . I wasn't sure I could put in words.

It was a strange feeling, but in a good way. There was no chaos in my head, no tangle of thoughts. As if finally talking to Winter and admitting my fears to him, admitting that I wanted to try pushing myself, and admitting we were now dating, it seemed to calm the noise in my head.

For the first time in my life, my heart was doing the talking.

When I finally climbed into bed, I grabbed my phone and typed out a quick internet search.

What does love feel like?

CHAPTER TWELVE
WINTER

ALL I COULD DO WAS sigh.

And swoon.

I showed Ro my phone screen. "He quoted The Beatles. The freaking Beatles." I sighed, not for the first time. "How is he even real?" I could have nearly cried.

If he fell in love with me, would I help him understand because love was more than holding hands.

"Could he be any more perfect?"

Ro shook her head at me. Also, it might not have been the first time I'd asked that today, or talked about him, or told her about the palm-tracing thing, or swooned.

"Go and get something to eat," she ordered. She tapped the watch she wasn't wearing. "I'm only here for an hour to cover your lunch break. The boys are at home by themselves."

I grimaced. "Did they hate the new crate?"

I didn't love the idea of a crate, but it was safer for them. Especially when they had to spend time at home by themselves. Like now.

She gave me a dead-eyed glare that told me I should know better than to doubt her, and she pointed to the door.

"Okay, okay," I grumbled, pulling on my coat and scarf. "I'm going."

Jeesh.

The diner was warm and busy, full of delicious aromas and happy chatter. Jayden was working today, and he looked up from the back of the kitchen when he heard me order.

He gave me a wave. "Hey, Win," he said, tucking a dish towel into his apron. "How you goin'?"

Uh . . . "Going? What's going where?"

"He means, how are you doing," Hamish said, suddenly appearing beside me. "It's an Aussie thing."

"Oh," I replied with a laugh. "Right."

Jayden came over, grin wide. "Is this a planned lunch break 'cause I didn't get the memo. Or the invite."

"Uh, no," I said. "Ro sent me on a break. Actually, it was more of a threat, but you know. Same thing."

Hamish grinned and pointed his thumb at me. "And I saw him walk in from across the street, so here I am. Here for all the goss." Then he shrugged. "And two lunch specials to go, please. I told Ren I was getting him food."

"Two for me to go as well," I added. "Whatever the lunch special is." I didn't even know what it was. But I hadn't had one bad thing from here yet.

We each paid at the register. "Sure thing, boys," Crystal said. "Take a seat, I'll bring it over."

Surprising me, Jayden slid into a booth with us. "I can take a fiver."

"Do you ever rest?" Hamish asked. "Between here and the bed and breakfast, you are one busy man."

He shrugged. "I'll rest after the holidays. Plus, it's not really work when you love it."

"True," I agreed.

"How is the bookstore going?" Hamish asked me.

"Great. Surpassed my expectations. Though, to be honest, I do expect it to quiet down after Christmas."

"Well, yes. Such is retail. But," Hamish said, "there is always something happening in this town throughout the year to base little events on and change up the display in your front window. There's Valentine's Day. Arbor Day is a big day in the park in springtime. We have tree-planting initiatives. We do stuff in the summer for the tourists." Then his eyes lit up. "Ooh, you know, we could organize a monthly farmer's market between your store and the youth center. I'm sure there's some local businesses and producers who'd love that. We could have stalls for jams and sauces, wood-carved stuff from the mill. Maybe the school could sell cakes to raise money. I dunno what else, but there's a lot of local farms and ranches who can showcase their goods. Pretty sure I heard Bryn telling Ren about her alpacas and using the wool for . . ." He made a confused face. "Or was it the goat's milk. I can't remember."

Jayden laughed. "That's a great idea. You should totally run for council."

He rolled his eyes and waved that idea off, but it got me thinking . . . "The market day is a great idea. It would attract locals and visitors alike," I said. "Something to think about in the new year, anyway. But before I forget, about your Christmas party dinner . . ."

Hamish looked at me, then he began to smile. "Yessssss. Will you be a plus-one?"

I couldn't help but grin. "Yes. He said he'd like to come along."

Hamish gripped my hand and made a strange high-pitched *eeeeep* sound. "This is the kind of conversation I'm here for. Tell me everything."

It was hard not to laugh because I was still so damn happy and giddy and excited, but I tried to compose myself. "Okay, so he said he wants to come with me, but," I said, high emphasis on the but. "We might not stay long. He doesn't like being in unfamiliar situations, and meeting a bunch of new people can be overwhelming. But he wants to try. For me. He wants to try for me."

"Aww," Hamish said. "He's so sweet."

Sweet? They had no idea.

I whipped out my phone. "Look at this," I said, pulling up his texts. "Every morning he sends me a line of poetry."

Hamish gasped and gripped my forearm. "Shut up. He does not."

"He absolutely does." I scrolled up, showing him.

"That is the most romantic thing ever," Hamish breathed.

"I know! That's what I told him."

Jayden was smiling at me. "I'm telling ya, this Cupid thing needs to be studied."

I sighed dreamily. "And this is probably going to sound lame to you guys, but it's huge for him . . . He wants to practice holding my hand."

Jayden stared. "He wants to practice—"

There was a muted thud, and I was sure Hamish kicked him under the table to shut him up.

"That's really sweet," Hamish said gently. "It is a big deal for him. When I first took Chutney to the vet for a checkup, Ren told me not to expect a handshake or anything like that. Said he doesn't like being touched."

Pretty sure he said this for Jayden's benefit, not mine.

I nodded. "It's a whole thing." I turned my hand over on the table and drew my index finger over my palm. "But he did this last night."

Hamish put his hand to his heart. "Oh my word."

I sighed again. "He's the sweetest man I've ever met."

"You're perfect for each other," Hamish whispered. There was no judgment or sarcasm, just complete understanding. Then he put his hand to his heart and leaned in so only we could hear. "I *totally* get why you don't—asexuality is one hundred percent valid—but personally, I love the big D. If you know what I mean—"

"Jesus," Jayden mumbled.

"Looooove the D," Hamish continued. "Hard, fast, slow, I don't care. Any way I can get it, and lemme tell you, Ren is—"

"Okay, we get it," Jayden said.

I burst out laughing. "So happy for you."

Hamish beamed. "Me too." But then he reached over and gave my arm a squeeze. "And being serious, I'm happy for you too, Win. Queer love in all its forms is a beautiful thing. It really makes me so happy that you and Deacon have been mowed down by the Christmas Cupid like the rest of us. We've got two more little rainbow babies in our family now, and it just gives me life, ya know?"

I nodded. "Family, huh?"

"Abso-fucking-lutely," Hamish mumbled.

Thankfully, no one close by seemed to hear him.

I smiled at them both. "Moving here was the best thing I ever did."

"Same," Hamish said.

"Same," Jayden added.

"Here you go, boys," Crystal said, bringing over two bags: one for me, one for Hamish.

"Yeah, I better get back to work," Jayden said.

"Same," Hamish said.

"Same."

"Okay, so remember dinner is potluck," Hamish said.

"We all have to bring something so Jayden doesn't feel the need to cook on what's *supposed* to be a night off for him."

I smiled at Jayden. "Totally fair."

"I think we have most of it covered," Hamish said. "Though a vegetable side would be great."

"Perfect. I can bring a Mediterranean vegetable thing," I offered. "No one has any allergies, right?"

"None," Jayden replied. "Though Clay and Gunter get totally weird when anyone mentions garlic bread."

Hamish snorted. "Yeah, do me a favor and ask Gunter about that."

They both laughed.

"Oh," Jayden said, as if he'd just remembered. "And no gifts," he said, directing that straight to Hamish. "Handmade or otherwise. We're not having a repeat of last year."

Hamish grimaced again, then sniffed and raised his chin. "Well, yes. However well-intentioned I may have been at the time, that's not a mistake I ever intend to repeat."

I didn't know what that was about, but it made me laugh anyway.

They had such a history, all these small inside jokes that close friends seemed to have. It was so lovely, and the fact they were now including me into their circle—their little queer family, as Hamish had called it—made me incredibly happy. Hartbridge already felt more like a home to me than Boise ever did.

I'd never really had the queer-friends-only group thing before. Sure, I'd had queer friends back in Boise, but nothing like this. Here, these guys made a point of catching up often, had regular meals together, they helped each other, they supported and cheered each other on. It was awesome.

I just hoped Deacon was ready to be included too.

Small steps. Remember, Winter, small steps.

Yes. Absolutely, I reminded myself. Small and patient steps, and I knew there might be the occasional step backward, but I was excited for what our future might look like.

Whatever that might be.

"COME IN," Vicky said, opening her front door. "Deacon's just . . ." She glanced over her shoulder. "He's a bit nervous."

Oh.

I kept my voice down. "Is he okay? Can I do anything?"

She gave me a soft smile. "No, no. He's fine." Then she whispered, "He told us that you're dating."

"Oh."

Oh god.

She put her hand to her heart. "That's very exciting. He was beaming."

Pure relief made my legs feel a little weak. "I'm glad. And yes, exciting. For me as well. I thought for a moment—"

She leaned in and whispered in a rush, "Vegetables can touch vegetables but not meat. Sides should never touch anything."

Uhh, what?

It took a second for her words to click . . .

"Ahhh, okay. Understood."

"I suggested he eat something small before you got here but . . ." She shook her head and gave me a pensive smile. "He wants to do this properly."

"I want to do this too," I whispered. "For him, and for me."

We heard some mumbling and footsteps and turned to find Deacon and his dad coming through the house. Deacon stopped so abruptly when he saw me that his Dad ran into him, Deacon's smile instant and honest. "Hello. Sorry if I kept you. Dad was trying to distract me," he said. "Which usually means I was being insufferable."

"Not at all," Wayne said, giving me a look that said *yes*.

I couldn't help but chuckle. "I just got here. You didn't keep me at all."

"We should leave," he said, checking his watch. "We're going to be late and I don't like being late."

"Me either," I said, still smiling. I turned to Vicky. "Thank you."

Vicky grabbed Deacon's coat off the rack and handed it to him. "Have a good night."

Deacon pulled his coat on, then his gloves. He opened the door for us, and we walked to my car.

"We'll leave the front light on," Wayne yelled out as we were getting in. He gave us a wave, and their smiling faces were the last thing we saw before they closed the door.

I started the car. "Your parents are the cutest ever."

He buckled his seatbelt. "Cute?"

"Totally." I buckled up and cranked the heat. "They're so excited. It's cute."

He flattened down his coat and pressed his hand against his stomach as I began to drive. "I'm nervous."

"I am too," I told him.

"You are?"

"Sure," I said, smiling at him as I drove. "They're all established friends, and we're both the new guys here. Actually, you know them better than I do. You're a local. I'm a newbie."

"They like you already though."

I glanced from the road to him. "They'll like you too. Hamish already does like you. And Jayden, from the diner."

His brow furrowed. "You spoke to them about me? What . . . what did you say?"

I hated that his first reaction is to think it wasn't a positive conversation. "Of course I told them about you. I told them that we're officially dating, and that you were awesome, and how happy I was that we were on the same page now."

He tried not to smile, and even I could see his blush from the dashboard light. "Oh."

"I think a few nerves is a good thing," I added. "Being excited is a positive thing, right?"

"Hmm."

"And you know Hamish and Ren, and all the others."

"All the gay couples."

"Yep! How amazing is that?"

His brow furrowed as he seemed to consider this . . . "I guess . . ."

I knew his nerves were the outlier here. He wanted to do this. He was excited to do this. It was a big deal and his nervousness was expected.

"Hamish called it family," I said. "Have you heard of the term *found family* before?"

Deacon shook his head.

"It's when people find their own people to belong with. Like a family but not blood related. Because not everyone has blood family. Especially queer people."

His mouth drew down. "Their parents didn't accept them."

I nodded. "Yeah. Like me and my mom. Me being gay wasn't the entire problem—she never wanted to be a mom, I don't think—but she could never deal with it. And of course, then add to the fact that I'm asexual. She could never understand why I'd call myself gay if I never experienced sexual attraction to guys. She said there was no reason I couldn't just say I liked women if I never intended to sleep with them."

He stared at me. "That's not how it works. I've done a lot of reading and research since you told me, and she's wrong. Either willfully or ignorantly, and that's not fair to you."

Oh my god, I could have kissed him for saying that. Instead, I raised both hands. "Exactly!"

"Please don't take both hands off the wheel."

I gripped the wheel again. "Sorry." But then I grinned at him. "Thank you for saying that."

"Driving safety is important."

I chuckled. "Yes, it is. But I meant what you said about asexuality. But willfully ignorant sums up my mother."

His face did a displeased thing. "I can't understand why a mother would do that to her own child."

I loved that he couldn't fathom it. It told me he was loved so unconditionally by his parents, and I loved that for him. "Your parents are awesome," I said. "You're very lucky."

He gave a nod. "And your aunt Ro is your found family?"

"Well, yeah, I guess. Even though we are technically family. She's like my found mom." I slowed down and indicated to pull into Ren and Hamish's driveway. "Not everyone is so lucky. I think a few of the guys here tonight don't have family, which is why this kind of Christmas dinner is important."

He nodded again, and I could see his cogs turning in the hard set of his eyes. I pulled the car up alongside the others and cut the engine.

"Tonight's going to be fun. But we can leave at any time. If you want to leave, just give me a sign."

"A sign?"

"Yep. A signal that tells me you'd like to leave."

"Such as?"

I had to think . . . "Uh . . . Tug on my sleeve. Then you don't have to say anything, but I'll know and we can make a run for it."

His eyes went wide. "A run for it? I don't think running is an appropriate social response."

I laughed. "I didn't mean run literally. Because honestly, if you ever see me running, please know it's either a dire emergency or I'm being chased by a bear." Then I thought about it. "Or the tickets to a queer book convention go live when I'm not in front of my computer. Or if they release a never-seen-before J. R. R. Tolkien book. I would one hundred percent run for that."

Deacon's eyes met mine, and he smiled.

And if anything, this whole conversation had taken his mind off his nervous tummy. "Are you ready to go inside?"

He looked up at the house. It was a wooden-cabin-style rambler, the windows glowing from the warm light inside. There were Christmas decorations and colored lights along the porch, the Christmas tree visible inside the window. It looked fantastic and inviting.

Deacon's eyes met mine and he gave a nod. "I'm ready."

CHAPTER THIRTEEN
DEACON

I WAITED by the car as Winter retrieved a covered dish from the backseat. Was I ready to go inside and meet a whole group of people at once?

Yes. Yes, I was. I'd prepared myself for this. I knew what to expect.

Was I ready to be the one who went up the steps first on my own?

No. I would wait for Winter for that.

He could be the one to knock, the one to greet them first. He was braver than me in that regard.

He was braver than me in a lot of ways.

I was ready to do this, though. I was ready to step out of my comfort zone and be Winter's date for the evening. I wanted that more than anything. More than my nerves could stop me.

Winter closed the car door and, with a bright smile, held out the dish. "Can you please carry this for me?"

I took it. "Of course."

That way he could knock on the door . . .

I was almost certain he had the same thought as me.

We went up the steps, and before he could knock, Hamish opened the door. "Hello and welcome," he said. "Please come in."

Hamish was wearing a pink Christmas sweater that was . . . Perhaps garish was a strong word.

"Love the sweater," Winter said.

Hamish laughed. "It was the most perfectly hideous one I could find."

Well, I'm glad it wasn't a stylistic choice.

"Hello," I said.

"Deacon, I'm so glad you're here," Hamish said. He looked at the tray I was holding. "Bring this through to the kitchen."

There were a lot of faces.

Ten in total, and they all stopped their conversations to watch us, which is the part I hated the most.

"Guys," Hamish said. "This is Winter and Deacon. Pretty sure you've met everyone before," he said to Winter.

Winter gave a nod. "Yes, I think so."

I put the tray on the counter, trying to avoid outright introductions. I knew they all knew who I was and that they knew I was autistic. Everyone in town knew. I knew that they knew. In a lot of ways, it helped me that they knew, but in times like this, it felt like a neon sign above my head.

If I hadn't met them directly, I still knew who they were. It's what happened in small towns; everyone knew everyone.

Gunter from the youth clinic and Clay Henderson from the sawmill. Jayden from the diner and Cass from the bed and breakfast. Braithe was the schoolteacher. Deputy Price, though he looked different. I couldn't recall ever seeing him out of uniform. Soren the fireman and Doctor Rob. And Ren from the hardware, of course.

They were all standing around or sitting on the sofa,

and they all smiled and waved, and said a greeting of some sort.

"Win, Deacon," Gunter said. "Can I get you guys a drink?"

"Ah, a soda or a water for me," Winter said. "I'm driving."

"No worries." He pulled a can of soda from the fridge. "Deacon, would you like a drink? Soda? A beer? Glass of wine?"

Oh.

I liked that he offered me alcohol. Not that I had ever drank much of it before, and I had no intention of drinking it now, but I liked that he offered it. It made me feel . . . normal wasn't the right word. Included, maybe? "Just a soda for me too, thank you."

Conversations around the room had begun again, our arrival not the spotlight it was a moment ago, thankfully.

Gunter handed me the can of soda with a grin. "Been busy at the clinic?"

"Yes," I answered. Small talk . . . ugh. I didn't enjoy it and wasn't particularly good at it. I tried to be more conversational. "The colder months aren't usually any quieter for us; typically, it just means that the cases we see and treat are different than in the warmer months."

"Ah, that makes sense," Gunter replied. "Come on over to the living room, and we can chat."

Winter gave me an encouraging smile, so I went with him over to the couch. There were two spots available on the three-seater, so I deduced they were for us. Winter gave me the end seat so I wasn't between him and Braithe, as he and Jayden were talking about the annual Christmas fun day at the school—it had always been my favorite week at elementary school. Making all the fun Christmas crafts and a break from the typical lessons. I never performed in the class plays, but I did enjoy painting the backdrops and props.

Jayden was talking about his and Cass's kids practicing for their class plays, Braithe laughing along. By the fire, Deputy Price was talking to Soren and Clay about felling trees from roads, from what I could ascertain, and on the other sofa, Rob and Gunter were quick to include Winter in their conversation about the bookstore.

And me?

I was very happy to sit and watch.

Happy to sit this close to Winter. Our hips and thighs were touching. It didn't bother me so much, like it might have if it were someone else. But this was Winter, and this was a smallish sofa and seats were limited. It couldn't be helped.

And it was Winter. I trusted him, and . . .

It felt nice. A comfort, even. In this new-to-me social situation with new-to-me friends, having Winter beside me was a security I'd tried to convince myself I didn't need, but clearly I did.

Because I felt safer.

Until Chutney saw me. She trotted over, wearing a sweater matching Hamish's, and I gave her a pat. "Hello there," I said to her, and she then jumped up on my lap.

Winter turned, surprised at seeing her little pink sweater. "Oh my goodness, what?" He gave her a pat, smooshing her little face. "Is she not the cutest thing ever? Look at her sweater." Then his eyes met mine, wide with excitement. "I need to get sweaters for the boys."

"Good luck trying to get a sweater on Bright," I said.

Winter laughed. "Good point. Okay, so maybe one sweater for Merry."

"Oh, Chutney, hop down," Hamish said from the kitchen.

"She's fine," I said.

"She soon picked you out in the crowd," Ren said.

It was hard not to feel special. Animals always liked me, and even as a vet, that was a flex. My dad always said it was my energy. Animals felt safe with me.

Winter gave me the brightest smile. He was so close. Closer than I would normally allow, but it was different with him.

I was different with him.

Having him in my personal space wasn't a bad thing. The way it was with my parents. I was safe with him; I trusted him. Much like how Chutney felt with me. My body felt at ease, not tense and alert. There was no pressure building up, needing an outlet. There was no panic brewing in my belly. Even in this new environment: a strange house surrounded by people I didn't know well.

I smiled back at Winter, and Chutney plonked herself down and closed her eyes. Conversation around me resumed, and I sat there, listening. Not actively involved but included all the same.

Dinner was laid out on the kitchen counter, a serve-yourself affair. I stood beside Winter and he was so happy. I'd been nervous all day about the food situation. My list of dislikes was long, but I'd mentally prepared myself for what to expect and told myself whatever was served was fine, and I should expect foods I wasn't familiar with, especially if I intended to go on dinner dates with Winter.

And I wanted to do that.

There were some dishes I wouldn't eat, but there was a selection of roast beef, potato au gratin, green beans. Food my mom served often, and I stuck to those. Most of the guys' plates were piled heaps, but I noticed Winter tried a little of each, and he plated his carefully, creating little valleys between small hills of food. No food touching other food.

Like mine.

And I noticed Braithe's plate was similar.

I wasn't the only one, the odd one out.

The table was set beautifully. A Christmas centerpiece of gold and garland, gold candles, and each setting had a gold Christmas cracker.

"This is so perfect," Winter said.

Jayden and Cass were first to pop their crackers, taking out the paper crown and putting them on their heads. It was probably a bit childish, but it was fun. Everyone laughed when they popped their crackers, they wore their crowns, they read out the lame jokes.

Winter took his cracker and held it for me to pull apart with him. It popped loudly, and then we did mine. We wore our paper crowns, read aloud our silly little jokes, and not for one second did I feel out of place or overwhelmed.

Ren stood up at the head of the table and raised his wine glass. "To friends, old and new. To the family we choose. Merry Christmas."

Everyone raised their drinks and chorused, "Merry Christmas."

I looked at Winter and he was smiling, but his eyes were glassy. Was he sad? Was he about to cry?

I was shocked to see it, but he let out a soft laugh and shook his head. "Happy," he murmured. "Just really happy."

Oh.

Okay then.

Everyone else began eating, though I noticed Gunter was watching Winter and me. His smile was warm, and the way Gunter looked at Winter reminded me a lot of the way my dad looked at me.

I liked Gunter, and I was glad he'd befriended Winter.

Eating dinner was pleasant. General conversation, happy and decidedly normal. Soren asked Winter about the kittens he'd helped rescue, and Winter's whole face lit up as he talked about Merry and Bright.

"Deacon named them," Winter said.

All eyes went to me—the attention wasn't great, but Winter's gentle smile told me it was okay. "It was written on the box he brought them into the clinic in," I explained, sure my face was red. "Christmas decorations, I believe."

"Perfect Christmas names," Deputy Price said.

"Ah, I love it," Hamish said. "We should totally get a second dog. A little brother or sister for Chutney to play with."

"We have an adoption drive in the new year, late January," I volunteered. "The end of the holiday season usually has a high surrender rate."

Hamish made an excited buzzing noise and gave Ren a wide-eyed grin.

Ren deflated. "Awesome."

Everyone laughed.

"We were talking of organizing a market day," Hamish said. "To get people downtown near the youth center and the bookstore, and for local producers and crafters to sell their products. Once the weather warms up a bit, that is. But maybe the vet clinic could have an adoption stall? You know how they do those photos with the dogs and cats wearing scarves or hats?"

Oh . . .

I wasn't sure about that.

I wasn't expecting this.

I didn't particularly like how everyone was looking at me. I put my fork down and put my hands in my lap, trying to rein in the feelings, the emotions, the panic . . .

But then Winter slid his hand beneath the table and held my shirt sleeve at my wrist, the way I'd held his. The way he'd liked. The way I needed.

Not touching my skin, not gripping my arm or holding my hand.

The gentlest of reminders that he was there, and that it was all okay.

"It could help educate people about pet ownership," Winter said. "Buying puppies or kittens for a holiday gift without considering the sleepless nights, the training, the cost, only to then dump them afterwards. Believe me, I became a sudden cat dad at the worst possible time with my new business. Round-the-clock feeding, taking them to work with me."

"The baby carrier you had them in at the Christmas tree lighting was just adorable," Braithe said.

Conversation moved on, the focus swiftly off me, and I could breathe again. Winter let go of my shirtsleeve and gave me a reassuring smile as if he hadn't just saved me from freaking out.

I hated that I did this.

But you didn't freak out. You didn't lose control.

Thanks to Winter, but still.

It gave me time to think about the market day idea though . . .

When dinner was finished and the table cleared away, Hamish and Ren served Christmas cookies with a pot of coffee. I'd kind of lost my appetite and my mood had soured a little. Not through anyone's fault but my own. Everyone here had been so great, but I wanted to leave.

And once I had it in my head that I was leaving, it needed to happen.

"Winter, Deacon, coffee?" Ren asked.

"No, thank you," Winter said, patting his tummy. "I'm

so full. I think we're ready to go." He looked at me and I nodded, because how he knew I needed to leave was beyond me. "I have two little gremlins waiting for me at home that will be wondering where I am."

I stood up from the table and ran through my manners. "Thank you so much for dinner. It was a pleasure to be here. Merry Christmas to you all."

"Aww, you are the sweetest," Hamish said. Then he looked at Winter. "He is just the cutest."

"Pleasure to have you," Ren said. "Thank you for coming."

We went to the door and put on our boots and coats. Everyone said goodbye and waved. "Merry Christmas."

I felt the need to say something, to fix my mistake. "I'll speak to my dad about the market adoption idea. The decision will be his."

"Of course," Hamish said. "No pressure. It was just an idea. We need to take it to the city council yet."

"Hamish needs to run for council," Jayden said, and everyone laughed and agreed.

"Thank you again," Winter said to Hamish and Ren. "Goodnight, all."

"Oh, here, have this," Hamish said, bringing over Winter's empty dish.

"I want the recipe," Jayden yelled as we left.

We went down the steps to his car and got in. He started the engine and adjusted the heat, and we both buckled in.

I was afraid to ask, but I needed to know . . .

"Did I ruin it?" I asked, not wanting to look at his eyes. Not wanting to see his disappointment.

"Ruin it? Deacon, no. What did you think you ruined?"

"When they asked me about the adoption stall, I—"

"No, no, Deacon, look at me."

I did, for just a second, but had to look away.

"You were so great tonight," he said. "Perfect, even. I'm so proud of you."

"Proud . . ." I shook my head because that didn't make sense.

"Absolutely. You did great."

I swallowed hard. "I liked it. Everything was good until . . . I didn't mean to get so . . . weird."

He reached over and took my coat sleeve. "You weren't weird. Tonight was fantastic."

"You knew," I said. "When you held my sleeve. When you smiled at me. You knew what to do. What I needed you to do."

He smiled at me. "I needed that too."

He what? He needed it? "You did?"

"Of course. Social gatherings are a lot. Even with the nicest people."

I couldn't begin to describe the relief I felt. "They are nice people. It wasn't overwhelming like I thought it would be."

"Did you have fun?"

I tried not to smile *too* big. "I did."

Winter did a little happy dance in his seat. "I'm so happy. Look at us, being all social and stuff."

I laughed at that. "I feel . . ." I tried to name it. Relieved. Happy. I was both of those things, but they weren't the word I was after. "I uh . . . I'm proud of myself too."

Winter looked at me and beamed.

I was disappointed when he pulled into my driveway. I didn't want tonight, this feeling, to end.

He slowed to a stop out front and kept the engine running. I deduced that meant he wasn't getting out. He turned to me, his face lit up by the dash. "I had a really great night," he said. "It wouldn't have been the same if you weren't there with me."

My throat was dry, my heart thumping. "I had a great night too. I'm glad I did this. I was nervous, but you made it all okay."

He grinned, but then, taking a deep breath, he pulled his glove off his hand and laid it on the center console between us, palm up.

I knew what he wanted me to do.

So I took off my glove as well. My heart beat so hard it almost hurt, but I traced my fingertips across his palm, leaving them there for a second. His hand was warm and soft, and with a bravery I didn't know I had, I slipped my fingers between his and held his hand. Our fingers laced, my palm to his.

For half a second before I had to let go.

His eyes shot to mine and I needed to leave. "I'm going now," I said before rushing out of the car. I raced up the steps and opened the front door, but before I closed it behind me, I saw his face in the car.

Grinning.

I shut the door and leaned against it, out of breath like I'd run a race; my heart was thrumming, my lungs needing more air.

Dad appeared in the foyer, concerned. "Deacon, is everything okay?"

And I couldn't help it. I laughed. "Yes. Better than okay, actually."

His smile matched mine and he nodded. "I'm happy for you, Deac. Want me to make us some hot chocolate? You can tell me all about it."

I nodded, my heart finally calming down. "Yes."

CHAPTER FOURTEEN

WINTER

THERE WAS NOTHING, and I mean nothing, that could ruin my mood. Nothing. Not two little ginger demons who were legit mad at me for leaving them. Not the blustery freezing cold wind that blew through all the next day. Not the customer who I think was also legit mad at me because I couldn't name the book they were after when their entire description was, "I can't remember the author or the title, or much about it at all, really, only that I loved it and the cover was green."

Not even then.

Not even when Merry realized he too could escape the playpen at work with his brother. I wasn't bringing the crate to work, but keeping the playpen in the storeroom would have to do. Not even when the only way I could get any work done was when they were asleep or with Merry in the baby carrier and Bright perched up on my shoulder like an orange-gremlin parrot.

My customers thought it was the cutest thing.

Gunter and Rob dropped in to tell me they could see me smiling through the window from across the street.

"Jokes aside," Gunter said. "I'm happy for you both. Deacon's a sweet guy."

I whipped out my phone and found this morning's text, showing them the screen. ". . . like sunshine after rain." I wasn't about to tell them it was a partial quote from Shakespeare. The full quote was, "Love comforteth like sunshine after the rain," and I was doing my best not to unpack the L-word he didn't use but kind of did. I looked at Gunter and Rob in turn. "I'm sorry but could he be any more romantic?" Then I drew my finger across my palm as if they were supposed to know the relevance of that.

And then I swooned.

"Ohhh," Rob said, shaking his head pitifully. "That Christmas Cupid got you goooood."

Gunter laughed, and I couldn't even be mad.

Because maybe they were right.

I wasn't mad about the freezing cold wind or the snow flurries swirling around my car on the drive home. I wasn't mad about the color Ro wanted to paint the kitchen.

I held up the paint swatches. "It will look like a tequila sunrise threw up in here," I said.

This, apparently, was the best answer. "I love that description! I want it to be funky and light and colorful and fun. And there's a lime-green appliance set I have my eye on."

Of course there was. And of course it was lime green.

I gave her a quick hug. "Then you should absolutely do it."

Still in a great mood, I cleaned out the boys' crate and kitty litter, washed all their bowls, and sat on the floor with them as they ran, jumped, and skidded around the room. I loved them so much. They were the two sweetest little things ever, and I already couldn't imagine my life without them.

I managed to catch a great video of them wrestling and hopping, using me as a launching pad in their game of crazy parkour, and I sent it to Deacon.

Looooooook at them

He read the message and didn't reply.

I waited and waited.

And waited.

My mood deflated with every passing minute.

I checked the time. It wasn't dinnertime. Maybe he was watching his show with his dad . . . Maybe he was busy. Maybe . . .

Maybe I was overthinking things. Okay, so there was a very good chance of that. In fact it was highly likely.

But did he not know that I could see he'd opened the text and not replied?

Did Deacon not know that I could see he'd left me on read?

"What's wrong?" Ro asked.

"Hmm, maybe it's nothing."

"If you're worried, it's not nothing."

"Deacon didn't reply." I had to unstick Bright off my sweater without pulling a thread. "He never doesn't reply. I can see that he read it. Does he not know I can see he saw my text and he chose not to reply?"

Ro's smile was patient and warm. "He's not the kind of guy to do that deliberately. He would have good reason. Maybe he's on a call on a farm. Maybe he's tending to some poor, sick animal."

Oh.

"I didn't think of that."

She held up her arm. "Maybe he's up to his elbow in a cow or a horse."

"Okay, I didn't need to think of that." I grimaced. "Yeesh. Do you think he's done that before?"

"He's a vet in a small town surrounded by ranches and mountains. I can almost guarantee he has."

"Dear god."

She laughed. "You're welcome."

"What for? The images in my head are nothing to be thankful for."

"At least you're not overthinking the text message anymore."

Except now I was thinking about that again because she just mentioned it, and she could clearly tell because she sighed. "Call him, Win. You're both grown adults. There is no reason whatsoever to play guessing games. If you need him to not leave you on read, then he should know that."

Then his text bubble appeared. "Wait," I said, relieved. But then it disappeared. I frowned at my phone. "Oh."

I thumbed out a quick text.

> Everything okay?

His reply was instant.

> No

My heart sank, and before I could overthink some more and hit panic stations, I hit Call instead. "Deacon, what's wrong?"

There was a beat of silence before he answered, his voice quiet. "It was not a good day."

"Oh, Deacon, I'm so sorry. Is there anything I can do? Want me to come over?"

Another beat of silence. "No. It's late, and the weather isn't good. As much as I'd like to see you."

"I can come over—"

"I'd rather you didn't," he murmured. "I would only worry. I'm in my room anyway. I had a shower and I'm in my pajamas, so I'd have to get changed again and I'd rather not do that either, so . . ."

I sighed. "I get it. I understand. As much as I want to see you too. I'm sorry you had a bad day."

Ro relaxed when I said this, knowing he was okay. I smiled for her.

"Was it a bad day in general, or did something happen?"

He was quiet, and I could picture him frowning. I could imagine his anguish.

"It's okay," I offered. "You don't need to tell me."

I knew that too much pressure to do something he wasn't comfortable doing wouldn't end well, and I didn't want him to feel overwhelmed. "I'll tell you about my day if you like?"

More silence followed by a soft hum, which I took for a yes.

"Well, you see, it all started with this really cute boy I'm dating. He sends me poetry every morning and he does this amazing thing where he runs his finger over my hand. Sometimes he holds my sleeve. It's the cutest thing ever."

There was more silence for a beat, but then there was a soft sound that could have been a laugh. "Are you talking about me?"

"Why, yes. Yes, I am."

"That's absurd."

"*Every absurdity has a champion to defend it,*" I quoted.

"Is that a quote? I'm not familiar."

"Yes, it is. Oliver Goldsmith, Irish poet."

He was one hundred percent smiling. I could tell.

"And I'll have you know, that guy I'm dating? He is very cute. And very sweet."

He sighed quietly and, after a long beat of silence, murmured. "One of my customer's dogs passed away today. Mrs. Stevens. She's an elderly lady, and she loved that dog so much. He was all she had. She lives alone, and she was so upset. I know it's part of my job. We train for this. My dad has told me all my life that it's part of his job, and it *is* a part of life. I deal with it all the time but today was . . . not good."

Oh, my heart . . .

Ro seemed to understand that this was meant to be a private conversation. She gave my shoulder a pat as she walked out.

"Deacon, I'm so sorry. I can't imagine. It's not easy, and you're allowed to feel sad. Poor Mrs. Stevens. She must have been so upset."

He swallowed hard. "Yes. She was. I think that's what is harder for me. To see her so upset. She's been my client since I started. She trusted me with his care."

"Oh, Deacon. I'm sure you did everything you could."

"He was old. Sixteen, to be exact. And he'd had liver issues. It wasn't unexpected. But she was so upset. I . . . I can't deal with that. I don't know what I'm supposed to do or say in these situations. When it's a ranch and livestock go down, it's not like this. It's to be expected, and ranchers and farmers know it's a part of farming. It's not ideal, but they understand the cycle of life. But poor Mrs. Stevens. She has no one." He sniffed. "And I can't stop thinking of her by herself. In her empty house."

I wished I could see him, sit beside him, comfort him somehow. Not that I could touch him or hug him. But something . . .

"She was Dad's client before," he continued quietly, "and she was one of the first to agree to see me. Some folks in town didn't want me to be their vet. Not at first. I know my people skills aren't . . . I know what people say. What they think of me."

"Oh, Deacon." I shook my head, not sure what else to say. "It's only because they don't know you. If they knew how sweet you are, how deeply you care. Remember when I first met you? When I brought in the stray momma cat? What you told me was the sweetest thing."

"Because you like books."

"Well, yes. But you didn't know that then. You said what was in your heart and it really helped me."

"I wish I could help Mrs. Stevens. I wish I knew what to say or what to do. I wanted to console her, put my hand on hers, but I couldn't. I couldn't do it. Like how I want to hold your hand but I can't do that either."

Oh, his pain hurt me.

"Then let's help her another way," I offered gently. "Why don't we go see her tomorrow. We'll take some Christmas cookies and have a cup of coffee with her, or tea. And we'll see how she's feeling. You and me. I'm sure she'd appreciate that."

A long beat of silence. "You'd do that with me?"

"Of course I will. On your lunch break. I'll ask Ro to mind the store for an hour. I'm sure she won't mind. We can go together. I'm sure she'd appreciate the company."

"I'd like that," he whispered. "Thank you."

"You're welcome, Deacon. Thank you for telling me what was bothering you. I'm glad we talked."

"I am too. I feel better now."

"Aww, I'm glad about that too. Now, I'm not an expert on dating or anything, but I'm pretty sure this is what dating people do. They talk about what's bothering them and they try and make each other feel better. A trouble shared is a trouble halved, or something like that."

"I'm not an expert on dating either."

"Just as well we found each other then, isn't it?"

He made a contented sound. "Yes. The video of Merry and Bright was cute, by the way. I can appreciate it more now. Sorry I ignored you. I didn't want to burden you—"

"You're never a burden, Deacon," I said. "If you're ever sad or having a bad day, you just have to tell me, okay? I only worry when I don't know what's going on."

"Okay," he murmured. "Thank you."

"Feel better now?"

"Much."

"Good. I'll buy some cookies or something from the diner tomorrow morning and we'll go see Mrs. Stevens. You can come pick me up from the store and we'll go together."

"Okay."

Bright and Merry were now curled up on my chest, purring loudly. "Can you hear this?" I put the phone close to them so he could listen before putting it back to my ear. "Their little electric motors are running hot."

"They sound very content."

"They're asleep on me," I said. "I can't imagine my life without them," I said quietly. "For little purry, furry gremlins, they totally own me."

"I'm glad it was you who found them. They're very lucky."

"I'm lucky too. Because if not for them, I wouldn't have met you."

He was quiet again before he made a happy sound.

"Are you smiling?" I asked.

"Yes."

"Then my work here is done. I'll let you go now, and I will see you tomorrow at lunchtime."

"Okay," he whispered.

"Oh, and your text in the morning. Let's not forget that."

He chuckled. "I won't ever forget it."

"Night, Deacon."

"Goodnight, Winter."

I ended the call and totally would've hugged my phone if two sleeping kittens weren't on my chest.

Ro poked her head in. "Everything okay?"

"It is now," I said with a smile. "He had a bad day and wasn't sure how to talk about it. Or if he should talk about it at all. I think he didn't want to bother me with it." I sighed. "He's such a gentle soul. He had a customer's dog die today."

"Oh no," she murmured.

"And it wasn't even the death of the dog that upset him. It was how upset the customer was. It was an elderly lady. He struggles dealing with heavy emotional stuff."

Ro frowned. "Is he okay now?"

"Yes, we talked and he was smiling in the end. And I told him I'd go with him to check on his customer. We'll take some Christmas cookies and have a cup of coffee with her."

"Oh, that's really sweet, Win."

"I'm glad you think so because I was hoping you could mind the store while I go with him. It won't be for long. An hour max."

She pretended to be put out for half a second before she smiled. "Of course."

"He's the sweetest guy I've ever met," I said simply.

Ro's smile was warm and maybe a little proud. "You're a good one, Winter Atkins."

"I had the best role model," I said, giving her a pointed look.

She got a little teary, but she fanned her hand in front of her face. "Don't you make me cry. I just put my night cream all over my face, and that stuff is expensive."

I laughed. "I'm gonna put these two to bed. Can I get you anything before I turn in?"

"No, I'm fine. Get some sleep."

I yawned right on cue. "I plan to. The sooner I sleep, the sooner I get Deacon's poem text in the morning."

She snorted. "You sound like a kid going to sleep early on Christmas Eve, thinking it will make Santa come quicker."

"It totally does. And anyway, my eight a.m. poem is way better than Santa. I get this every day, not once a year, and it's poetry. About how he's feeling, or what he's thinking. It tells me more about him than he ever could, and I think tomorrow's is going to be the best yet."

I wasn't wrong, and I wasn't disappointed.

"My heart is stronger now you're in it."

Ghibli. He'd gone and quoted *The Secret World of Arriety* by Studio Ghibli and fixed himself a permanent place in my heart.

CHAPTER FIFTEEN
DEACON

I'D SPENT most of the morning overthinking a lot of things. Dad assumed it was about Mrs. Stevens, and although he wasn't entirely wrong, I didn't correct him.

Yesterday had not been a good day.

For the most part, I'd managed to keep it all in check while Mrs. Stevens was there. Dad knew though; he always did.

Highly emotive scenes had never been great for me. Emotions made people unpredictable and that always made me anxious, and when emotions were already running high in stressful situations, having me add to that was never ideal.

Dad said he was certain Mrs. Stevens hadn't even noticed that I'd needed to leave. He'd taken her into his examination room for some privacy while he consoled her, and I dealt with her beloved dog.

At least death was predictable.

I could deal with that.

Buddy had been a great dog. A great companion to Mrs. Stevens since her husband had died, and I knew from experience, as my dad had told me years before, sometimes people weep, not so much for the lost pet but for the grief of a loved one that pet helped them through.

They relive that grief all over again.

It wasn't a rational response, but very few things humans did were rational.

It's why I preferred animals. They acted on instinct and there was a predictability in that. There was no subterfuge, lies, or insults disguised as sarcasm in animals.

Winter's suggestion to drop by and check on Mrs. Stevens was a great idea, and I was so grateful he offered to come with me.

I was so grateful for him.

For his phone call last night. For his letting me talk without judgment. For listening. For making me smile.

I didn't know I could need someone like I needed him.

It was different from the way I needed my family.

It made my heart feel too big and happy.

So the line of poetry I sent him might have been too much, which was part of my morning of overthinking, but I couldn't bring myself to regret it.

Was it a declaration? Was I saying too much?

It was very likely *yes*.

His gif reply of a black-and-white movie star clutching a letter to her chest while she swooned told me he liked the poem, but still . . .

Overthinking was my specialty.

His blinding smile when I walked into his store at lunchtime told me he was happy to see me.

Maybe he felt for me what I felt for him.

Though I was certain what I felt for him far exceeded his feelings.

If the online definitions of love were anything to go by.

He made my heart skip a beat, my breath would catch, and my brain would stop processing . . .

It was either love or a medical condition.

Given it only presented when I saw him, or spoke to him, or thought of him, I was sure it wasn't medical.

"Hey," he said softly, his eyes scanning mine. "You look great. I haven't seen that coat before."

I looked down at my coat. It was a navy peacoat. Nothing special. I had a white button-down underneath. Not my usual work attire. "I wanted to dress appropriately to see Mrs. Stevens," I replied.

"Well, you look very dapper."

Dapper.

That word made me smile.

Or maybe it was just him.

"Let me grab my coat," he said.

"Hello, Deacon," Aunt Ro said, coming out from the storeroom. She was carrying some books. "Well, don't you look very handsome today."

Oh.

I was not a fan of compliments, and two in as many minutes was my limit.

"I've already embarrassed him," Winter said, coming over, now wearing his brown coat and orange beanie and holding a box of cookies. He grinned at me. "Ready?"

"Yes."

I held the door for him and he ducked his head as he walked by me.

We walked to my truck and I opened the door for him there as well. "Oh," he whispered. "Thank you."

His smile made my heart thump, and when I got in behind the wheel, his eyes were on me, his cheeks pink. "Are you cold?" I turned up the heat.

"No."

"Your cheeks are flushed."

He laughed and fanned his face. "Because . . ."

"Because why?"

"Because you held the door for me twice just now, and that's a first for me. Plus the poem you sent me this morning was possibly the best ever. It made me very happy, and seeing you just now, being so handsome and cute. That made me happy too. It's a happy blush."

My face grew warm. "Oh."

He chuckled. "Are you cold?"

"No."

"It's just that your cheeks are flushed."

I narrowed my eyes at him and he laughed. "I'm just kidding, Deacon. I'm very happy today, that's all."

I met his eyes. "I am happy too."

He looked away first, which I think was a record for me. "You know, if you keep this up," he said, looking out the window, "I just might think that silly story about Hartbridge's Christmas Cupid is real."

Goodness.

"I would be inclined to think it's *not* real. The idea of mythical beings with a bow and arrow lacks any foundation in reality."

He laughed before his eyes met mine. "What about fate?"

"Fate?"

"Yes. The predestination of people meeting, of paths crossing."

I thought about that for a second. "I . . . I'm not sure. Can I get back to you on that?"

"Yes, you can." Then he held up the cookies. "I bought the raspberry shortbread cookies. I hope Mrs. Stevens likes them."

Oh, yes.

Right.

Mrs. Stevens.

"Yes. We should go." I pulled the truck out and set off toward Pine Street. It wasn't a long drive. We probably could have walked, but the air was cold today and I didn't want Winter to catch a chill.

Mrs. Stevens's house was a small bungalow, painted cream and white. Her shrubs had been covered for the winter, though her path had not been shoveled in a day or two. I spotted the shovel on the porch and made a mental note to do it for her when we were leaving.

I knocked on her front door and could hear her shuffling before she answered. "Oh, Deacon, is that you?" she said.

"Yes, Mrs. Stevens, it is. And this is Winter Atkins. We wanted to come see you today, to check if you were okay after yesterday."

She got teary again.

I hadn't thought for one second that she might not appreciate this. "If this is not appropriate, I will understand—"

"No, no," she said, opening the door. "Please come in. It's very sweet of you, Deacon. Please come in."

She led us into her kitchen, to the round dining table in the middle of the room. Her house was warm, and there were a few Christmas decorations here and there to brighten the place up. "Please, take a seat."

"We brought some cookies," Winter said, offering her the box.

"Then I best put the kettle on."

"I love your gingerbread house," Winter said.

It looked as if a child had decorated it, and I wasn't going to mention it.

"Oh, thank you," she said with a smile. "My grandson made it."

Thank goodness . . .

We sat and had a cup of tea, which was not my favorite, but the cookies were delicious. And Mrs. Stevens did seem to appreciate the company.

We didn't speak of Buddy much, but like how Winter had talked to me on the phone last night, just talking in general seemed to help.

She was smiling by the end of our visit, and that made me happy.

I was glad I'd done this, and I was even more grateful for Winter now. It was his suggestion, after all, and his ability to make conversation looked easy. Small talk was not something I excelled at, or even enjoyed, but he made it look effortless.

I checked my watch, realizing it was past time we left. "My dad will be wondering where I am," I said.

"Thank you, boys, for stopping by," she said as we walked out. "It was very sweet of you."

I picked up the shovel. "I will do this first," I said, quickly shoveling her path while Winter stood by the door, still chatting with Mrs. Stevens.

Then I collected her mail and gave it to her, leaned the shovel on the porch wall, and again held Winter's car door for him. Because he seemed to like it so much.

When I got in behind the wheel, he was looking at me, cheeks pink, eyes bright.

"Everything okay?" I asked, starting the engine.

"Just you," he said. "You are all kinds of wonderful, you know that?"

I stopped and blinked. "Wonderful?"

"Yep. Wonderful. The way you shoveled her path, collected her mail. She said you were just like your dad. Kind, thoughtful, and handsome."

I stared at him. "She did not say that."

He laughed. "Okay, well, I added the handsome part. But she totally did say you were kind and thoughtful, just like your dad. She said she made the right decision in making you her vet."

Oh.

He reached over, very quickly patting my arm. "You did great today, Deacon. You really helped her and totally brightened her day."

"It was your idea, and I wouldn't have done this had you not suggested it. And I wouldn't have come on my own."

"Then we make a pretty good team, huh?"

I met his eyes. "Yes." I tried to hold his gaze but had to look away. "I think we do. Make a good team."

He pressed his hands to his thighs and inhaled deeply. "We better get back to work."

"Yes. I'm late already."

As I drove down Main Street, and just as I was about to park the truck, Winter cleared his throat. "Sooo," he drew out, in a way that often preluded something uncomfortable. "I was thinking . . ."

I put the truck into Park and held my breath.

And waited.

"Thinking about what?" I asked, suddenly not feeling very well.

He reached over to where I had my hand pressed to my stomach, and taking my sleeve, he whispered, "Hey."

I looked at his face then. He was smiling, which confused me . . .

"So I was thinking," he said, his eyes locking with mine. "That dating is awesome and all, and I'm very happy with where things are at, but I was wondering if you would want to upgrade to boyfriends?"

I blinked.

Boyfriends . . .

"Totally cool if you don't want that," he added quickly. "If you're happy with how things are progressing between us. If you think it's too soon. But I really like you, Deacon. You're the most amazing guy I've ever met—"

"Yes. Yes, to boyfriends. Yes, to upgrading. Yes, to everything you said. Except the moving too fast part. That's a no. I don't think we're moving too fast." I winced. "But yes. To being boyfriends. I've never had a boyfriend before, nor have I been one. Which kinda negates the whole never-had-a-boyfriend part, because I can't have had a boyfriend if I've never had one. Which doesn't include girlfriends, because I've never had one of those before either."

He laughed, eyes bright, cheeks pink. "You just might be the best boyfriend ever." He still had hold of my sleeve, which he only just seemed to realize. Instead of dropping it, he slid his hand over mine, giving a quick squeeze before letting go. "I'll call you later tonight."

All I could do was nod, before he was gone.

My heart was racing, my tummy now full of butterflies and jitters that didn't feel achy at all.

Boyfriends.

I had a boyfriend.

I am a boyfriend.

I drove back to work and walked in floating on cloud nine. Dad was at the reception desk, holding a white rabbit. He took one look at me and stopped talking to Courtney.

She looked at me too. So did the rabbit, and the two clients in the waiting room.

"Deacon," Dad said cautiously optimistic. "Everything okay, son?"

I rocked up on my toes, as if the excitement was too much for standing still. "Yes."

"Mrs. Stevens was okay?"

"Oh yes. She was fine. She appreciated the visit."

"Good, good."

Courtney stood up, smiling at me, and handed over a file. "Your one o'clock."

I read the name and turned to Mr. Sanchez and his dog, Buffy. "Come on through," I said, gesturing to my examination room.

Dad eyed me as I went inside, but I closed the door so I could concentrate on my work. It was hard enough to stop smiling, but focusing on my patients did help.

I still hadn't stopped smiling when Dad came into my examination room at the end of the day. I was disinfecting the stainless-steel table, which he didn't even seem to notice. "Okay, tell me what happened?"

I tried to play it cool.

Which was futile because I'd never been cool in my life.

"You haven't smiled this much since you beat me at D&D. I take it things with Winter went well," Dad said, prompting me to talk.

"Yes."

He waited. "And? Yes, what?"

"He asked me if I'd like to be his boyfriend."

Dad's eyes went wide. "Oh . . . well, that's great, Deac. I'm happy for you."

"I am happy for me also."

He chuckled. "And you said Mrs. Stevens was okay?"

"Yes. She said she appreciated me stopping by. I didn't tell her it was Winter's idea. She was upset in the beginning, but Winter is good at talking and asking questions to distract her. He was much better at it than I was. I'm certain if he hadn't been there, I'd have sat there awkwardly and she'd have grown more upset. He has quite a knack for making people feel comfortable."

Dad's smile softened. "He's a good guy," he said.

"He is."

He was quiet for a moment, studying me. "So, boyfriends, huh?"

That rush of excitement, even at simply hearing the word. "Yes. He asked me. He said he was very happy and comfortable with how things were progressing, but he wondered if I'd be interested in upgrading from dating to boyfriends. He said he really likes me, and that I'm all kinds of wonderful. This was after I shoveled Mrs. Stevens' path and collected her mail for her. I think he liked the fact I did this without having to be asked. He said I'm sweet and cute. And handsome in this coat. I think he likes this coat."

Dad's smile grew wide. "It's a great coat."

"It's just a coat."

"I'm happy for you, Deac. I think Ernie White was a bit concerned about you smiling so much. He wondered if you were okay."

"Mr. White . . . I did wonder why he was staring at me. He seemed confused. Is he okay?"

He laughed. "He's fine, son." He gave me a quick clap on the shoulder. "Let's go home. Your mom is gonna be so happy when you tell her. Her smile might even match yours."

I was still smiling. "I think I might be in love with him."

Dad stopped, stared at me, and blinked. "Oh." He blinked again, gaining some composure. "Oh, well, that's . . . that's great. Maybe a little fast, but I can see it."

"Fast? Is there a quantifiable allotment of time for falling in love? Some parameter I should meet first? Because I did google—"

"No," he said, amused by something I'd just said. He chewed on his bottom lip. "You googled, huh?"

"Simply to determine if there was a reason my tummy aches were only prevalent around him. And the heart palpitations, and my inability to think."

His grin widened. "And Google diagnosed the big L-word, huh?"

"Well, it was a process of elimination."

He nodded sagely. "You know, you could have just asked me. I feel that way whenever I see your mom."

I rolled my eyes but . . . still smiling.

"Well, I'm glad you're not anxious about your feelings anymore. There was the initial confusion and uncertainty."

"Those were a different kind of tummy ache."

"I remember it well," he said. "From when I first met your mother. Speaking of which, we still need to figure out what we're gonna get your mom for Christmas."

"Books. We get her books every year."

"Yeah, I know. And I'm all for that, but I thought maybe we should get something else this year. What do you think?"

I stopped cold; that dreaded icky feeling was suddenly back in my tummy.

"Deac, what is it?" Dad asked, concerned.

"Christmas gifts."

I could feel the blood drain from my face.

"What am I supposed to get Winter for Christmas? I've never . . . I've never bought anyone a Christmas gift before. Well, apart from you and Mom. You don't really count."

"Thanks, Deac."

"I mean a boyfriend. What am I supposed to get him? Just what does a boyfriend do for a Christmas gift? Surely there are expectations." I put my hand to my forehead, light-headed and panicky. "This was a terrible mistake."

Dad sighed, put his hand on my shoulder, and looked into my eyes. "Son, it'll be fine. We are Clark men. Well-educated, somewhat socially inept but that's subjective, and we are nothing if not lateral thinkers. We will do what we've always done."

"What's that? What have we always done?"

"We'll go home and ask your mom. She'll know just the thing." He clearly thought this was the best idea because he brightened, even raised his index finger. "She always knows."

MY MOTHER'S advice wasn't as helpful as I'd hoped.

I'd reasoned that perhaps Winter and I should set parameters on both monetary value and expectations. Dad wholeheartedly agreed with me.

Mom's suggestion, however, was more philosophical.

"A first Christmas gift to someone you love should come from the heart," she'd said.

Which was all fine and reasonable for fine and reasonable-minded people.

Of which I was neither.

How was I supposed to give him a gift from my heart? Jitters, palpitations, and an entirely weird, full, squeezy feeling were hardly something I could bottle and wrap to put under the tree.

Instead of overthinking and spiraling, as I wanted to do, I referred to the good, sometimes-misguided information on the internet.

"HELLO," Deacon said, coming into the store a few minutes before closing. He dusted off his coat and pulled off his beanie, looking windswept and incredibly handsome.

"This is a nice surprise," I said, unable to stop grinning.

"Oh." He froze. "Should I have messaged you first?"

"Not at all. Come in, come in," I said, ushering him away from the door. "Ugh. It's bitter out there today."

"Yes, it is."

He was watching me with those intense eyes, but when I caught his gaze, he looked away, cheeks flushed. "So what do I owe the pleasure of this visit?"

He winced. "Can I be honest with you?"

Oh dear.

Because no good conversation ever started with that.

"Yes, of course."

"I'd like to invite myself to your house."

Uh, what? I almost laughed, because that was not what I was expecting.

"Oh. Okay."

He quickly became flustered. "I'm sorry . . ."

I took hold of his coat sleeve. "It's okay, Deacon. You can come to my house. That's what boyfriends do, after all, right?"

He let out a little laugh, cute as hell, but he was antsy.

"Tell me what's bothering you," I prompted gently.

"Christmas gifts."

Okaaaay. Also not what I was expecting.

"It was brought to my attention that the exchange of Christmas gifts would be expected," he said. "Mom's suggestion of something from the heart, while well-intentioned, was not entirely helpful. Dad's suggestion was to ask Mom. The internet suggested many things. Most of which were not appropriate, or *in*appropriate. I've seen things I could've lived happily never seeing." He grimaced and I did my very best not to smile. "It was also disheartening to see how many times books made the top three suggestions. Which I would normally agree with, but . . ." He gestured around us, to the walls lined with books and grimaced. "Other suggestions were something for your house or your room, but I've seen neither. I realize this eliminates any hope of a surprise, but would it not be worse to get the wrong gift? What if I got you something that you already have. Or have ten of? I don't know. Do you collect anything? Do you like plants? LEGOs? These are things I feel I should know. But I don't, because I've never been to your house. I've never seen your things, your room. So I thought I could remedy that by inviting myself over; however, I realize now that it was rude, so I explained the whole gift conundrum, and—"

My smile eventually won out. "You are so cute."

He blinked.

"But yes," I went on. "Christmas gifts. We should discuss. And maybe set some guidelines—"

"I suggested parameters to my parents. Dad said yes.

Mom told me to go with my heart. But surely if we have parameters, we'll have a better idea of expectations, and then I can apply the suggestion of meaning."

He was just so stinking cute.

"One hundred percent agreed."

He let out a big sigh of relief. "Good."

"I'm glad we talked about it," I said. "Thank you for bringing it up."

He was smiling, eyes bright, his cheeks a rosy pink. "It really is best to talk about things."

"It totally is. And look at us getting it right." I went to the front door, locked it, and pulled the blind. "Let me just get closed up here, then we can go. I think Ro was making lasagna for dinner. Do you eat that? Or should we grab a pizza on the way home?"

"Lasagna is fine," he said.

"I'll just shoot her a quick text to let her know you'll be joining us," I said, taking out my phone and thumbing out a quick text.

"She won't mind? I feel bad. Maybe we could leave it until tomorrow and give her notice—"

My phone beeped while he was still talking. I held it up so he could see the screen. "She already said it's fine." Then I read the message. "Actually, she said how exciting; first dinner date as boyfriends, so I'd say she's more than okay with it."

He blushed and let out a cute little bubble of laughter. "Oh."

"I haven't stopped smiling all day," I admitted. "And your line of poetry this morning . . ." I sighed dreamily. "Okay, so I may have gotten that text when I met Gunter out the front of the store this morning. I swooned and he saw. I had to tell him about the boyfriend status, but I told him to keep it on the downlow because I wasn't sure how public you wanted to be."

"Oh." He made a face. "I wasn't hiding it. I should have asked you that, but it didn't occur to me. I also fail to see how it's anyone else's business, but I don't care if people know."

Now it was me who did a cute little laugh. "Me either."

"Apparently I was grinning so much I scared Mr. Sanchez."

That made me laugh.

I closed out the till for the day and locked the money away while Deacon perused the bookshelves. "Is this new?"

I poked my head out of the storeroom to see him holding a book on Cambodian history. "Yes. Came in yesterday."

"My dad would like this," he said.

"Great Christmas gift idea," I said with a laugh.

"Have you been busy?"

"Steady, yes. The weather made it quieter today though. I didn't mind. It allowed me to catch up on some paperwork."

He nodded. "Are you still happy here?"

I came out then so he could see my face when I answered that. "Are you kidding? Coming to Hartbridge, opening this store, adopting Merry and Bright, and meeting you? Best decision of my life so far."

He smiled, his eyes meeting mine. He didn't look away this time. "I'm glad you moved here."

"Me too." I sighed. "Well, speaking of Merry and Bright, I better get home. Poor Ro has had them all day. She said it was too cold for them to be transported around, even in their blankets and baby carrier."

"She was probably right."

"Which means they've been running her ragged all day. We should go save her."

"Okay. I'll follow you in my truck."

"Okay."

It was ridiculous how giddy he made me. Driving home, I was almost dancing in my seat, excited and thrilled at how things were progressing between us.

Gunter had joked again this morning about the Christmas Cupid, and I didn't even bother correcting him anymore. Because I was thinking maybe he was right?

Deacon was perfect for me. All his idiosyncrasies and quirks matched my own. Like a patchwork of odds and ends, of bright colors that at first glance might look out of place, but together we made a cohesive, happy picture. Once we'd figured out how we should communicate—once we'd understood each other a little better—things between us were easy.

I didn't care what society might think of us.

I didn't care what other couples thought of our minimal-contact, sexless lives.

We were happy. And we were complete. Nothing was missing. Nothing was lacking.

Sure, it was incredibly new and still quite early in the relationship. But I had a very good feeling about us. I could definitely see myself with him long-term.

He made me happy.

I liked that he'd dropped into my store unannounced. I got the feeling he didn't do much, if anything at all, sponta-neously. He must have driven himself to the point of distraction with the whole gift-giving thing. He'd googled things.

But what he hadn't done was spiraled. Instead, he'd referred to the internet and his parents, and when he wasn't satisfied with that, he came to me and asked.

It felt like a big deal and I wanted him to know that I appreciated his effort.

I waited for him by my car as he pulled in behind me, and we hurried through the front door together. We took off our coats and boots, the warm house a welcome reprieve from the bitter wind outside.

"There'll be a good dump of snow by the morning," Deacon said. Then he looked up at me, alarmed. "Do you have someone to plow your driveway? You could be late to work, or worse, stuck or isolated."

I smiled at his concern. "I think Ro has that all set up, but I'll double-check." I nodded through the entrance. "Come this way."

It was a gorgeous old farmhouse. In dire need of some love and modernization, but the white wooden paneling and pale cream walls, high ornate ceilings were rarely found outside of old homes such as this.

"In the kitchen," Ro called out.

I followed my nose, leading the way. "Dinner smells amazing," I said as we walked in, Deacon a step behind me.

Ro gave us a warm smile. "Deacon, welcome. I hope lasagna and salad is okay for dinner?"

"Yes, thank you," he said quietly.

"Where are the boys?" I asked. "I hope they weren't too much for you today."

"They're in their crate. You know, they'd be monsters if they weren't so adorable. They tired themselves out and fell asleep, but—" She glanced at the clock on the wall. "—it's getting to be their dinnertime. And they'll hear your voice, no doubt."

I smiled at Deacon. "Let's go check on them."

The living room was small and cozy. And by that, I mean with one three-seater lounge, a coffee table, a wood burning stove, a Christmas tree, and a crate, not much else would fit.

Small and cozy, yes. But we loved it.

Bright was sitting at the front gate, as if he were a time warden and I was half a minute late. Merry came plodding over with the cutest little squeak, demanding freedom immediately.

"They've grown," Deacon noted.

They really had. "Grown into their own little personalities too. Bright is still a terror-gremlin, and Merry is a sweetheart. But I love them both equally."

I opened the crate door and scooped them both up. Merry's meows were *daddy, I missed you* and Bright's were more like *where is my food, peasant-human.* "I better feed them or Bright will knife me with his murder-mittens."

Deacon smiled as I handed them both over. He was so adept at handling them. He was gentle but firm, in a way a veterinarian should be, I guessed. Bright tried to follow me by launching himself into mid-air. Deacon was also good at catching, as it turned out.

It made me laugh.

Once they were fed, it was our turn to eat. Dinner was delicious, as always. Ro had watched us both serve up our own, keeping the lasagna and the salad apart on the plate.

"You like your foods not to touch either," Ro said.

Deacon nodded, then talked about the complexities of lasagna and a bowl of salad. When food, such as lasagna, was made up of many parts, it was fine for *those* parts to touch. Necessary even. They had to be layered to make the dish. Same as a sandwich.

And a tossed salad was a whole unit. Now, if the individual components had been served separately, they would stay separate on the plate and shouldn't touch. But served as a complete dish, a tossed salad was a whole entity.

Made total sense to me.

"One hundred percent agree," I said. "But the salad and the lasagna should never touch."

Deacon nodded. "Correct."

"When Win was a boy," Ro said, smiling, "he used to say the food was the hills and there should be enough space between them, like a road for the fork."

Deacon's eyes met mine and he laughed, warm and throaty.

The sound made my heart skip a beat. The light in his eyes when he looked at me shot a thrill through me that felt a lot like love.

The realization that I might actually love him made my dinner hard to swallow. Ro's foot nudged mine and it prompted me to try again.

"You okay, Win?" she asked.

I sipped my water, cleared my throat, and nodded. "Yeah. I'm fine."

The look she gave me told me she saw straight through me.

Between her smug smile and Deacon making my heart happy, I didn't dare make eye contact with either of them. It was hard enough to eat while trying not to grin like a lunatic.

"Leave the dishes," she said, giving me a fond, all-knowing smile. "Go on," she said, nodding to the living room.

I checked the clock. "Oh, Deacon, your show is about to start."

I found *Antiques Roadshow* on TV and we sat on the sofa, not touching, but almost. I looked down at the space between us, barely an inch. "Is this okay?"

He swallowed hard, and not meeting my eyes, he nodded. "Yes."

I was ridiculously giddy. Ugh. It was surreal that I should feel like this.

Had I been in love before?

Sure.

Well, what I *thought* was love.

This surpassed any of that. This was different somehow.

"Eighteenth century," Deacon said. "French, £500."

Oh, the show . . .

"Ummm," I hedged. "I have no clue about clocks . . . German, £1,000."

It was eighteenth century, French, and worth £500.

"You're so good at this," I said.

He beamed.

The next item was a painting by a Scottish artist I'd never heard of. "£2,000," Deacon said.

"£500," I guessed.

It was £2,000.

He guessed the next one too.

"Hey," I said, nudging him. "Have you seen this before?"

He blushed.

"Oh my god, you totally have!"

Deacon laughed, his cheeks bright red, and he nodded. "Yes."

I laughed with him, surprised by his sense of humor. I got up. "Come on then, I wanna show you my room."

I almost tripped over Bright as he attacked me in the hall. I scooped him up and Merry squeaked as he ran-hopped behind us, trying to catch up. Deacon picked him up, and we went inside.

Thank goodness I'd made my bed and hadn't left clothes hanging over the hamper.

"It's a work in progress," I said. "I have plans. I want bookshelves all along this wall and a reading chair in front of the window. This room is bigger than my old room, so . . ."

"I can help you build the bookshelves," he said, holding Merry to his chest and petting him.

"Uh, build? I'm um, not really the building type. I'm more of a buy-it kind of guy."

"Flat packs are easy," he said. "If you buy them and have them delivered, I can come over one day and we can do them together. It could be fun."

"Or," I suggested, "one day we could go to some thrift shops and check out some secondhand ones. Ooh, and we could go looking at some antiques. Might find a Rembrandt or Ming Dynasty vases or something, like they do on *Antiques Roadshow*."

His eyes met mine and he grinned. "I would like that."

"Me too! It could be so much fun." The more I thought about it, the more I liked it. "Oooh, secondhand books! I love secondhand books."

He chuckled. "Do you not have enough?" he said, gesturing to my one very lonely bookcase. "This does not include your bookstore."

"But those aren't technically mine," I countered. "I'm like their foster parent waiting for someone to come in and adopt them."

He laughed just as Bright fought to escape my hold. I gently threw him onto my bed, the way he loved, which apparently activated his gremlin mode. He did little kitten zoomies, attacking the bed covers, then trying to attack me.

It made us laugh. "He's in a mood," I said. "And did you say I had another year of this?" I gave Merry a gentle pat in Deacon's arms. "Not like this sweet little angel."

"They are cute," he said. "Playful and funny. It doesn't last too long. You'll have a good ten or twelve years or more where they're much more chill."

Hmm. Even that didn't seem long enough. It made me

think though . . . "Do you think Mrs. Stevens might like to go to the pet-adoption day in the new year? I can drive her down if she needs. It's a month or two away. I don't mean to just replace her dog, but she might like some company by then."

Deacon sat down on the end of my bed. "Maybe. That's a very nice offer." He put Merry down on the bed, which Bright understood as fair game. He tackled Merry and they wrestled for a moment before Deacon saved the day. He extracted Bright, who decided Deacon's hand was also fair game and chomped his little milk-vampire teeth into the skin.

Deacon barely winced—clearly used to handling tiny feral gremlins—and he put Bright on the bed. Bright then decided to launch into attack number two on Deacon's arm, but I caught him just in time.

"Excuse me, little mister," I said, holding him up near my face so I could speak sternly to him. "No attacking the guests. We have manners in this house."

Deacon chuckled. "He's fine. I've had worse."

When he turned his palm up, I could see puncture marks and a scratch. "Oh my goodness," I said, turning Bright around so he could see his handiwork. "Look at what you did. Say sorry to Deacon."

Bright was, in fact, not sorry.

He was ready for attack launch number three.

"Nope. Bedtime for you, mister. Solitary confinement until you calm down," I said. "I'll put him in the crate, then please let me take a look at your hand."

I put Bright in the crate, which displeased him greatly. If we had a cat-translator, I was sure his tiny angry yips were a string of four-letter curse words.

Deacon was holding Merry up to his chest and I went to him, looking at his palm. "It's fine," he said again.

"Please let me have a look. I'll feel terrible if it gets infected or something."

He showed me the punctures and there were two tiny spots of blood. I sighed. "We can add Dracula to his résumé. I'm so sorry." I gestured to the table. "Come take a seat."

He sat, still holding Merry, and I retrieved the antiseptic spray and swabs. "It's not that serious," Deacon said, amused.

"Yet. It's not serious *yet*. God only knows where his mouth has been."

Deacon seemed to find that funny.

I put the spray and swabs between us and met his eyes. "Can I touch your hand?"

I didn't want to just grab him, especially knowing he had issues with touch and consent. Being prepared was key.

Deacon's smile faltered, his eyes serious, and he gave a single nod.

So, holding his fingers with one hand, I sprayed the cotton swab and then his puncture marks, then I lightly dabbed his skin before applying a bandage. It only took a second, but when I was finished, I kept my fingers on his, and he didn't move away either.

He was watching me though, and this time it was me who couldn't look at him. My heart was strumming and I was almost too scared to breathe. "Is this okay?" I asked quietly.

He gave another nod and whispered, "Yes."

Then he turned his hand over, and I kept mine still. Our palms were almost touching, our fingers almost entwined.

And my heart was almost bursting.

He skimmed his hand over mine, our palms, our fingers, then traced his fingertips across my skin. He was watching his movements, as if he were both fascinated and scared.

"Do you like it?" I whispered.

He nodded. "Yes. Do you like it?"

"Yes."

Then his fingers slipped through mine and he held them. Warm, gentle, soft.

Perfect.

He pulled his hand back and he let out a quiet laugh.

I was so freaking happy. And yes, I was definitely falling in love with him. "Thank you," I murmured. "For coming into the store earlier, for coming here for dinner. For being you."

His eyes met mine then. "Me?"

I could still feel the ghost of his touch on my hand. "Yes, you."

Just then, the wind howled outside and we both turned to the window. "Hmm," he said. "I should get home before it really starts coming down."

"Good idea." As much as I didn't want him to leave, I'd rather he not drive in a blizzard. "I'll take this little one," I said, taking Merry. I put him in the crate with his now-behaving brother and walked Deacon to the door.

He pulled on his boots and coat, found his beanie in his pocket, and put it on too. "So," I said. "About our Christmas gifts . . ."

"I think I know now what to get you."

"But we didn't set any parameters," I said.

"Have you not any ideas for mine?"

The truth was, I'd ordered him something already, but now it didn't feel right.

I made a face. "Well, I thought I knew what I was going to get you, but now I'm not sure. I've never had to buy a boyfriend a Christmas gift before, so . . ."

He grinned at the word boyfriend. "Okay. Parameters are a spending limit of forty dollars. This will eliminate one of us outdoing the other and making it uncomfortable between us."

"Great idea. I love that. Look at you making awesome executive decisions."

He laughed before he put his hand on the doorknob and stopped. "Are you going to the Christmas light festival on Christmas Eve when they close the street off. It's a lot of fun." Then he shrugged. "I've always gone with my parents. I've never had someone else to go with, so . . ."

"I think going together sounds like the boyfriend thing to do, don't you?"

His grin was back and he nodded again. "Yes. Okay, I'll . . . I should go. Please tell Ro I said thank you for dinner."

"Anytime. Next time I'll cook . . . or order takeout. Probably safer. But dinner again, yes?"

"Okay."

"Drive safely," I said. "I'm already looking forward to your poem tomorrow. No pressure or anything."

He laughed. "I already know what it's going to be." With a grin and bright eyes, he ran out into the snow. I watched him start his truck before I closed the door, and when I turned around, Ro was standing there watching me.

I swooned. Actually freaking swooned.

"He is a bit cute," she said.

I laughed. "Isn't he just? Oh my god."

Her smile was half happy, half sad. "You are so in love," she said quietly.

"I think I am, yes."

"I'm happy for you, Win."

"I'm happy for me too." I sighed dreamily. "Thank you for everything tonight. I'll bring us home dinner tomorrow night as repayment."

"Sounds good."

"And you have to help me figure out what the hell I'm supposed to get him for Christmas."

She gasped. "You haven't gotten him anything yet?"

I grimaced. "Well, I have but . . . what I ordered for him doesn't feel right now. I got him some noise-canceling head-phones. You know." I shrugged. "It can really help when he gets overwhelmed."

"And now you don't think that's a good idea?"

I shook my head. "No. I mean, I can still give them to him, but I don't want him to think I'm trying to fix him. Because he's not broken. Now I understand him better. He just needs reassurance. The headphones might still be okay as a side gift, but I need to get him something . . . more. Something better. Something that tells him how grateful I am for every little line of poetry he sends me. How happy he makes me, that tells him, shows him how I feel."

"It's five days till Christmas, Win," she pointed out.

I made a pitiful noise. "That's not helping."

She gave me a look that told me to stop being a whiny baby and let out a long-suffering sigh. "You really are the Winter of our discontent."

I gasped, hand to my heart. "Ouch."

But then we googled ideas. Did we find anything?

Nope. Not one thing.

I went to bed confused and a little deflated, but I woke up excited for his morning poem.

Unlike my ability to think of the perfect gift, he did not disappoint.

"To touch can be to give life."

I had to google that quote, and boy, did he ever keep surprising me. Now he was quoting Michelangelo, and my heart . . . well, my heart was his.

❄

"GOOD MORNING, EVIE," I said as she came into the store. "Ro, are you sure you're okay to take these?"

She was juggling the online-order packages. "I got it all under control."

"Yeesh, it's cold out there today," Evie replied. She then looked at Ro. "I can help you if you want. I'm not doing anything today. I'm free as a bird."

"No, thank you," Ro said. "It's fine. I've got it."

The door opened again, bell chiming, and in walked Toni. She was the mail lady who came in every weekday at the same time, like clockwork. She was a tall woman, big-boned, and handsome in a womanly way, if that was even a thing. "Morning," she said in her brusque voice, handing over my mail. Which was mostly window envelopes, my very least favorite kind of mail.

"Morning, Toni," Evie said.

"Hi," Ro said softly, sweetly.

It made me stop and look at her.

Toni gave Ro a nod, looking at the packages she was holding. "Need a hand with those? I'm heading back to the post office now."

"Oh," Ro said, her cheeks blooming with pretty pink apples.

Uhh . . . excuse me? I beg your finest pardon . . .

"That'd be very helpful," Ro said, voice soft. "Thank you."

Toni took all but one package and Ro followed her out the door like a lost little lamb.

And I was left standing there . . .

Ummm.

What the hell just happened?

Evie laughed. "Your face."

I pointed to the door. "You saw that, right?"

"Oh, yes. Your aunt Ro is so cute."

"Cute?"

"Sure. In a hot and trendy sexy momma kinda way."

I stared at her, unblinking. Not computing. "Uhhh. What?"

Evie laughed again. "It's true. And Toni is a sweetheart. She has the mail run and owns a small ranch out of town. A bit rough around the edges, but maybe Ro's into that."

I think I need to sit down . . .

I slumped onto the stool behind the counter, my hand to my forehead. "I need answers," I said, specifically not answers to what Ro might and might not be *into*. "Like what the hell just happened? And when? And why she never told me. And what the hell?"

Evie chuckled, seemingly unperturbed, gesturing toward the storeroom. "Are the boys here today?"

"No, they're at home. It's too cold, and Bright's entered into his feral-gremlin era, I'm afraid."

She sighed. "Then I do have nothing to do all day." She looked around. "Need a hand with anything?"

And it struck me then what a great idea that could be.

"Yes. Evie, do you want a job?"

She stared. "Here?"

"Yes, here." I nodded. "Casual, probably just for the rest of the holiday period, maybe an afternoon here or there in the new year. You won't need to open or close the store for me, or anything like that, but it's been busy and I have things I need to do, and I rely on Ro for far too much. And you've been a great help at the center, Gunter speaks so highly of you, and you look after my boys—"

"Yes," she cried. "Yes, I would love that! I leave for art college in Billings in the new year. So I need some money, and the experience, of course."

"Perfect!" I clapped my hands together. "I will get some paperwork and forms for you to fill out."

She did a happy, excited little buzzy dance. She was so cute. "Yay!"

"Okay, lemme show you how the point-of-sale system works . . ."

Two hours later, she'd filled out all the paperwork, served some customers, restocked the shelves, and straightened and tidied everything, and had a pile of flyers for our first book club meeting in her hand, ready to be mailed out.

She was a gem, and I wish I'd thought of asking her if she wanted a job sooner.

Like I wish I'd thought of a lot of things sooner.

I took out my phone and shot Ro a text.

> I just gave Evie a job over the holidays, and she's crushing it

> That's great news

Then it got the better of me . . .

> Okay so you're going to tell me everything about your crush on Toni because watching you blush like a schoolgirl has been burned into my brain

Her reply made me roll my eyes.

> I know not to which you're referring, kind sir

> I will have details, all of them, young lady

> I didn't blush like a schoolgirl by the way

I scoffed at that.

Do I need to remind you that I have camera footage in the store?

Winter Theodore Atkins

I grimaced at my phone, because getting full-named was never good.

I need to ask a favor

Ask away

I want to ask Deacon if he has any free time this week and I'll need you to look after the store for me. That okay?

Of course. Doing anything exciting?

I've thought of the perfect gift idea

Oooh, spill the details

You first

Winter

Theodore

Atkins

I laughed and typed out a reply.

Let me check with Deacon. It might not be able to happen yet

Sigh. Fine. Remember dinner tonight. Pizza sounds great

Done

Then my phone beeped with a text from Deacon.

> Dad reminded me that our clinic is closed Christmas Eve, so I have the day off. I know the store will be busy so I can help if you need

I could have hugged my phone.

> Yes please and thank you! You're the sweetest boyfriend ever for offering. I really appreciate it

Then without thinking, I added a heart emoji and hit send before I could stop myself.

I mean, it was just an emoji. It didn't have to mean anything . . .

Except it did.

I wondered how he'd take it. I wondered if he'd overthink it, just as I was overthinking it on my end.

"What's wrong?" Evie asked. "You're staring at your phone in horror. Is everything okay?"

"I sent him a heart emoji," I whispered. "By accident. He's seen it but hasn't replied."

"Is it a lie?" she asked. "I mean, I send heart emojis all the time. It doesn't have to mean anything, but if you love him . . ."

"I do," I said.

"Then don't revoke it. If he questions it, tell him."

I grimaced; my impending spiral was imminent in three . . . two . . .

My phone beeped with a message.

From Deacon.

I may have let out a high-pitched keening sound that concerned a customer enough to look at me.

"It's fine," I said. "I'm fine. Everything's fine."

I turned my phone around for Evie to see, and she grinned when she saw the heart.

Then, for some stupid reason, my eyes burned and I wanted to cry. "I'm fine," I said again, waving my hand in front of my face. "Totally fine."

Thankfully I had customers to help, which was a great distraction, and I managed to get a lot done in my office while Evie manned the service counter. I kinda lost track of time when there was a quiet knock on the door. I looked up to see Deacon standing there, smiling, nervous, cheeks flushed. He was wearing that blue coat again with a sweater underneath, his hair tousled, no doubt from the beanie stuffed into his pocket.

My god, he was so handsome.

I stood up. "Oh, hey."

"Hello. I seem to be making a habit of stopping in unannounced. I apologize if it's inconvenient."

"No, it's perfect," I replied, breathless for some reason. "I'm always happy to see you."

He swallowed hard, fighting a smile. "My dad told me to finish early. I was unhelpful, again, apparently."

"The heart emoji?" I asked.

He nodded. "Yes."

"I sent it by accident but I'm not sorry. I mean, I panicked at first, but like Evie said, if it's true, then don't tell him it was a mistake." I shrugged. "Because it *is* true."

He grinned at me, then at the floor, then at the wall, then back at me.

I went to him, not touching, but close, and with a courage I didn't even know I had, I held up my palm.

He stared at it, then ever so slowly traced his finger

across my palm and then my fingers. He blinked a few times quickly, then slid his hand across mine and threaded our fingers.

I didn't even dare breathe.

It was wonderful and beautiful, and . . . it was everything.

I wanted to tell him in actual words how I felt.

Not just an emoji, not what the heart represented, but my actual heart.

But then he pulled his hand free and opened and closed his fist a few times, then wiped his palm on his sweater. He laughed. "Makes my skin feel all funny."

I chuckled too. "Same."

He swallowed hard again, still grinning. His eyes were the most fantastic blue. "I want to get used to it."

My eyes did that burning thing again, and I tugged gently on a button on his coat. "You can practice on my hand any time you'd like."

So he took my hand again, holding it in both his. He pressed our palms together again, sliding our fingers through, but then he scrunched his nose up in the cutest way that told me he might have had enough hand-holding for now. But then he linked our little fingers.

"Pinky promise," I whispered.

He chuckled. "I've never . . . I've never pinky promised anyone anything before."

I grinned at him. "Then let's make it your first. What do you want to promise?"

His eyes met mine ever so briefly, a flash of striking blue, before he stared at our hands again. "I promise to try."

"Try what?"

He winced. "To be a good boyfriend. To try and hold your hand. To try and make you happy. I won't always get it right, but I will always try."

Oh, my heart.

"Deacon," I murmured. "I don't want you to change a single thing. I want a boyfriend who is just like you, just the way you are."

"You do?"

"Yes."

"I want to hold your hand. I want to do that."

"Then we'll work on it together," I said gently. "If it's what you want."

He nodded. "I do."

"No rush though, okay?" I said. "We have all the time in the world. To me, you're already the greatest boyfriend ever, so everything else is a bonus."

His eyes met mine and held my gaze, so intense and honest it made my heart squeeze. "Okay."

"My pinky promise to you," I said, holding up our hands, still joined by our pinkies. "Is to make you as happy as you make me." Then I remembered. "Oh, and about our Christmas gifts. I had an idea."

CHAPTER SEVENTEEN
DEACON

THE LINE of poetry I sent to Winter at eight o'clock wasn't the one I really wanted to send him.

But it was Christmas Eve and the line 'Twas the night before Christmas, when all through the house, not a creature was stirring, not even a mouse'

It was cliché, yes, but it was relevant for one day of the year.

It was fitting and wholly appropriate, which meant the one quote I wanted to send him would just have to wait.

Like he'd said, we had all the time in the world.

Even though what I felt for him sometimes was a balloon inside me that would expand so much it could burst.

Love was such an immeasurable thing.

I'd read countless books and poems and quotes about love. I'd read those words then, as if reading any fiction; words on paper that held little meaning because I'd never experienced it.

Well, I understood it now.

I'd been watching my parents my entire life. I knew

what love could be. I'd see them laugh and cry together, cook together, read together, be happy to be together. I'd always wanted that depth of understanding for myself.

Never once thought it'd be a reality for me.

But now . . . now maybe it could be.

I really wanted to hold Winter's hand.

I liked it. Not with anyone else—never with anyone else—but Winter was patient and understanding. He didn't mock me like the kids at school had, and he hadn't pressured me like the guys at college had tried to.

Winter let me be me.

On my own terms, in my own time.

And that trust unlocked something in me.

Something small, like a tiny seed that, with the right conditions, could sprout.

I wanted to try, anyway. Small steps.

The fact I'd held his hand at all was huge for me, but Winter seemed to understand the gravity of it.

He didn't dismiss me or hurry me. He wasn't disappointed or impatient or frustrated.

He'd looked at me in wonder, as if he were amazed and proud.

We'd made a pinky promise.

An actual pinky promise, like the kids in elementary school did, like I never could.

My promise to him was to try.

And with him, I felt like I could try a whole world of things. One measured, carefully thought out, over-analyzed step at a time, of course.

"Earth to Deacon," Dad said, waving his hand in front of my face.

Oh.

"Sorry. What were you saying?"

Dad rolled his eyes, smiling. "I said we're done here. I'll

stay and finalize some orders and do one final check on the patients before I come back later this afternoon." He shooed me toward the door. "You need to go. I hope you're more helpful at the bookstore than you've been here."

I winced. "I'm distracted, sorry." We'd stopped by the clinic to check on the overnight patients. Even though we were closed barring emergencies, we still needed to provide care.

Dad put the folder on the counter and leaned against it and gave me a smile I couldn't quite place. "You know, Deac, it's okay if you want to take some time off work."

"What?" I was not expecting this. *What did he mean?* "Why would I want to take time off? Are you saying you're not happy with my work? I know I've been distracted, but I can—"

He put his hand up, still smiling. "No, no, Deac, not at all. I didn't mean anything bad by it. I'm just . . ." He sighed and ran his hand through his hair. "I'm not very good at talking about this. It's more your mom's forte."

"Talking about what?"

"About most things." He smiled at the floor. "You know, when we found out we were having you, I freaked out. I was not ready. Your mom took it all in stride, the way she does everything, but I . . . I didn't have a clue what I was doing. But jeez, we lucked out with you."

Lucked out?

He smiled fondly at me. "You were the perfect baby. Slept, ate, rarely cried. You were a great kid: super smart, inquisitive, always reading. Never argued, never put a toe out of line. Even at college, never did drugs or alcohol. During veterinary school, clinicals, and residency, you easily managed the rigorous courseload. And now, as an employee, you're pretty damn perfect. Since you've started here, you've never missed a day. Not one sick day, not one holiday. You've done every single thing I've ever asked and never complained. Not once."

I wasn't sure why he was telling me this. "Dad, why . . . why are you saying this? If I did something wrong, just tell me."

He shook his head. "What I'm trying to say is that I'm proud of you. Not *just* proud of your work. I know sometimes the lines can get a little blurred between work and home." He gave me a fond smile. My favorite kind. "Deacon, I am proud of the man you have become."

Oh.

A strange, heavy lump formed in my chest, hot and burning, and it made me want to cry.

"You're a good man, Deac. And I'm happy for you. I'm happy that you met Winter. He's a real nice young man. So, what I'm saying is, what the point was to this whole story, is that if you ever want to have some time off work to spend the day with Winter to go do something fun, you just have to ask, okay?"

I really wasn't sure what to say. I still had the strange urge to cry and didn't dare to look at him. I could barely even nod.

"Okay, enough of the sappy stuff," he said. "It's Christmas Eve. We should be talking about holiday cheer. And the light festival tonight is going to be fun. Your mother and I will see you there. You have a good day with Winter, okay?"

I nodded again. I did need to leave because it was almost time for the bookstore to open. I wanted to say something, a response to his kind words, to tell him that I was proud of him too, that I was lucky to be his son, but I couldn't say the words.

I had an overwhelming supply of love and gratitude that I wasn't quite sure what to do with. But I needed to do something. I had to. I needed to give it an outlet. I needed him to know.

So, I crossed the floor, and for the first time since I was a very young boy, I put my arms around my dad and hugged him. Just for a second, long enough to hear him suck back a shocked breath, before I let go and took a step back and hurried to the door.

I glanced back at him for a split second. He was stunned, his hand to his mouth, eyes teary.

I didn't dare stop though.

I hurried to see Winter. I was so excited when I got there. He let me through the door and eyed me cautiously. "Are you . . . is everything okay?"

"Yes," I said, grinning. "I hugged my dad."

He understood the significance immediately, without me having to explain. He grabbed my coat sleeve. "Oh, wow. Deacon, I'm so happy for you."

"He said he was proud of me, and I . . ." I trailed off as I noticed his sweater. It was red and white, Christmas themed, of course, with Rudolph and holly and snowflakes. "Oh, that's . . ."

He laughed. "It's my ugly Christmas sweater."

I grimaced. "Well, I wasn't going to use that word, but I'm glad you're aware . . ."

He laughed and laughed. "Oh, you're funny. Come through here; can I make you coffee before the rush? I left Merry and Bright at home again today because I'm expecting this morning to be super busy—well, I hope it will be—and it wouldn't be fair to the boys. And then this evening is the light festival, which I'm super excited for, so I won't be home until later. But I'll be home all day with them tomorrow to make up for it, to give them lots of cuddles and playtime."

I followed him through to the storeroom. There were

boxes of books, newly arrived, which would need to be inventoried and cataloged. *Which I should start on immediately . . .*

"Evie will be here soon. She's working this morning, helping out as well," he said. "She's been a godsend this week, actually. And I got her a little Christmas gift." He nodded to a gift bag on the desk. "Oh," he said, his perfect smile aimed at me. "Your poem this morning was lovely," he said.

"It wasn't the one I wanted to send," I admitted. "But it was Christmas Eve, so . . ."

"Which one did you want to send me today?"

I shook my head. There was no way I was saying it out loud. "One I've now saved for another day."

He laughed. "That's fair. I know I keep going on about them, but I don't expect you to do daily poems forever, I mean, that would be a lot. And it's unreasonable. If you want to pare it down to once every other day or once a week, I'll understand."

I shrugged. "Would you mind if I wanted to send you one every day forever?"

He grinned, eyes sparkling. "Oh, I wouldn't mind at all," he murmured. "I'm really glad you're here today."

That weird, burning lump in my chest was back. "I am glad I'm here also."

Just then, someone came through the door, bell chiming above them. Winter gave my arm a quick brush as he went to greet them. "Good morning, Evie," he said.

"Morning!" she replied. She came into the storeroom to hang her coat up. "Oh, Deacon. Good morning and merry Christmas Eve!"

She was so bubbly and loud. Normally I would avoid such types, but it suited her, and I almost envied her carefree energy. "Morning, and merry Christmas Eve to you also."

She grinned as the doorbell chimed again, then she was gone to greet them. "Merry Christmas Eve," she said brightly.

Winter came in, smiling, collected a pile of books with a customer's name on a Post-it note, and disappeared into the store. He was busy, non-stop, and always smiling.

I listened to Winter talk to the customer about the books they'd requested. I loved how passionate he was, how perfect he was. I listened as Evie hummed what I thought was the Smurf song as she worked.

I stood there for a second, so unbelievably happy, unrecognizably happy, taking it all in for just a moment. Then I got to work.

"SO DO you want your gift tonight or tomorrow?" Winter asked. We were closing up the store. It was dark outside now. Main Street was closed off in preparation for the light festival, people busy setting up stalls and making the whole town look more Christmassy than it did before.

It would be an understatement to say I was excited for the light festival. It would be my first time attending with a boyfriend. It would be my first time going to a public event as part of a couple.

I was nervous, but mostly excited.

His question surprised me, because I hadn't even thought of that. "Will I see you tomorrow?"

He pulled the blind down on the front door. "Well, yes. If that's okay? I can come over, or you can come to my place if you want. It'll just be me and Ro, and Merry and Bright, of course. Do your folks do anything special?"

"Dad and I will go to the clinic in the morning. We have two admitted patients who will need tending, twice tomorrow at least."

"Oh no! Are they okay?"

"They will be," I replied.

"I guess I never thought there'd be animals hospitalized over the holidays. Of course there would be." He frowned. "Those poor little things."

"They don't know it's Christmas. Though my mom made them little stockings to hang on the front of their cages."

He smiled then, his eyes glinting. "Cute." He handed me my coat and pulled his own on, then his beanie and gloves. "So, gifts tomorrow then."

I nodded. "It'll be Christmas Day, after all."

"Ro and I always have a quiet day on Christmas. We do a big lunch, then we usually watch sappy Christmas movies all afternoon. It's quiet and lovely."

"Do you not see your mother?" I asked, then realized far too late that I probably shouldn't have. "Sorry if that was insensitive."

"It's fine, really." We went out through the front door, and he locked it with the key. "I will call her, and I did send her a card with some lottery tickets. But we're not close. Ro is more of a mother to me, and we'll have a lovely day together."

"I'm glad you have her," I said.

He grinned at me. "So am I." As we reached Main Street, he stopped walking. "Oh my word. Look at how beautiful this is. Isn't this the prettiest town ever?"

Main Street was always pretty but the holidays were something special. The lights, the decorations, the people.

"Evening, Deacon," Mr. Piper said as he walked past. "Merry Christmas."

"Merry Christmas," I replied to him, nodding to his wife and kids.

Winter grinned at me when they'd gone past us. "You're so cute," he whispered.

My face burned despite the cold. I pulled my beanie down and fixed my glove, embarrassed but happy. "As are you," I replied.

He beamed, then rubbed his gloves together and blew out a puff of steam. "Boy, is it cold tonight." Then he saw some food stalls. "Ooh, let's go see what goodies Jayden has tonight."

Turned out, Jayden had spiced-meat-on-a-stick things, which I didn't want to try, but the cups of tomato soup and grilled-cheese sandwiches were delicious. Perfect for this weather. We strolled as we ate, stopping excitedly only when something caught his eye. "Oh my goodness, Deacon, look! I have to get them, obviously," he cried at one craft stand. He held up two small, crocheted orange-and-white cats. "Oh, these are just like my boys."

Seeing him so happy did something to my heart. I was sure it was physically impossible for it to increase in size, but it felt like it had grown two sizes.

Then he spotted some familiar faces in the crowd. "Oh, it's some of the guys. Come on, let's go say hi."

It was indeed Hamish and Ren, Clay, Gunter and Doctor Rob, and Braithe. They were by the Winter Wonderland area. "Evening all," Winter said. They turned and all said hi to both of us, smiling.

"Deacon, good to see you again," Gunter said.

"Hello," I replied, nodding. It was a lot of people, and for the most part, their attention was on us. I tried to smile. Not just for Winter's sake, but for mine as well.

I wanted to do this.

"Merry Christmas," I added.

This seemed to please them because they eagerly replied in kind.

"I was talking to your mom and dad earlier," Ren said. "They were by the animal pen."

Oh, of course.

I looked down the street, but there were too many people to spot them. Still, I liked knowing they were here.

"We're all here for our annual Santa photo," Hamish said, nodding to the Winter Wonderland where Santa Claus sat on his big chair for photos.

Clay groaned. "You sit on my dad's lap and you're uninvited from New Year's."

They all laughed. Hamish laughed the loudest.

Gunter slid his arm around Clay's waist. "Cliff was saying he might hand the baton over to Clay next year."

They all stared at him. Hamish gasped.

"Yeah, I don't think so," Clay said.

"You must," Hamish said. "Oh, Clay, you must."

"I agree," Braithe said, putting his hand up.

Gunter found this funny for some reason. "Told you, babe."

Clay grumbled, just as Deputy Price came over. He was in full uniform, so working, obviously. "Oh good, glad you're here," Clay said to him. "We need some crowd control, starting with these two." He gestured to Braithe and Hamish.

Deputy Price shook his head. "Don't wanna know."

Everyone laughed, Winter included. I wasn't entirely sure I *fit in* with them, but it was nice to be included, and for some reason, they had included me in their circle of friends.

"Busy day?" Ren asked Winter. "A few customers told me they went to your store today. Said it was crowded."

"Oh, yes," Winter replied. "It's been three and a half weeks of busy days. Not complaining though. I love it."

"And he had you working today," Ren said to me.

"I offered," I said.

"I couldn't have done it without him," Winter added, smiling up at me.

Everyone smiled at me.

I tried to smile again, but it was all a bit much. Too many people, too much attention. I felt as if all eyes were on me, as if they expected me to say something, and I didn't like that.

That not-good jittery feeling began to creep in, and I wondered if I should make an excuse to leave. But then Winter tugged on my sleeve.

A little reminder that it was okay.

He was with me.

Some kids ran past saying hello to Mr. Branson, and Braithe called out for them to not run. Rob made a joke about school-teaching mode, and the conversation moved away from me.

And I could breathe.

Winter never let go of my sleeve.

We were close enough that no one would have noticed, but that contact, that comfort was what I needed. He was a tether before the storm could roll in.

How he knew, I'll never know.

But I was so grateful.

"You okay?" he asked me quietly.

I gently pulled my arm free from his hold.

"Oh, sorry," he murmured.

But then I took his hand in mine.

His eyes met mine and his smile made everything okay.

We were wearing gloves, so there was no skin contact, and I think that helped. There was no clammy skin feeling, even if the gloves meant our fingers were bulky. Even if it was in public.

I needed to do this.

I wanted to.

For him, for me.

Everyone chatted some more, but after a while, Winter leaned in. "Want to go find your parents to say hi?"

I nodded. "Yes."

"Okay, guys," Winter announced. "We're just going to catch up with Deacon's folks. We'll see you in a bit."

They waved us off and we headed further down Main Street to where there was a crowd of mostly children. I kept hold of Winter's hand the whole time. I knew my parents would see, and they'd understand the significance for me.

How big this was.

As soon as they saw us, Dad grinned at me, and I remembered that I'd hugged him earlier today. "Oh, Deacon, love, there you are," Mom said. "Winter, hello."

"Merry Christmas," he said. "Isn't this all so magical?" He looked around, and it was only then that Winter seemed to realize where we were, or more to the point, what was in front of us. "Oh my god, is that . . . is that an *actual* reindeer?"

I chuckled at his reaction. "Yes, it is. Toni Beltran has a breeding pair."

His eyes were comically wide. "Toni, the mail carrier?"

I nodded. "Yes."

He looked around then, at the crowd, searching for someone . . .

"Ro!" he called out.

His aunt Ro turned around, and seeing him, she waved. She was talking to Toni, said something to her, then made her way over to us.

"Remind me to tell you about this later," Winter

murmured to me before he greeted his aunt. "Hello there, fancy seeing you here. At this stall in particular."

"Oh, shush," she said to him, giving him a nudge. "Hello again, Deacon." Then turned her attention to my parents. "Hello again."

"Oh, lovely to see you," Mom said, and they all exchanged pleasantries and small talk.

"I cannot believe that's an actual reindeer," Winter said to me, bewildered, almost.

"Have you not seen one before?"

"Only on TV." He couldn't take his eyes off it. "That's . . . that's incredible." Then he looked at me. "Do you tend to them?"

I nodded. "Yes. If we have a scheduled house call to the Beltran ranch, you should come with us. You can see all her animals. She has quite the menagerie."

He nudged Ro with his elbow. "I'd love to go to Beltran ranch one time."

She leveled a tight smile at him, which he seemed to find funny. I wasn't sure what that was about.

"Did you have a good day?" Mom asked me.

"Yes. I had a great day."

"Me too," Dad added, his smile aimed right at me. I was certain he was referring to the hug . . .

"Ah, the Clarks," Mrs. Phillips said, coming over. "Merry Christmas to you all."

Then the Jacksons stopped by to wish us a merry Christmas, then my parents got chatting with Mr. Hayes and his two boys, then the mayor, then someone else, then someone else after that. And of course, people said hello to me too, and as Winter chatted with Ro, he included me as well, but throughout all the interaction, I was more than happy to stand back and watch.

It was as if I was a part of it all but not in the middle, and that suited me perfectly.

I noticed Mom watching me. She saw that I was holding hands with Winter, and her smile was pure joy.

"I'm so happy for you," she said quietly to me.

"Mm," I said, unsure what I could say. "I am too."

She gave my arm a quick squeeze. "Your dad told me you hugged him today. He's been on cloud nine all day."

"I, uh . . ." I winced. "I didn't know what else to do. I was . . . it was . . . a lot."

Her face softened. "I'm so proud of you."

And now this was a lot.

I must have squeezed Winter's hand because he turned to me, giving me a smile. "You okay?"

"Hmm."

Just then, the mayor called everyone's attention over the microphone, and I was glad for the distraction, for all the attention to be off me.

We walked down to the big Christmas tree, along with the entire town of Hartbridge, as we did every year. The mayor wished everyone a joyous holiday, the carolers sang, and the massive Christmas tree's lights twinkled.

Only this time I had Winter.

A funny name, really. Because he was the warmest person I'd ever met.

The wind sent flurries of snow around us, making everyone cheer, and despite the cold, I was filled with nothing but warmth and happiness.

As the night drew to a close, I wanted this feeling to last forever.

"What are you boys doing?" Mom asked.

"Oh." Winter turned to me. "I didn't bring my car because the street was being closed off. I was going to go home with Ro."

"I can drive you home if you like?" I offered.

Winter nodded, smiling, his cheeks and nose the cutest pink.

"Okay then," Dad said. "We'll see you both later. Don't be out too late," Dad added with a wink.

Oh dear.

"I might see you tomorrow at some point," Winter said to my parents. "But in case I don't, have a wonderful Christmas Day."

"Same to you," Mom said, giving his arm a squeeze.

We watched them walk up toward the fire station, where they'd parked their car, no doubt, then Winter and I headed back up toward his store. He slipped his hand back into mine, letting me do the holding, not being held, so I could control when I let go. "Is this okay?"

I nodded. "Yes. I think the gloves help."

"Awesome." He grinned at me. "Tonight was so much fun. I can't believe this happens every year."

I agreed, but there was something he'd said earlier. "You wanted me to remind you of something to do with your aunt Ro," I prompted.

"Oh, yes. Well, I think she has a crush on Toni."

I stared at him. "Really?"

He laughed, delighted. "She was so flustered and cute the other day, oh my god. You know, I think there might be some credence to that Christmas Cupid thing."

I chuckled. "Do you honestly believe that?"

He stopped walking, his eyes meeting mine. "I didn't, but now I'm thinking maybe, yeah, I do."

"Because of your aunt Ro?"

"No, because of you." He smiled up at me, eyes bright, the tip of his nose pink. Then he put his hand to his heart. "I think that little Cupid got me good."

"Oh."

"Maybe just because it's Christmas and how incredible and romantic this night was," he said. "But I want you to know that I think you're amazing, and I'm so happy you came into my life. I'm falling in love with you. Maybe I've already fallen, I don't know."

It seemed today was a day for declarations . . .

A lot of overwhelming declarations.

I wasn't sure what to say. I wanted to tell him how I was feeling. This overpowering, too-big-heart feeling. "Winter, I . . ."

His smile faltered. "It's okay. I don't expect you to say anything back. I'm just a big old sap, and tonight was perfect. And you should know how incredible you are."

I tried to speak but couldn't.

I tried to breathe and couldn't . . .

I considered turning and hurrying away. I couldn't do that either. My legs, lungs, brain couldn't catch up. So, for the second time today, bursting with too much emotion, I panicked and pulled Winter in for a hug.

Just for a second. A long, perfect, overwhelming second.

Then I let him go, just as abruptly.

"Oh," he squeaked, flustered, fixing his beanie. "Wow, okay, so that just happened."

"I'm sorry. I don't know why I keep doing that. That's twice today." I held up two fingers. "Twice in my life, actually. It's just that my insides get too much." That didn't sound right. "My heart . . ."

He held onto a button on my coat, maybe so I couldn't turn and hurry away, his smile becoming a grin. "My heart too, Deacon."

I laughed and put my hands to my face to stop myself from grinning too hard. "I'm sorry."

He laughed again, his eyes shining. "Don't be. It was . . . perfect."

A big old logging truck pulled up on the street and the window rolled down. Gunter stuck his head out, grinning, and waved. "Merry Christmas, boys."

We both laughed and it served as a good distraction, a break in the intensity.

I had rational thought back, at least. My truck wasn't far, so I nodded to it. "We should go. It's cold out."

"We should."

The drive out of town was slow as long lines of traffic made their way home. Winter pulled the two crocheted cats out of his pocket. "I can't believe I found these tonight. Even their markings are similar."

He held them in his hands as if they were the real things. When we pulled up at his house, he turned in his seat and held out one of them to me. "I want you to have him. Put him in your little tray of collectibles as a reminder of tonight."

I blinked in surprise but took the little cat. "Thank you. Though I don't need a reminder, because I won't ever forget tonight."

"Me either," he said. He put his hand on the door handle but stopped. "Thank you, Deacon. I'll see you tomorrow. I'll wait for your text at eight." Then he laughed. "No pressure."

Yes. No pressure at all.

He climbed out and held the door open and looked back at me. "Merry Christmas, Deacon," he whispered.

I nodded, my heart hammering. "Merry Christmas, Winter."

CHAPTER EIGHTEEN
WINTER

I WAITED for Deacon's text at eight o'clock.

8:01

8:02

"It's Christmas morning," Ro said. "Give him some grace. He's probably having breakfast."

"No, he would've had breakfast at like six or something. They're morning people. He was going to check the overnight patients at the vet clinic—"

"Well, there's your answer. He's busy. Maybe one of the sick little animals needed him."

I sighed and held Bright a little tighter. They'd already been up, had breakfast, played, and were about to have their first nap of the day. He was just so cute when he was all cuddly and sleepy.

Twenty minutes ago he was doing burnouts in the hall and using the sofa as a parkour launching pad.

I had to take the cuteness whenever I could get it. My sweet little Merry was playing with a toy mouse he got for Christmas.

As cute as they were, I just couldn't stop thinking about

Deacon. "I know, I just . . ." I sighed and pouted like a child. "We had such a good night last night. I told him I was falling in love with him and—"

Ro gasped. "You did?"

I nodded, smiling as I remembered his face. "He was so excited. He hugged me. Like an actual hug. And he'd hugged his dad earlier yesterday."

"He did? Wow. I thought he didn't like physical touch."

"He doesn't. That's why it's a big deal. Maybe it was all too much. Maybe he—"

Ro cocked her head. "Is that a car?"

I got up and Bright and I peeked out through the curtains. A truck with Hartbridge Veterinary Clinic written on the door was coming down the drive.

"Eeep. Look who it is, Bright. Can you see?"

Bright let out a tiny meow, which I was fairly sure meant *please put me to bed*.

"Glad you didn't overthink anything and assume the worst or anything," Ro deadpanned.

"Oh, shush. And you still have details to spill about a certain reindeer-owning postal carrier. Don't think I've forgotten."

Then I stopped and looked down at myself.

"I'm wearing my pajamas. Dear god. Why?"

"Because it's Christmas morning," Ro said. "Give me the child and go and put your robe on."

I handed Bright over and raced to my room and was pulling on a hoodie when there was a knock at the door. A hoodie was better than a robe, right?

I opened the door with a little more gusto than was probably necessary. "Deacon, this is a lovely surprise. Come in."

"I'm sorry for stopping by unannounced," he said.

"I'm getting used to it," I said, but I think he missed the

joke. He looked kinda stressed. "What happened? Is everything okay?"

"Yes, it's just . . ."

"Come in and sit with me," I said. Having a conversation inside the front door wasn't a great idea.

Ro was putting the boys in their crate. "I'll just go take a shower," she said. "Let you boys talk. Merry Christmas, Deacon."

"Oh," he said, blinking. "Yes. Merry Christmas to you as well."

Once we were alone and sitting on the sofa, I turned to give him my full attention. "What happened? Was something wrong with the overnight patients at the clinic?"

He was momentarily confused. "Oh no, they're okay. Doing well, actually."

"Oh, good."

"I missed the eight o'clock text," he said.

Oh no, was *that* what he was upset over?

"Deacon, it's fine."

He shook his head. "I had one ready to send but it wasn't right. It was a Christmas Day one . . . What if Christmas, he thought, doesn't come from a store. What if Christmas, perhaps, means a little bit more'." He winced. "It is Christmas Day, after all."

"It's a beautiful line," I said gently. "Seuss, right?"

He nodded.

"I love that movie. It's on our list to watch today."

He frowned. "It's not the one I wanted to send. Like yesterday's as well. That was the Christmas Eve one so I had to send it, even though my favorite line is the sugarplum one. I was going to save this one until tomorrow, but I wanted to send it today. But then I'd have missed the Christmas Day one, and I was trying to decide all morning, but then I ended up missing it and sending none . . ."

I reached over and gave his hand a gentle squeeze, not for long, just a moment. But then he was quick to grab my hand before I could pull it back.

"Love looks not with the eyes, but with the mind," he whispered. "And therefore is winged Cupid painted blind."

I stared at him.

"Is that . . . what you wanted to send me?"

He nodded and gave me a tortured, embarrassed smile. "To reference your Cupid. It wears a blindfold so it can only know by heart."

"Shakespeare, *A Midsummer Night's Dream.*"

"You know it?"

"Of course I do," I said, my eyes burning. "It's only the most beautiful words ever written." A stupid tear escaped my eye, and I scrubbed it away. "Deacon, it's beautiful."

"I don't know if I believe Cupid found us, but . . . it's how I feel. I'm not good with expressing myself," he whispered, gripping my fingers now, his hand trembling. "I get overwhelmed, and the words get stuck in my head. But these poems say it for me. Each one I've sent you is what I wished I could say."

My chin wobbled and I had to wipe away another tear. "If you want to quote poems of love to me, that's more than okay. In fact, it's almost better."

"Then why are you crying?"

I let out a super classy snotty laugh. "Because I'm a sap. And I'm a romantic, and I love books and poetry, and you combine them all. You're so perfect for me. I love you, Deacon. There, I said it. It's true. You're just," I shrugged. "Like the best of Shakespeare and Byron and Keats and Dickinson all combined, just for me."

He smiled, blushing and shy. "I didn't want you to be mad or disappointed. I hadn't forgotten to text you. I just . . . it wasn't right and then I got all caught up in my head."

"I could never be mad or disappointed. I thought you might have got busy at work, that's all."

Ro scoffed as she walked out, clearly having heard my little white lie. "I'm making Christmas pancakes. Deacon, would you like to stay for breakfast?"

He looked at me, as if asking for permission. "I like pancakes," he whispered.

"Yes, he'll stay," I said, giving his hand a squeeze.

Then he frowned. "What are Christmas pancakes?"

"Normal pancakes shaped like Christmas trees. And you can add toppings to decorate it. It's a thing we do."

His smile was blinding. "Then yes."

"Ooh," I said, remembering. "Your gift. Would you like it now? Or should we exchange later?"

He grimaced again, suddenly awkward. "Well, I . . . what I got you . . ."

"Will be perfect. What you've given me already today is all I could ask for, Deacon."

He seemed somewhat relieved. "Good. Because I got you a scarf that is the colors of the asexuality flag but without the dog wormer logo, and a flat pack bookcase, which now seems grossly inadequate."

I laughed. "Really? That's perfect!"

"It will fit along the wall you wanted it to," he added. "I thought we could make it together."

It was my turn to grimace. "Well, my furniture building skills are non-existent, but I can hand you the tools and offer moral support and cookies while you build it?"

He chuckled. "Okay."

I took his gift from under the tree. "Speaking of grossly inadequate gifts, I have this for you. It's okay if you want to take it back or exchange it for something else. I kept all the receipts."

He opened the gift slowly, perfectly, and pulled out the box and then the items in turn.

I explained as he inspected them.

"They're noise-canceling headphones. In case we have to go somewhere where there's a lot of noise and people. I'm sorry if they're inappropriate, but I thought they could help. If you don't like them, I—"

"I like them."

"I asked your dad if I should get in-ear or over-ear and he told me," I added quickly. "I don't want you to think you need them or that I think you *should* use them, because I don't. I just read that some people find them helpful . . ."

He smiled at me. "I'll try them. Thank you."

The next was a journal, pages blank. "I thought we could make our own keepsake journal, of us, to keep on your bookcase. We could take photos, or stick in movie stubs, or an awesome shaped leaf we find, or little quotes, or hearts. There are special pens as well, and some different washi tapes and crafty things to make them pretty. It'd be like your tray of keepsakes but in book form." I shrugged, uncertain.

His eyes met mine. "I love this so much. This idea. This journal." He swallowed hard. "You."

My heart skidded and thumped, my breath caught.

He just . . .

He just said that . . .

"I love you too," I whispered.

"Christmas pancakes are ready, boys," Ro called out from the kitchen. "Fresh coffee too."

I gave Deacon's hand another gentle squeeze and let out a shaky breath so I could speak. "Merry Christmas, Deacon."

"Merry Christmas, Winter."

EPILOGUE
WINTER

SPRING HAD ARRIVED EARLY for Valentine's market day. It was unseasonably warm, though the air had a chill, the sky was blue, the sun was warm.

It was gloriously beautiful.

Short Street was full of craft and food stalls, and a marquee set up as a pet-adoption stall hosted by Hartbridge Veterinary Clinic in conjunction with the Humane Society.

"Oh, what a splendid day," Mrs. Stevens said.

She had her arm linked through mine as I walked her from my car to the mall.

"It is indeed," I replied.

I was thrilled to see her at my first monthly book club meetings, and she'd said she was ready to adopt again. So I'd offered to escort her down to see if she could find a little doggo in need of a new home.

Deacon and his parents were busy, and by all accounts, it seemed the day was a success. Even Mildred was there with a pink Humane Society bandana. Deacon was showing an information brochure to someone, but he looked up as we walked in, smiling at me before addressing Mrs.

Stevens. "Good morning," he said. "Thank you for coming today."

"Good morning, Deacon," she said. "Winter here was just telling me you gave him flowers and have a Valentine's Day date tonight. How exciting."

Deacon's gaze shot to mine. "Did he, just?"

I grimaced. "I was making conversation," I said quickly. "So, the dogs . . ." I said, grinning at him. "Shall we make some introductions?"

"Hmm." He led her around the area set up with crates and cages to where all the dogs were waiting. There were big dogs, little dogs, fluffy dogs, short-haired, happy and yappy, and sleepy dogs.

Mrs. Stevens took her time, meeting them all, one dog at a time. I could tell by her expression she wasn't feeling it.

Maybe she wasn't as ready as she thought she was.

I suggested we sit a while and ponder, and she was clearly disappointed. Only her chair was beside a cage with a tabby cat in it. He was a big, chonky boy, and immediately began meowing at Mrs. Stevens. Then he stood up and tapped the cage, still meowing at her.

"I think he's trying to say hello," I said.

"Oh, he's very vocal, isn't he?" she said.

"I have two cats," I said. "Well, kittens. They're like three months old now, and I love them to pieces."

Deacon took the cat from his cage. "Maybe he's trying to tell us something. You know, it's common for an animal to choose the human, not the other way around."

He gently placed the cat on her lap. I worried the cat might try and run, or worse, claw her in the process. Deacon kept close, but there was no need to worry. The cat put his paws on her chest, leaned up to nudge her chin, then lay down, settling in right there, closed his eyes, and began to purr.

Mrs. Stevens looked at me, her mouth pulled down, and she had a little cry. "Oh my goodness," she said.

I got teary right along with her. "I think he found his human."

"I came for a little dog," she said.

I read the details for her. "His name is Rupert," I said, "and he's five years old."

She pet him. "Rupert, huh? That's a very gentlemanly name."

"It is," I agreed. "What a sweetheart."

She looked at me. "He chose me, didn't he?"

Considering he was like a loaf on her chest, purring contentedly, eyes closed, I'd say yes. "He did. I think he's got a lot of love to give."

And that was that.

Mrs. Stevens was now a cat mom to a very happy, chonky boy, and the adoption day was a great success. The whole market day was. Local producers were happy to sell their wares, and the town residents were very happy shoppers.

It was all over by mid-afternoon. I helped Deacon and his parents pack up their stall, and when we were done, we headed to the diner for a milkshake and some of Jayden's peanut brownies.

Deacon was positively shining.

We sat in a booth, our legs touching. He even put his hand on my thigh a time or two.

We didn't need to sit this close, there was plenty of room, but this was us now. Occasional touches, hand-holding. One time, he even put his hand on my lower back when he'd held a door for me.

I was on cloud nine every single day.

The best way to describe how Deacon loves is quietly. There's no extravagant fanfare or excessive parades of attention or declarations. His love is honest and sincere and with the entirety of his whole heart. It's so deep and consuming that it could be almost overwhelming if it weren't so gentle and pure.

I could read a thousand poems about the depth of the ocean, the immense force of its ebbs and flows, the undercurrent of emotion. Or the vastness of stars, infinite and perfect, full of wonder.

But not even the words of Keats, Shakespeare, or Dickinson could capture the way Deacon loves me.

He was a single flower. Not a field of flowers. Just one. It might seem simple to some, but it was anything but simple. It was complex and beautiful and had just waited for the perfect moment of sunshine before it could bloom.

That was how Deacon loved me.

And I counted myself as the luckiest man on the planet to be loved by him.

"I'm glad today went well," I said. "But I should get back to the store and close up for Ro."

"Okay, thanks again for your help today," Wayne said. "Don't you boys be out too late tonight."

It was a given that Deacon would be coming with me. We were pretty much inseparable these days.

Ro was happy to see me. "Oh, I was beginning to wonder where you were?" she said.

"Hmm," I hedged. "Late for something? Have a hot date tonight? Did I see Toni in here earlier today?"

She leveled me a mind-your-business glare and grabbed her bag. "Don't wait up for me tonight."

I gasped. "I want details!" I called out, but she was already out the door.

"Do you really?" Deacon asked. He was straightening up some merchandise. "Want details? That seems an odd thing to want. She's your aunt, after all."

I laughed. "I'm just teasing her. But yes, I want to know. Not the intimate details, of course, but the swoony romantic stuff."

He smiled, distracted, but before I could ask him if he was okay, he nodded to the front window display. "Your Valentine's Day theme will need to be changed."

"I have the best Easter one ready to go up this week. It's a Peter Rabbit theme, and there are 3D paper bunnies and little paper Easter eggs. It's going to be amazing. Though I will miss the Valentine one."

The hot air balloon in the shape of a love heart will definitely be back out next year.

Deacon smiled again, but his eyes flinched and he didn't seem to know whether to keep his hands in his pockets or by his side.

"Everything okay?" I asked, closing out the till.

Something was definitely not okay.

"Yes. Are you almost done?"

I locked the money away and took one last look around the store. There was nothing that couldn't wait until tomorrow. "Sure."

He waited for me to lock the door, and when I gave him a big smile, he quickly looked away. "Walk with me?"

Oh . . .

"Of course," I said, and we headed toward the river.

The sun was getting low, rays of fading golden sunlight filtered through the green trees. Birds were chirping, people were walking dogs, laughing.

It was utterly perfect.

Except for whatever was wrong with Deacon. He was antsy and nervous. I took his hand gently and he stopped walking.

"Is everything okay?" I asked.

He shook his head. "No."

"What is it? You can tell me."

"It's Valentine's Day."

I nodded slowly. "Yes. Your poem to me this morning had me smiling all day."

"Yes, but I . . ." He screwed up his face. "I've been thinking a lot. And I tried finding a poem to ask, but they all felt so inadequate. Well, perhaps 'Love's Philosophy' by Percy Bysshe Shelly. I do like the line about moonbeams—"

"It's a wonderful poem," I hedged, unsure of where he was going with this. I knew the poem, and I knew what it meant. Could he possibly want . . . ? "Deacon," I whispered.

"But still," he went on. "It's still not enough. What Shelly wrote is not adequate."

I was about to argue because, uhhh, what? "I'm fairly sure Percy—"

"Stay very still."

I froze. "Why?" I hissed. "Is there a bee? A wasp?"

"No," he whispered, possibly closer than he'd ever been. "Stay still. Please."

I stayed very still.

"I think I would," he breathed, then blinked a few times. "I would very much like to kiss you. 'As the moonbeams kiss the sea.'"

Oh.

Oh my god.

I somehow managed to nod.

He put his hand to my cheek, his fingers tracing my jaw, and he lifted my chin a little. I realized he was *actually* about to kiss me.

He was doing this.

He's going to kiss me.

He leaned in slowly, his focus on my lips, and I didn't dare breathe. Then he pressed his lips to mine, soft, sweet.

Perfect.

For one time-stopping, perfect moment before he pulled back. My eyes fluttered and my heart hammered.

His smile stole my breath.

He laughed and put his hand to his forehead, looking around, agitated but in a good way, as if he had too much positive energy and no outlet.

Then, when it was all clearly too much, he threw his arms around me and hugged me, like he did when he was too overwhelmed with happiness and didn't know what else to do.

It made me laugh.

He let me go, grinning, blue eyes wide with wonder. "I kissed you."

"You did," I said, a little teary. He never stopped surprising me. "Wow."

Then he stopped. "Was it . . . ? I've never kissed anyone before. I've wanted to kiss you for a while now, and today's Valentine's Day. I wanted to make it special for you."

"You did," I said. "The poem this morning. The beautiful flowers. We're doing pizza and a movie tonight, and now this."

"A kiss," he whispered.

I nodded. "A perfect kiss. 'And the moonbeams kiss the sea.'"

THE END

ABOUT THE AUTHOR

N.R. Walker is an Australian author who loves her genre of queer romance. First published in 2012, she now has over 80 books, many which are also audiobooks, and numerous translations done in nine different languages.
She loves writing and spends far too much time doing it but wouldn't have it any other way.

nrwalker.net

Cronin's Key IV - Kennard's Story

Exchange of Hearts

The Spencer Cohen Series, Book One

The Spencer Cohen Series, Book Two

The Spencer Cohen Series, Book Three

The Spencer Cohen Series, Yanni's Story

Blood & Milk

The Weight Of It All

A Very Henry Christmas (The Weight of It All 1.5)

Perfect Catch

Switched

Imago

Imagines

Imagoes

Red Dirt Heart Imago

On Davis Row

Finders Keepers

Evolved

Galaxies and Oceans

Private Charter

Nova Praetorian

A Soldier's Wish

Upside Down

The Hate You Drink

Sir

Tallowwood

Reindeer Games

The Dichotomy of Angels

Throwing Hearts

Pieces of You - Missing Pieces #1

Pieces of Me - Missing Pieces #2

Pieces of Us - Missing Pieces #3

Lacuna

Tic-Tac-Mistletoe

Bossy

Code Red

Dearest Milton James

Dearest Malachi Keogh

Christmas Wish List

Code Blue

Davo

The Kite

Learning Curve

Merry Christmas Cupid

To the Moon and Back

Second Chance at First Love

Outrun the Rain

Into the Tempest

Touch the Lightning

EWB - Enemies With Benefits

Holiday Heart Strings

Bloom

The Men from Echo Creek

Method Acting

The Bait

Nothing Left to Lose

Deck the Fire Halls

Benji

Fitch

Kylan

The Team

Code Word

Titles in Audio:

Cronin's Key

Cronin's Key II

Cronin's Key III

Red Dirt Heart

Red Dirt Heart 2

Red Dirt Heart 3

Red Dirt Heart 4

The Weight Of It All

Switched

Point of No Return

Breaking Point

Starting Point

Spencer Cohen Book One

Spencer Cohen Book Two

Spencer Cohen Book Three

Yanni's Story

On Davis Row

Evolved

Elements of Retrofit

Clarity of Lines

Sense of Place

Blind Faith

Through These Eyes

Blindside

Finders Keepers

Galaxies and Oceans

Nova Praetorian

Upside Down

Sir

Tallowwood

Imago

Throwing Hearts

Sixty Five Hours

Taxes and TARDIS

The Dichotomy of Angels

The Hate You Drink

Pieces of You

Pieces of Me

Pieces of Us

Tic-Tac-Mistletoe

Lacuna

Bossy

Code Red

Learning to Feel

Dearest Milton James

Dearest Malachi Keogh

Three's Company

Christmas Wish List

Code Blue

Davo

The Kite

Learning Curve

Merry Christmas Cupid

To the Moon and Back

Second Chance at First Love

Outrun the Rain

Into the Tempest

Touch the Lightning

EWB

Holiday Heart Strings

Bloom

The Men from Echo Creek

Method Acting

The Bait

Deck the Fire Halls

Benji

Fitch

Kylan

The Team

Code Word

Series Collections:

Red Dirt Heart Series

Turning Point Series

Thomas Elkin Series

Spencer Cohen Series

Imago Series

Blind Faith Series

Missing Pieces Series

The Storm Boys Series

Gay Sex Club Stories

Free Reads:

Sixty Five Hours

Learning to Feel

His Grandfather's Watch (And The Story of Billy and Hale)

The Twelfth of Never (Blind Faith 3.5)

Twelve Days of Christmas (Sixty Five Hours Christmas)

Best of Both Worlds

Translated Titles:

Italian

Fiducia Cieca (Blind Faith)

Attraverso Questi Occhi (Through These Eyes)

Preso alla Sprovvista (Blindside)

Il giorno del Mai (Blind Faith 3.5)

Cuore di Terra Rossa Serie (Red Dirt Heart Series)

Natale di terra rossa (Red dirt Christmas)

Intervento di Retrofit (Elements of Retrofit)

A Chiare Linee (Clarity of Lines)

Senso D'appartenenza (Sense of Place)

Spencer Cohen Serie (including Yanni's Story)

Punto di non Ritorno (Point of No Return)

Punto di Rottura (Breaking Point)

Punto di Partenza (Starting Point)

Imago (Imago)

Imagines

Il desiderio di un soldato (A Soldier's Wish)

Scambiato (Switched)

Tallowwood

The Hate You Drink

Ho trovato te (Finders Keepers)

Cuori d'argilla (Throwing Hearts)

Galassie e Oceani (Galaxies and Oceans)

Il peso di tut (The Weight of it All)

Pieces of You - Missing Pieces 1

Pieces of Me - Missing Pieces 2

Pieces of Us - Missing Pieces 3

Code Red

French

Confiance Aveugle (Blind Faith)

A travers ces yeux: Confiance Aveugle 2 (Through These Eyes)

Aveugle: Confiance Aveugle 3 (Blindside)

À Jamais (Blind Faith 3.5)

Cronin's Key Series

Au Coeur de Sutton Station (Red Dirt Heart)

Partir ou rester (Red Dirt Heart 2)

Faire Face (Red Dirt Heart 3)

Trouver sa Place (Red Dirt Heart 4)

Le Poids de Sentiments (The Weight of It All)

Un Noël à la sauce Henry (A Very Henry Christmas)

Une vie à Refaire (Switched)

Evolution (Evolved)

Galaxies & Océans

Qui Trouve, Garde (Finders Keepers)

Sens Dessus Dessous (Upside Down)

La Haine au Fond du Verre (The hate You Drink)

Tallowwood

Spencer Cohen Series

Thomas Elkin One

Lacuna

German

Flammende Erde (Red Dirt Heart)

Lodernde Erde (Red Dirt Heart 2)

Sengende Erde (Red Dirt Heart 3)

Ungezähmte Erde (Red Dirt Heart 4)

Vier Pfoten und ein bisschen Zufall (Finders Keepers)

Ein Kleines bisschen Versuchung (The Weight of It All)

Ein Kleines Bisschen Fur Immer (A Very Henry Christmas)

Weil Leibe uns immer Bliebt (Switched)

Drei Herzen eine Leibe (Three's Company)

Über uns die Sterne, zwischen uns die Liebe (Galaxies and Oceans)

Unnahbares Herz (Blind Faith 1)

Sehendes Herz (Blind Faith 2)

Hoffnungsvolles Herz (Blind Faith 3)

Verträumtes Herz (Blind Faith 3.5)

Thomas Elkin: Verlangen in neuem Design

Thomas Elkin: Leidenschaft in klaren

Thomas Elkin: Vertrauen in bester Lage

Traummann töpfern leicht gemacht (Throwing Hearts)

Sir

So Unendlich Viel Liebe (To the Moon and Back)

Thai

Sixty Five Hours (Thai translation)

Finders Keepers (Thai translation)

Chinese

Blind Faith

Bossy

Japanese

Bossy

To the Moon and Back

Portuguese

Sessenta e Cinco Horas